ALSO BY ANTHONY DECASTRO

Everything is Broken

NORTH COUNTRY GIRL

A FUZZY KOELLA MYSTERY

ANTHONY DECASTRO

Cover illustration by Anton Rosovsky

ISBN-13: 978-1-7336533-0-5

Published by Palmetto Pulp Mill, Greenville, SC USA

www.palmettopulpmill.com

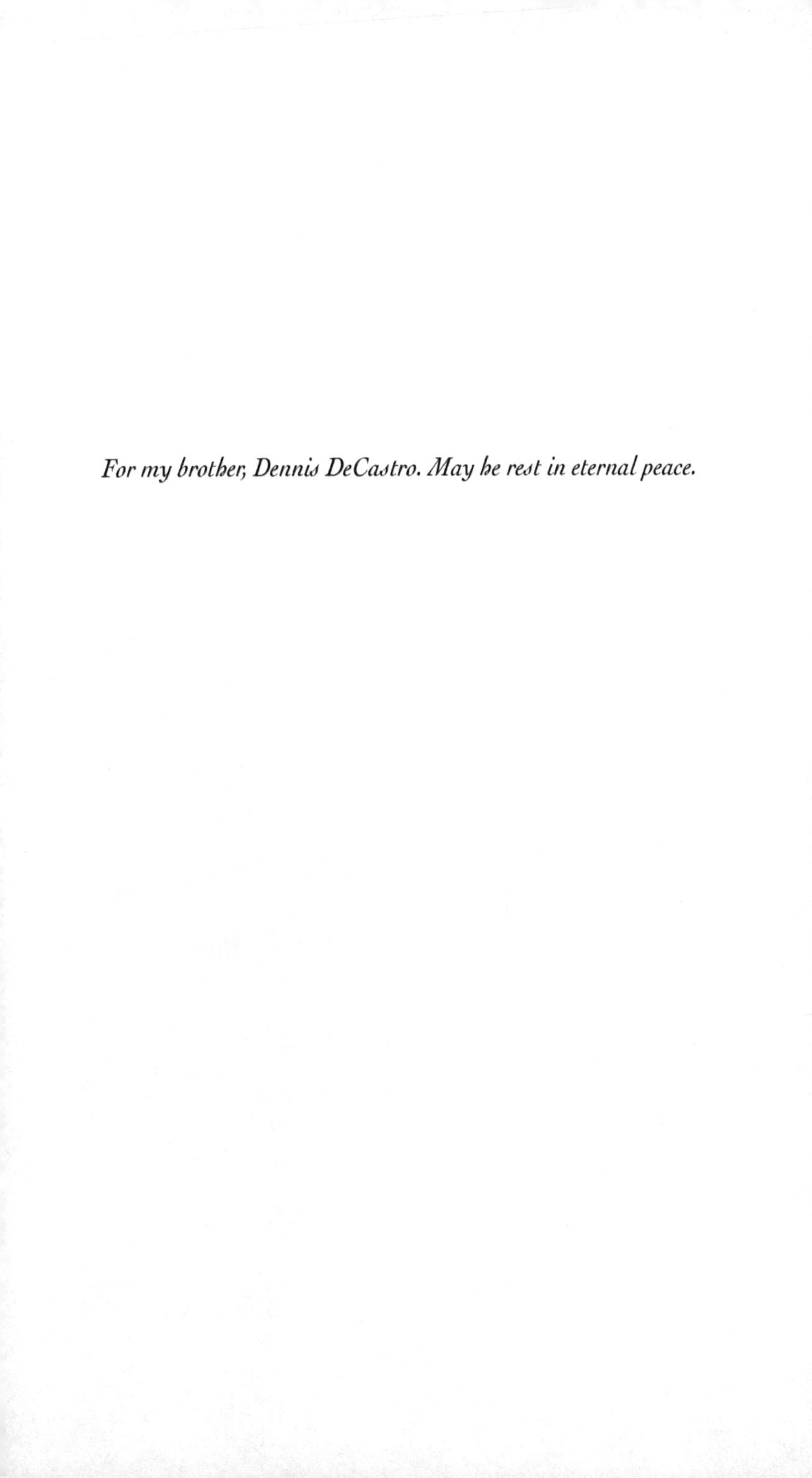

For my brother, Dennis DeCastro. May he rest in eternal peace.

AUTHOR'S NOTE

Fort Covington, NY is a peaceful, picturesque town on the Canadian border. In the writing of this book I have fictionally used actual locales as authentically as possible and have drawn on common surnames of the people of the "Fort" and the neighboring region. None of my fictional account reflects upon these people. In fact, I married into the Lapage (little P) family. There is one exception, Fuzzy Koella's gradual acceptance and love of the town and its people reflects my own.

1

———

The night after Christmas, I spent sitting in my truck in the parking lot of a barbecue joint across the street from a rundown convenience store called The Whiz. The night was pleasant. I had the window down to enjoy the crisp air and the lingering aroma of smoked meat and the chatter of middle America visiting The Whiz for their post-holiday beer, junk food, and lottery tickets. I hated stakeouts, but the stars in the skies, memories of gift giving with my girlfriend, and the fading pain from my last bullet wound kept this old bear in the yuletide spirit.

Old bear.

That's what Veronica called me. Old bear. I'd never asked her how old she was. I was too smart for that. I am a private investigator after all. But she seemed only a couple years younger than me. Yet, I was her old bear.

I was employed by an Indian-American entrepreneur named Hab Singh, who owned five other Whiz's throughout the Strand. Someone had vandalized all his stores with anti-Muslim graffiti over the last couple of months. Mr. Singh did not understand why, he, a Sikh, was being attacked with anti-Muslim hate. I understood perfectly.

People were stupid.

I had staked out three different stores over the last week. No luck. Fortunately, no other attacks had happened during that time. I planned this stakeout to be at the store less than a mile from my home the night after Christmas.

When the store lights shut off after midnight, I took more interest in observing the building. A few minutes later, the clerk appeared from around the back of the store in a twenty-year-old, gray Chevy Celebrity sedan. He signaled right and turned onto Business Highway 17 towards Myrtle Beach. The action died at the Whiz with his fading tail lights.

Two hours later, I spotted movement in the vegetation behind the store. I pulled across the street with my headlights off and slid past the south side of the building. As my truck nosed around the corner, the tires crunched on the remains of a broken beer bottle.

They crouched with spray cans poised at the back door. Two of them. Dressed in black. Wearing ski masks. They looked in my direction and sprung to their feet and sprinted to the safety of the woods.

I threw the gearshift into park, and jumped out of the truck. I hit full speed within a few steps. When I hit the woods, however, I faced the challenge of running in the dark through a path carved by people a lot shorter than six and a half feet. I soldiered on.

Branches lashed out at my cheeks. Sensing a disaster that could end up with me blinded, I held my right hand out in front of me to ward off the danger. Within seconds, thorny brambles bloodied my hand.

I could not see my prey, but the trees were alive with their passing. I continued in their direction. Just as I felt the cold clench of exhausted lungs, the branches ahead went dormant.

I should have heeded that warning.

Ten steps later, a vandal clothes-lined me with a forearm across my throat.

I flew from my feet. Time suspended. I wind-milled my arms, as if I could somehow tread air. I sank. My back slammed against the leafy floor of the path. My head followed and found a tree root. What little breath I had left in my lungs, expelled in a blast of air. I gasped trying to recover the lost oxygen. No luck. It felt like my lungs were clamped off. No air could enter. I rolled back and forth, gasping for air.

My attacker dropped beside me and sprayed paint into my face. It stung as it coated my eyes. The world went black.

I kicked and swung my arms, like a kid in a tantrum.

His partner said from my left, "Dude, let's bolt, now!"

"Shut up, Mason. I think we got a fuckin' rag-head lover, here."

I kept kicking and swinging, but with him straddling my torso and me blinded, I made no contact.

I felt his weight lift from me momentarily, and one of his knees shifted up onto my right bicep.

As the weight of his knee settled down, I rolled enough to the right to lift my left hip off the ground. I pulled my piece from the clip-on holster at my waist. Blindly, I jabbed the revolver up into where I believed his midsection would be.

"Ugh," he said.

From his groan, and the brush of his thigh on the back of my hand, I knew I had jammed my gun into his groin. I pulled the hammer back with my thumb. "Come out from the bushes. Hands up and empty, or your friend spends his life as a Eunuch."

"A what?"

"I will scatter his nuts all over the bushes here," I said. "Now get out here with your hands up!"

"Jesus, Mason. Come out," squealed the voice above me. "He's got a gun."

I heard bushes rustle over my left shoulder. Footsteps.

I ground the end of my gun against my attacker's crotch. The steel sight at the end of the barrel caught in his denim covered scrotum.

He whimpered.

I pushed harder against him. "Stand up slowly."

I kept continual pressure on his genitals as he crawled to his feet and I got to my knees. "Mason, I have the hammer pulled and my finger is on the trigger. You try anything and your buddy here has made sweet love to his lady for the last time."

"Mason, don't fuck around," his buddy said. "This motherfucker is crazy."

All the adrenaline had pushed air back into my lungs. Now, I wanted to make these two suffer for the hate they'd unleashed on Mr. Singh and his employees.

But I was no vigilante.

I fished my phone out of my pocket and held it out to my left. "Take that Mason. Remember, no funny business."

Mason's hand closed around the phone and my fingers.

I rotated the barrel ninety degrees against his buddy's crotch.

He breathed in harshly.

"Why the phone?" Mason asked.

"I want you to scroll through my contacts and find 'Uncle Rod'. Dial him up, and tell him you are with Fuzzy, and you want to turn yourself in. I want you to tell him we are in the woods behind The Whiz in Murrell's Inlet, down the road from Fuzzy's place."

He slid the phone free of my hand. The only sound as he searched my phone was the heavy breathing of his friend above me, and the chirping of crickets.

"Found it."

"Mason, Rod will have questions. He always does. Just put the phone to my ear when that happens."

He must have reached Rod, because he said, "Ah, yeah is this Rod?"

"No funny business," I reminded.

"So yeah, Rod. I'm here with Fuzzy. And he wants us to turn ourselves in." Mason paused. "Um, here let me let you talk to Fuzzy."

Mason must have knelt beside me to put the phone at my ear because I felt his breath warm on the side of my face. It smelled like corn chips.

"Fuzzy, what are you up to now?" Rod asked.

My Uncle Rod was a detective with the Myrtle Beach Police Department. I gave it to him in as concise terms as possible. When I got to the proceedings in the woods, I punctuated the action with little jabs to my spray-painting buddy's groin. I explained, as best I could, where we could find us. He said he would send cruisers over to retrieve us.

2

One cruiser took the vandals into the department. The other escorted me to the emergency room at Grand Strand Medical Center. You would think halting the execution of a crime would buy some preferential treatment at the hospital, but you would be wrong.

The cop who brought me over, checked me in and guided me to a hard, plastic chair in the waiting room. He left me there.

I blindly waited for what seemed like several hours. I wanted nothing more than to peel the enamel back from my eyes, but I feared the consequences of allowing more of the chemical into my eyes.

In my last hour of waiting, a meaty hand cupped my right shoulder.

"How's the shoulder healing," my Uncle Rod said.

A little over a year ago, I took a bullet from a small caliber pea-shooter, while working a case. The previous year, while working the case that put my mother in prison, I took a slug from something more menacing in the same wing. The shoulder was fine. The relationship with my mom still needed healing. "It's okay, Rod."

I tried to look up in the direction I thought Rod stood.

He must have just noted my blinded condition. "Whoa, Fuzzy, what happened?"

Before I could explain the spray paint, Hab Singh arrived. "Mr. Kola, I am so very sorry this mishap befell you."

Singh spoke in the quick, lilted diction common of his culture. So, when he said my name it sounded more like a soft drink, than the cuddly, tree hanging bear that most people mispronounced it as. I didn't like that Singh felt he needed to apologize. He'd lived in fear for the last month. "No worries, Mr. Singh. I don't think those guys will bother you anymore."

"I assure you there will be a bonus in a jiffy for you," he said.

"Fuzzy, how long have you been waiting?"

I shrugged. "I can't see a clock, Rod. A typical emergency room wait though."

"Oh dear, I have a nephew who is a doctor here. Let me see if I can expedite this for you," Mr. Singh said.

And he did. In a manner of minutes, a nurse with a cute voice wheeled me back to an observation room.

She had the paint removed from my eyelids and my eyes flushed with saline solution and then covered with gauze patches in less time than it took Mr. Singh to get me brought back. Before she put the patches on my eyes I had enough blurry vision to realize my nurse wasn't as cute as her voice promised. A doctor visited the room long enough to record that he had observed me, and then the nurse wheeled me out of the hospital.

Uncle Rod drove me home.

3

———

Against doctor's orders I removed the patches from my eyes once Rod left me to rest. My vision cleared in only a few minutes, and the humble environment of my little shanty off the back of the main boathouse at the Murrell's Inlet Marina came into focus. Ten foot by ten foot stretched reality, but it still housed a small kitchenette (pushed to one side, with microwave, sink and hot plate), a hide-away sofa bed, and a TV. I took my showers and trips to the John at the marina's main bathhouse.

The last few months, Veronica had shacked with me most nights. So, the place was tidier than usual. She hadn't waited around on me. So, I went about messing the place up by emptying my pockets onto the Formica kitchen countertop. In amongst the insurance card, spare change, and hospital paperwork, was my phone.

A few voicemails showed on the screen for phone numbers I did not recognize.

I played the first message.

"Fuzzy Ko-ell-a, what is up my friend? It's been a long time. It is your old teammie. Jo Jo Bigtree. Look, I need you to call me back. I need a good P.I., and I understand that is your game, now." He repeated the number on the screen and cut the connection.

Jo Jo Bigtree.

I hadn't seen him in over eight years. He was an enormous, first baseman recruited out of the Mohawk reservation in Upstate New York. We called him the F.B.I. — Fucking Big Indian. He could hit a fastball a country mile, and a curve ball not at all. He also failed remedial math, so we were only teammates for his red-shirt season, before he dropped out and headed back north.

I remembered Jo Jo's love of women, drink, and the fights that came with them. Nothing good could be behind this call. Voices from the past are often best left there.

I wasn't wise enough to heed my own advice.

4

—————

Two mornings later, I sat in the back row of a commercial prop plane. The row spanned the entire width of the fuselage, and I was in the seat centered on the aisle. The cockpit neglected to pull the curtain closed on their quarters. So, I had a clear view of the flat white expanse of the snow-covered runway as we made our descent.

I'm not a big flier, my height makes it problematic, but all the snow and size of the plane had me taking deep breaths and trying to imagine Veronica stepping out of the shower. Anything but the picture playing out through the windshield before me. I squeezed the armrests tight in both hands and closed my eyes.

The thump of the landing gear setting down was nearly imperceptible. In contrast, the rush of air encasing the fuselage, as we braked, assaulted the ears with sensory overload. My head flung forward as we came to a near stop.

I opened my eyes. The sky outside was the color of dirty dishwater flecked with crystals of a light falling snow. My southern blood chilled at the thought of stepping out into it.

The plane's ass-end shimmied on the slick, packed snow.

That continued, as we trafficked to the one gate at Massena International Airport. The co-pilot reminded us to remain seated with our seatbelts fastened. Two minutes ago, I would have done just about anything not to be on the plane. Now, I was content to sit in its relative warmth for as long as they would let me. I realized my worst fears when the pilot stopped us a football field short of the gate, and the grounds crew wheeled out a metal staircase for our de-boarding. The co-pilot stood and watched the ten of us from the cockpit's curtained entry. He beamed like a game show host as he took the PA radio in his hand. The plane had no "Fasten Seat Belt" sign to illuminate. So, we were at his mercy. When the exit door slid open, and he received a thumbs-up from a crew member on the stairs, the co-pilot informed us we may unfasten our seat belts, gather our things, and depart. "Please use care as you descend the stairs, as they may be slippery."

I had checked my bag plane side. So, I waited in the spitting snow, as they wheeled my bag and a handful of others around on a luggage cart. I retrieved it, and rolled it down a slick path to the terminal under a sign proclaiming, "Gate One". I saw no similar sign for a "Gate Two".

As I entered, Jo Jo Bigtree greeted me. He was a little beefier in the jowls, and a lot bigger at the waistline which meant he went about three hundred pounds and could look me eye to eye. FBI, indeed.

He held out a hand the size of a first baseman's mitt. "My man, Fuzzy. How was the trip?"

I took his hand. The calluses of thousands of swings per day in the batting cages were long gone. Replaced with the smooth hands of the man who worked a desk job and washed his hands with fancy soap. "Let's just say it's good to be on solid ground again."

He beamed a wide smile. "That bad, huh? Look I booked you at the Traveler's Rest in the Fort. Are you sure you won't stay at my place? We got the room, and I gotta say the Rest is a roach bag motel. But that's pretty much all we got."

"I'd rather have my own place, Jo Jo. I'll make do."

"Ok, are you good to get started? Or do you wanna check-in first?"

"Nah, I'm good to start earning my keep," I said.

He beamed again. "All righty then, we'll head to my office on the Rez."

The Massena International Airport looked like most rural railroad stations. People sat in ganged, molded plastic chairs, that lined a narrow passage through Gate One. Most of them were on the verge of nodding off, but two pre-school aged boys sat Indian-style in the center of the room racing Matchbox cars on the worn, patterned carpet. Jo Jo and I split around them, as to not disturb the action. A grandfatherly type stood beside a blonde girl, who came up to his waist, in front of a vending machine selling chips, candy bars, and honey buns. The girl had a determined look on her face. Grandad looked frustrated. There wasn't room for a dining area. There were no charging ports for iPhones nor access to Wi-Fi. There was no gift shop selling I Love NY t-shirts and coffee mugs. The most disturbing thing missing? There wasn't a book in sight. I was truly a fish out of water.

We passed what must have been the first metal detection device. A woman with disheveled blonde hair and black roots on display as if she'd done the hydrogen peroxide job herself, argued with the TSA guy about the need for taking her boots off. I could see her point. I had little faith in the machines, either. If the terrorists learned of the Massena International Airport, it would be like finding the chink in Smaug's armored scales.

Jo Jo carried on about something at my side, but I was too busy people watching to follow the conversation. A barely legal, teen-aged girl flirted with a late middle-aged ticket agent, at the airport's sole ticket stand. She leaned into the stand, and tucked a strand of greasy red hair behind her ear, and giggled at some quip he fed her. The two of them were the only ones on this side of security besides those of us passing through. There were more plastic chairs, sitting on a scarred vinyl floor, and vending machines lined the walls. An expanse of aluminum-framed glass faced the runway. It was so in need of washing it was almost translucent. Yet, I made out an old, 70s era Nova speeding down the runway.

I cut Jo Jo off, "What the hell is that guy doing?"

Jo Jo laughed. "You will love this," he said. "That's how they test if the runway is suitable for take-offs and landings. They get in that car, floor it, and when they get the needle pinned, they slam on the brakes."

I searched his face for humor.

Jo Jo shrugged. "Hey, it works. They ain't ever had a bad landing."

The exit doors were standard, metal embossed swing doors. Jo Jo pushed one open and stood aside to let me exit.

The cold stung my face once again, but somehow, I felt more comfortable in the elements than inside the confines of the airport.

Mounds of snow lined the curbs, and a film of gray slush coated the road. I skated across the road and through the parking lot with my hand on Jo Jo's elbow, until we ended up at a half-ton, Chevy pickup truck, that would be the envy of any Southern boy.

Jo Jo looked down at my soaked Nike running shoes, "Didn't you bring any boots?"

"Don't own any."

"We may need to fix that. Otherwise, you will break your neck before we get to work."

The work he mentioned involved gathering information to support Jo Jo's case to prove the innocence of a young man arrested for the murder of a nun, or city councilwoman, or something. I don't know, I couldn't figure out who the victim was from Jo Jo over the phone.

Jo Jo, however, was convinced of the young man's innocence.

I questioned the logic of flying up an out-of-town investigator to help with the information gathering, but Jo Jo insisted that he didn't have the resources, and he needed my expertise. Never mind that he had no way of possibly knowing my expertise.

Jo Jo's offer of four hundred dollars per day plus expenses, twice my normal rate, sealed the deal.

5

Jo Jo's truck was comfortable with leather upholstery and plenty of headroom, even for two guys of our size. A faint smell of wet dog overcame the spearmint scents coming from an evergreen-shaped, cardboard air freshener hanging from the rear-view mirror. I wasn't sure what was worse, the dog or the mint. If it wasn't so damn cold, I would have rolled the windows down for some fresh air.

Jo Jo read my thoughts, and turned the dial, and poured heated air onto my lap and numb fingers.

We didn't talk shop. Instead, we made small talk, catching up on eight years of inane details. He skated around the touchy subject of my fiancée Angel's death. I didn't ask how a kid, who flunked out of remedial classes, ended up an attorney.

We passed signs announcing the Bridge to Canada, the locks on the St. Lawrence River, and entry into the Akwesasne reservation. We also passed the dying corpse of a shopping mall, and strip shopping centers gasping for life amongst choking weeds and cracked black top parking lots. This was the America that politicians pointed to every four years when we were all due for a fresh call for change.

About fifteen minutes later, Jo Jo made a right-hand turn at a stoplight in front of the Akwesasne Casino on the left. The Casino was the only building I'd seen with a fresh coat of paint since my arrival.

He pulled us into the lot of a gas station with a restaurant connected called the Howlin' Wolf. It looked like any other convenience store you would see in, say, 1979. It had putty-colored metal siding with vertical battens. Algae and mold climbed up the base of the siding. Mr. Singh would probably swoop in and buy the place if it wasn't a thousand miles north of his nearest store.

Jo Jo pulled us around to the back of the building, where there was a grimy, pink two-story addition, which stood out like a boil on the ass end of the beige convenience store.

He parked, and we climbed up rickety stairs. My hand slipped on the ice slick, steel-pipe handrail. I counted three wooden treads where they replaced the rusty metal.

When we reached the top, JoJo said, "Watch your step?"

He guided me around a hole in the concrete landing big enough to swallow your leg up to your crotch.

Jo Jo led us to the only door. It matched the pink of the walls. Centered, right where a peep hole belonged was a narrow, five-inch-long brass name plate. It read: Joseph J. Bigtree, Attorney at Law. He opened the door without using a key and stood aside to let me enter.

He tossed his keys on a dark mahogany desk and waved his hand at an ox-blood colored leather seat. "Have a seat, Fuzzy."

The lay-out was like a shotgun shack with I would presume a conference room, toilet facilities, and possibly a records room lined up along one side of a corridor leading back from the front room, where we stood. It was a pretty simple place, but Jo Jo had made the best of it. The wood-paneled walls each held a mounted deer's head, and all the furniture were hardwoods or upholstered in dark leathers. The place was unapologetically masculine, and it left me wondering if Jo Jo ever had any female clients.

I took my seat.

He took his.

He spoke.

I listened.

He splayed his massive hands on a calendar ink blotter on the desk. The dates were from two years ago. "Okay, I know I did not explain much over the phone, but I wanted to get you up here first." He reached into a drawer in the desk and produced a manila folder. He slid a 5-x-7 picture of a pretty blonde in her mid-to-late 30s across the desk. "Sister Katie Couture," he said.

She wore a white peasant's blouse with the collar off the shoulders. It wasn't low cut or anything, but I still had a difficult time imagining her in a habit. Her honey-colored hair brushed her tan shoulders. But, it was her eyes that held your attention. The iris was so pale as to be almost white, but ringed with a blue the color of the sky on a day with no clouds. She looked like no nun I had ever seen.

Jo Jo must have caught the curiosity in my eyes. "She was not an official nun. In fact, she had three children. All out of wedlock."

That caught my attention. "The good Sister got around?"

"Easy, Fuzzy. She had one of those come to Jesus moments. From all reports, Katie was no angel as a young woman. All of her daughters were born before she was twenty. There is not much to do around here, and a lot of girls feel trapped. It can sometimes lead to promiscuous behavior." He added, "Lord knows I have taken advantage of it from time to time."

He continued, "With Katie, yes, she was a bit of a tramp as a young woman, and she drank too much. Probably, smoked weed. Somewhere along the way, she grew up. She made it to church. Volunteered. Made something of herself instead of just some pin cushion for any boy or man passing through. Even here on the Rez, we all respected Sister Katie, because she showed more respect to us than any white man had before."

"So how did she end up murdered," I asked.

Jo Jo contemplated that by examining the scar tissue on his knuckles.

I recalled the late-night brawls in college when the legend of the F.B.I. had been forged. Jo Jo took on all takers, often swinging his frying pan sized fists effortlessly, while other college boys hung from his shoulders. If Jo JoBigtree hadn't flunked out of college, eventually he would have ended up in the J. Reuben Long Detention Center. The scars had faded, white, and smooth. Old. I guessed when Jo Jo took the books seriously, he matured in other ways, too.

"That is what I brought you up here for," he said. "State police arrested Gary Pressley. Local kid in his 20s. Orphan. Homeless. Probably a little retarded."

I grimaced at the word.

Jo Jo must have noticed my discomfort. "Sorry, mentally challenged."

I waved it off. "You said he was homeless. How is he paying you?"

"I am working it pro bono," he said.

There wasn't the slightest hint of humor in Jo Jo's voice or face. His face, in fact, had taken on the stereotypical intense dead pan of the Native American portraits you saw in your High School history books. Mouth a flat slash. Broad nose. Eyes, dark and penetrating.

"How are you paying me?"

"Out of my pocket," Jo Jo said. "I'm certain Gary Pressley did not do this, Fuzzy. When you meet him, I am sure you will understand. And like everyone else I loved Sister Katie Couture, I want to find out who did this."

"Okay, so give me more of the basics. How was she found?"

Jo Jo removed an 8-x-10 photo from the folder and placed it beside the picture of Katie Couture in life. It was not as pleasant to look at. She slouched in a rusty metal folding chair, her head cocked to one side. Her tongue limply hung from her mouth. Her blonde hair was dark and nappy. The killer had pulled her arms tight behind her, and bound her legs at the ankles with yellow, nylon rope. She wore a soiled, silky white slip and nothing else. I was ashamed of the way I admired how it clung to the curves of her corpse. Behind her was a large, iron vessel that looked like a relic from the last century or before.

"They found her in the boiler room of the abandoned Ft. Covington Public Library. Best they can figure, she had been there three or four days. Whoever did this to her restarted the boilers in that room and left her there with no water."

I looked up from the picture.

The flat slash of Jo Jo's mouth turned down. "They tortured her, Fuzzy."

"And the kid? Why did they charge him?"

"Anonymous call came in from the Fort. They saw someone enter the Library. Caller just figured it was a simple trespassing, I guess. State police made it there two hours later. They found Gary draped over Katie's thighs, sobbing. His story was incoherent, and he kept saying it was his fault. I could not get a clear line of thought out of the kid either. He does not think in a straight line like you and I, Fuzzy. I do not doubt that there is something that Gary Pressley blames himself for in the death of Katie, but I know he did not bind her up and lock her in the boiling room to die of thirst. Katie took care of Gary, like she did everyone else, but she was literally all that the kid had in the world. To everyone else, he was just like a stray dog. A pleasant one that does not compel you to call in to the pound. But you do not take it in, either."

I understood the type. We had some in the Strand. You always noticed them in the off season. The restaurants fed them free meals. The locals nodded to them and smiled. Not knowing their names, but knowing their friendly faces. When Spring break hit, they would disappear for the season. I'm not sure where they went, but somehow, they knew they were not welcome during the money harvesting season. Most of them seemed a little off. Mentally disabled. But like Gary Pressley, none of them seemed capable of what was done to Katie Couture. "I guess you'll want me to talk to the Kid first?"

He held his hands out, palms open, as if he were holding a large, imaginary bowl. "I'll leave that to you, but I figure I'll work the Rez."

"Don't you have lawyerly things to do?"

"You will not get far asking questions on the Rez. Besides, the crime happened off the Rez." He added, "And I do not think Katie's killer was Native."

"Yeah? And do you have any thoughts on who killed her?"

I lost him there for a second as he searched for something in the recesses of his mind. When he settled on it he gave a quick nod of the head, "Start with the Kid. After you've talked to him, let us share notes and we can talk about who I need you to talk to next."

I suspected Jo Jo was reluctant to have me speak to

someone, but he was paying me to interrogate the people he pointed me to. I didn't need to solve the crime. I needed to gather enough information for Jo Jo to cast reasonable doubt on the guilt of Gary Pressley.

It always sounds easier when you put it that way, but it never turns out that way.

6
___

Jo Jo put me in a primer coated Nova, much like the one they used at Massena International on the runway. He gave me directions to the Franklin Correctional Facility, where Gary Pressley was currently held, and told me I would see the Traveler's Rest Motor Court on my way, if I wanted to stop and check-in to the room he had reserved for me. The snow had picked up, and the Nova's wipers were about a year beyond their usable life. They sounded like a knife scraping against the sharpening stone, as they etched arcs, like interlocking rainbows into the windshield glass. Somehow the wipers kept the windshield clean of snow. The visibility was getting fuzzier with the growing storm, but I was at least able to see to the front edge of the Nova's hood. My sweat slick palms gripped the wheel tighter.

The speed limit hopped between 30 MPH and 45 MPH every half-mile on the reservation, and I counted four tribal police cars alongside the road in the five miles it took to get to the limits of the Town of Fort Covington. The joke was on them. You don't put someone who's lived his whole life south of the Mason-Dixon line behind the wheel in a snowstorm and expect him to go any faster than 30 MPH. The stop signs were illegible, just fuzzy red lollipops alongside the road. A convoy stacked behind me on State Route 37.

Fort Covington was much the same as the Reservation. A-frame houses with snow-capped roofs and single-wide mobile homes dotted the sides of the road, interspersed among wide expanses of farmland. I passed another gas station slash restaurant, called the Willow Creek, on the left. It had a shuttered shack propped up in the parking lot advertising ice cream. The parking lot was full of salt and rust covered cars, but they weren't there for the ice cream. Just beyond the Willow Creek, atop a berm alongside the road was the Traveler's Rest Motor Court. It looked like the kind of place the meth dealers set up in down home. I passed it by. If I stopped to check-in now, there was no way I was getting back out in this and getting to Malone to see Gary Pressley.

As I approached the town center, I passed under my first traffic light, and approached a green-sided building with a tall, turreted clock tower built into one of its corners. Graffiti covered the faint sign out front, but you could still read *Fort Covington Public Library*. More than half the windows of the library were broken, and no light shown in them.

I reached down and turned the heat up as high as it would go. But either the heater core on the Nova was failing or the chill I felt would not be cured by hot air.

I passed a small park with a frozen skating pond, an ancient church built of massive stone blocks, and another filling station. Then as quickly as I had entered Fort Covington I exited.

It didn't look like a town where nuns get tortured to death in seedy basements.

Forty minutes later, I had numbed to the sound of the wipers scraping the windshield, and settled in at a comfortable 35 miles per hour. Any faster and the world took on the appearance of an old tube TV unable to pick up a good reception on its rabbit ears. Before I had the pleasure of experiencing the Village of Malone, a green roadside sign directed me to the Franklin Correction Facility, hugging the snowy ground just off Bare Hill Road.

The Franklin Correction Facility looked like one of the cookie-cutter designs they used for public elementary schools. The entry building was a low-slung red brick building with a shallow hip-roof, which labored under the weight of the 6 inches of snow that blanketed it. Following the school motif, it even had what looked like a drop-off circle at the front of the main entry's glass storefront.

I pointed the Nova up the withered tree lined drive leading up to the drop-off circle. You had to look close to even see the chain-link fences that encircled the campus. The whole place looked far less intimidating than any prison I'd ever visited. I would not see my mom in this prison. That may have colored my emotions on the subject.

I took a right immediately before the circle, and parked in a vast, nearly empty parking lot. Stepping out of the car, I was greeted with a fresh case of pin pricks to the cheeks, and the crystallization of snot in my nose. I shuffle stepped quickly through the lot, up a salt encrusted concrete walk (that I still almost slipped and fell on), and in through the welcoming doors of the prison.

My business card didn't get me very far with the front desk, neither did my license. Apparently, New York corrections officers were not impressed with South Carolina private investigators. But, Jo Jo's card, and the call to him that followed got me into a cinder block meeting room at the end of a labyrinth of halls, offices, and similar rooms in the main building. The block walls were unpainted. The floor was unfinished concrete. A faint smell of sewer gas hung in the air. The only view outside the room was the narrow vision panel in the metal door. The door was the same homey gray as the Nova.

I sat at a wooden table, scarred with profanity scratched into its surface.

Across from me Gary Pressley slouched in a metal chair. His blond head lulled to one side. His chin rested on his shoulder. I couldn't be sure he hadn't nodded off to sleep.

I snapped by fingers under his chin. "Yo, Gary. Stay with me here."

Without lifting his head, his eyes rolled up. "Aren't you gonna take notes? Jo Jo always has a notepad."

It was an interesting observation. He couldn't seem to focus on who I was, and why I was there to see him, but he noticed that I didn't carry a notebook. I probably should. I admit, but I had always assumed that I would not forget anything important. It was my subconscious way of weeding through the chafe. At least, that was how I rationalized the laziness.

"We're just going to talk, Gary. Jo Jo and I will have to talk a lot with you over the next several days if we're going to help you."

He looked up at me now. His eyes were slate colored. His short cropped blond hair was plastered to his odd shaped head. It seemed incomparably oblong, from front to back. I once had a case to find a missing boy who had cerebral palsy. His head was similarly shaped.

"You talk like those cops," he said. His voice slurred like a drunkard's early in the night. "They are always talking about helping me too, eh?"

"Don't talk to them at all, Gary. You talk to Jo Jo or me, that's all. Do you understand?"

He looked beyond me to a rusted floor drain.

"Smells like shit," Gary said. He chuckled, as if he had just told an inside joke.

I stood up and went to the door and flagged down an officer walking in the hallway. I asked him to bring us two bottles of water.

From the door, I asked, "Gary, did you like Miss Couture?"

He searched my face, tilting his head back and forth as he did so. "Which Miss Couture? We have a lot of them."

"Kate," I said.

The corners of his mouth turned down. "Yes, I guess that's who you would ask about, eh?" He rocked forward. "I liked Sister Katie, yeah."

"Did you think she was pretty?" I didn't even know where I was going with this line of questioning.

"She was beautiful," he said. "But she was more pretty with her clothes on."

I swallowed a big glob of saliva that instantly appeared in the back of my throat. I stepped back from the table and slid into my seat. "What do you mean by that?"

His eyes were dead. He would be a hard one to read.

I snapped by fingers in front of his face again. "What did you mean, Gary? Have you seen Sister Katie with her clothes off?"

"Yeah," he said. It came out like a moan. "When I found her in the chair at the library, she was in her undergarments."

Right. That would make sense.

"And that's the only time you've seen her without her clothes?" I said.

There was the briefest of pauses. The dead eyes came alive long enough to shift to look over my shoulder. He stared at something back there intently, avoiding eye contact with me.

Maybe he wouldn't be so tough to read after all.

He nodded his head. "Only that one time."

"What were you doing at the library, when you found Sister?"

He continued to look over my shoulder. Moisture was building in his eyelids. "I went to save her."

I hated to see people cry. It didn't make me sad. It made me angry. Angry at them, for putting me in that uncomfortable situation. I reached over and took Gary's chin in my hand and yanked his face back. So, he would have to look me in the eye when he answered. "But how did you know she needed saving? How did you know she would be there?"

His lifeless eyes stared directly into my own. He grinned.

A dimple formed on his left cheek. He began rocking back and forward. "I knew," he said. "I put her there."

I could see why Jo Jo said it was hard to make anything out of what Gary said. "Help me out, Gary. If you put her in that chair why did you then try to save her?"

The waterworks showed up again in his eyes.

I wondered if Gary Pressley was brighter than any of us gave him credit for.

"Sister was my friend," he said.

"Then why did you put her in that chair, Gary?"

He wiped at the corner of one eye with the heel of his hand. "I think I'm done talking, now," he said.

"But Gary…"

He continued rocking back and forth in rhythm to music only he heard.

A knock came at the door.

"Done," he said. "I'm done. And take your hand off me, Mister."

I saw the officer through the door's vision panel. I waved him in.

He sauntered over and placed two plastic bottles of water on the table. His badge said Officer William Melton.

"Don't make a habit of this, dick," he said. "I ain't no goddamn waitress."

His shiny black belt and polished black leather shoes creaked as he walked off.

I twisted the top off a bottle and walked over to the floor drain and poured half of the bottle down the drain.

Melton must have caught me doing it in his peripheral vision because he stopped with the doorknob in his hand. "What the hell are you doing?"

"It smells like shit in here," I said.

I turned to wink at Gary Pressley, but he already had a

wide smile. One of his incisors was missing. Somehow, it made him look like an innocent kid.

8

———

The drive back to Fort Covington was much less of a white-knuckle event. A fuzzy, full moon provided greater illumination than I recalled during my daytime drive. Delicate flakes floated in the night sky like dust motes.

The Nova only had AM radio, but I found a public station that played a decent selection of Americana music. I listened to Jason Isbell sing about not wanting to die in a Super 8 motel and reflected on my meeting with Gary Pressley.

If first impressions were everything, I was in for a rough time. All I got out of Gary Pressley was frustration. I couldn't even place something as simple as his age. He could be twenty-five. He could be forty-five. I guess a look in Jo Jo's files would solve that mystery.

I did not share Jo Jo's conviction that Gary Pressley could not have done this. I hoped he wasn't wasting his good will by working this case *pro bono*. I didn't come away from my first encounter with Gary Pressley assured he didn't kill Katie Couture. On the plus side I didn't have a strong belief he did either. Jo Jo had said he would have more people to talk to after I spoke with Pressley. I figured that would wait until tomorrow. Tonight, I would check into the Traveler's Rest, and then find a local watering hole. You could learn a lot about the goings on in a small town in two places — the dining room table of one of the local families and at the elbow of the town drunk at a friendly neighborhood ginmill.

9

The Traveler's Rest Motor Court was a scattering of single-story buildings with cementitious siding scattered atop a short hill halfway between downtown Ft. Covington and the Akwesasne Mohawk Reservation. When I pulled onto the gravel drive leading up from Route 37, to the small shack with the neon office sign, the snow had stopped and the clouds dissipated. The occasional star winked with aspirations of a brighter morning to come.

I pulled up in front of the office. There wasn't a parking spot there, but as there were only two other cars visible in the entire court, I figured I was okay leaving the car there, while I checked in. The door to the office was as light as pressed paper. It felt like it could fall off its hinges with the slightest effort. Inside, there was a countertop covered with hunting magazines, Styrofoam fast food cartons, and torn open envelopes of what appeared to be utility bills. Light poured from a cased archway behind the desk. Tendrils of tobacco smoke flickered in the light.

On the top of a stack of magazines was the typical bell you expected at a hotel desk.

I gave it a ring.

She came through the archway waving smoke away with one hand. She pinched a filtered cigarette between the forefinger and middle finger of the other. A column of ash nearly an inch long clung precariously to the end of the butt. She flicked the ashes to the soiled carpet, and ground them into the rug with a pale-yellow work boot. She was average height, and had an impressive figure for her age, which was tough to place because she had the catcher's mitt face of a lifelong smoker. She had a jet-black page boy hairdo. The color probably came from a bottle, and it matched the heavy mascara she wore on her lashes. Her orange tanned skin also came from a bottle. No one got a tan like that in December on the Canadian border. She wore a tight-fitting long underwear top, that stretched tightly across a set of fake boobs. Her jeans had the knees cut out, showing off the same orange skin. As she stepped closer to the desk, my sinuses flared to the smell of her cheap perfume. She had a name tag pinned to one breast, that said, "Stefanie Charles."

"How can I help you?" Her voice sounded as if she had just gargled with charcoal. Just as I expected it would.

"I have a reservation for Koella," I said.

She smiled and raised her eyebrows in what would go for a flirtatious gesture on just about anyone. She made it look like a frightening glare from the Bride of Frankenstein. "You're the one from the Carolinas?"

"Yes, ma'am."

She reached over and gave my bicep a squeeze. "Yes ma'am? How sweet. Jo Jo told me all about you."

I had to remember to thank Jo Jo for sticking Lily Munster on me. "I bet he has," I said. "But don't believe everything that comes out of that Indian's mouth."

She laughed a little too hard at that. Moved her hand

from my arm to my chest and gave my pectoral muscle a pat. "That is so true!"

I was getting more than a little uncomfortable with all the feeling up I was being subjected to, and I was exhausted from the travel, the bad weather driving, and all the memories of college-life. All of that was conspiring to put me in a cranky mood, and I would have to cut short the proceedings here, or I would end up telling Miss Stefanie Charles to keep her fucking hands to herself. Pissing off a local on my first night wouldn't serve me well. So, I asked for my key.

"Not much for small talk, are you?"

She bent over and opened a cabinet door behind the desk. On the inside face of the door were a series of hooks carrying brass room keys. It was like a scene from an old black and white movie.

Stefanie handed me the key to Unit number 3. "It's right across the lot from here. So, I can keep an eye on you."

She winked, and her mascara nearly glued her eye shut.

"Well, thanks. Stefanie, and I'm sure I'll see more of you over the next few days."

That got more of her creepy smile. "I'm sure you will, Mr. Fuzzy."

I turned to escape, but thought better of it before I closed the door behind me. I called back to her, "Say where can a fella get a drink around here?"

Her eyes went wide. She propped one haunch on the countertop, leaned forward, and rested her chin in her palm. "Now you're talkin'. In the Fort, there's pretty much only the Legion. In fact, I'm planning on heading there after work."

The thought of escorting her for a night on the town terrified me. "Legion? You mean like American Legion? Because I'm not a member. I'm not even a veteran," I said.

She waved that off like she was swatting at a fly. "Sweetie,

I'm not a member there either, and I'm there every Thursday night for bucket night."

It was a Friday night. I didn't point that out because I really didn't want to hear an explanation of how she was making a special trip to entertain me.

"Ok, well, what time do you get off?"

"Ten o'clock," she said. "Is it a date?"

It was eight o'clock now. I could probably get an hour of uninterrupted time at the bar listening to the locals. "Sure," I said. "But listen, I could use that beer right about now. So, I'll probably head over soon. Why don't you meet me over there?"

She looked disappointed.

10

Unit 3 at the Traveler's Rest looked like something straight out of the Rockford Files. It had two full sized beds with mustard yellow vinyl headboards. It had gauzy sheets and blankets with a Parisian print. The TV had legs, and dials, and no remote control. The place smelled like an ashtray. And judging by the cigarette burns riddling the vinyl-tile floor, prior tenants had used it as one.

I wanted to take a quick shower, but there was a thin film of dust and insect legs coating the bottom of the tub. I decided against it.

I changed my shirt from the button-down, checked shirt I had been wearing to a black concert T-shirt for some band called Webb. They had been a Charleston metal band that built a small following due to their passionate live shows. The studio didn't suit them though. Almost immediately after they released their first album, they lost a couple members to internal strife. They found replacement members, but the small, loyal following wasn't that loyal, and they disappeared.

I contemplated the fans' reaction, if our local minor league team, the Grand Strand Gulls, ever decided to not re-sign me. Who was I kidding? We didn't have fans. We had tourists.

Katie Couture had fans evidently. I wondered what I would hear about her tonight.

There was only one way to find out.

11

___

The American Legion Post 1418 was a white clapboard building with a rust colored mansard roof, situated in an island strip of grass and gravel in between the lanes leading to and from Canada. The crushed stone parking lot was full of pick-up trucks, and SUVs, and sagging sedans from last decade. I parked beside a telephone pole on one side and a blue Chevy Corsica on the other. When I got out of the car, I noted that the driver of the Corsica was still in the car. She was a middle-age blonde with wild blue eyes. I caught her quickly tossing back a handful of pills. When she saw me, she frantically tossed a pill box in the glove compartment. The way she was acting, I seriously doubted she held a prescription for the pharmaceuticals she was taking.

Whatever, I was not one to judge.

I walked into the back entrance of the Legion vaguely aware that Patty Pill-popper was following behind at a safe distance. Inside the door, I hung my coat on an overloaded tree in a breezeway. The place smelled like a wood stove. I welcomed the heat.

I stepped from the hallway into the main hall. The Legion was done up in blond wood paneling, and was brighter than any saloon I'd ever visited. Missing were the neon beers sign, the smell of cigarette smoke, and the sounds of the jukebox playing decades old one-hit wonders. It looked like a well-lit recreation center. I entered beside the horseshoe-shaped bar. It was lined with a collection of lifelong drinkers, college kids in for holidays, and casuals just in for a beer and a game of billiards, or shuffleboard, or darts. Beyond the limits of the bar, the place opened up into a large hall with an empty dining area, billiards tables, and a shuffleboard set up along one wall. A young couple played darts at the wall on the far side of the hall. By the teasing the brunette was giving her bearded boyfriend, it was clear who was winning.

I took a seat at the only empty stool at the bar between a beefy guy with long red hair falling out of a red "Make America Great Again" hat and a short, wiry guy in his 50's, who had enormous ears and was dressed like the Fonz, in white T-shirt, black leather jacket, and starched blue jeans. One of them had body odor that smelled like spoiled milk.

The bartender was a tiny imp with a Pat Benatar hair-do, and blue eye shadow that arched halfway up her forehead above each eye.

"How are you?"

She had an enthusiastic smile, which almost forgave the eye shadow.

"I'm good," I said. "How about a Labatt's?"

"What's your name, honey?"

"Fuzzy."

"Alright, Fuzzy. I'm Jeanie. It'll be a buck-fifty."

She reached down into cooler below the bar top, and fished out an amber bottle of beer so cold that it was dotted with flecks of ice.

At the end of the bar, right under a sign for the

Restrooms, Patty Pill-popper slid beside an old Asian man with greasy, black and gray hair, and thick Buddy Holly glasses. She whispered something in his ear.

He leaned his head forward, and looked over his glasses at me.

Just great, I thought. Five minutes was all it took for me to make enemies in town.

Jeanie put my beer down on a cardboard coaster with Old Glory imprinted on it.

I handed her a twenty, and set about enjoying my beer. It was ice cold and crisp, and tasted like well water.

Halfway through the beer, or about thirty seconds later, the beefy guy with the Trump hat clapped me on the back.

"Damn, if you ain't a big son of a bitch," he said.

"You aren't so small yourself, partner," I said.

His bushy mustache crawled up his cheeks in what I assumed was a smile. It was hard to tell, as his mouth was buried under the ginger shrub blanketing his lower face. He patted his belly with two doughy, freckled hands. "I guess you got a point there, but I'm big in the wrong direction."

I held my beer bottle out to him. "And you aren't from around here, either."

He tapped my bottle with the neck of his Budweiser. "That's a fact, my friend, and neither are you."

"What brought you here?" I asked.

"A girl," he said. "What else would bring a Georgia boy to this godforsaken place? Six months out of the year I can't feel my toes."

"She must be some girl," I said.

"She was," he said. "Cancer got her last summer." His eyes latched onto a spot on the wall behind the bar. "Here I am stuck for another winter. Ain't life a bitch?" He took a handful of popcorn out of a wooden bowl sitting in from of him, and parted the way in his bushy beard, enough to shovel his mouth full. He chased it with a pull on his Bud, that would be the envy of any Spring Breaking college kid. When he turned to face me, popcorn crumbs clung to his damp beard. "So, what brings you here?"

"Work," I said.

His jaw dropped and pieces of popcorn dropped onto the lacquered surface of the bar in front of him. "Work? Dude, don't bullshit a bullshitter, there ain't no work here."

"I'm a private investigator working a case for an old college buddy of mine."

His mustache climbed again, then immediately went flat. "You ain't kidding?"

I was used to it. People either see Phillip Marlowe or Thomas Magnum when they think of a P.I. So, when they hear what I do for a living they think it's an exotic career.

I shook my head.

"Well, I'll be damned," he said.

"Trust me. It's not all it's cracked up to be."

"It's gotta beat working at the school bus garage," he said. "Let me guess. You're working on the Sister Katie case."

"How'd you guess?"

He shrugged his shoulders, and poured some beer into a recess in his beard. "What else is gonna bring a P.I. into town from," he paused. "Where'd you say you were from again?"

"I didn't say. I'm from Myrtle Beach."

He whistled. "Myrtle Beach? I bet it's a lot nicer there right now, than this shit."

I reached across him and grabbed a handful of popcorn. "I haven't felt my toes since I stepped off the plane."

"I know, right?"

I fed some popcorn in my mouth, and choked back the desire to upchuck. Some of the kernels were stale. The others were soggy, as if they'd already been in someone's mouth.

My new friend held out his hand. "Billy Howe," he said. "Like 'How you like me now.'"

I took his hand. It was firmer than it looked, and when he wrapped his fingers around mine, I could feel the bones of my knuckles grind. I tried to return the favor, but my grip was no match for his. "Fuzzy Koella."

I still couldn't see his smile, but his blue eyes were full of good cheer.

"Like I was saying, ain't much happening up here that's gonna draw a P.I. from South Carolina. Most of the crime is related to the border, but I couldn't see you up here for that. But the murder of a nun?"

I winked. "I ought to hire you."

He chuckled at that, and his pectoral muscles, or fat, bounced up and down like a show-off bodybuilder's. "That would be a trip," he said. "You know they arrested this homeless kid. Are you sure your ship hasn't sailed on this one?"

"I know. I'm working for the kid's attorney."

He broke eye contact with me, and shoveled some more nasty popcorn into his maw. His lips smacked as he munched away. He stopped occasionally to pull an un-popped kernel from his mouth, and dropped them to the bar. By the time he was finished, he had a dozen little hard, round soldiers lined up and ready for duty. He raised his bottle to let Jeanie know he was ready for another cold one.

His silence was getting the best of me. It had only been a minute or so, but Billy Howe didn't strike me as the introspective type. I didn't like him so much now. "Something wrong with me working for the kid's lawyer, Billy?"

He looked at me sideways, as Jeanie approached him. "Bigtree?"

"Yeah," I said.

He continued to look forward. Jeanie reached into the

cooler. "How 'bout you bring us a bucket, Jeanie? Half Bud, and half this Canadian shit, that he's drinkin'."

"Make it all Bud," I said. "He's right. It is shit." If I was going to drink shit, it may as well be American shit. I am a patriotic sort, after all.

Jeanie smiled. "You got it, guys." She sauntered off underneath the restrooms sign by my new Asian friend.

Billy stood up, and I'm pretty sure I heard a sigh of relief from his barstool.

"Let's grab a seat over there at one of the tables."

I was intrigued and optimistic. Billy obviously had something to get off his chest about Jo Jo Bigtree, Gary Pressley, or Katie Couture. Or all three. I felt like the decision to make the local watering hole my first stop was already paying off. I followed Billy to a table five rows deep, halfway back into the dining area. I dropped into the seat across from him.

"The relationship between Natives and Whites can get as nasty as the Blacks and Whites down South, Fuzzy."

I waited for him to continue, but he left it hanging there like that was all there was to say on the subject. Jo Jo had told me he would handle the interrogations on the reservation. Now, Billy seemed to be questioning the logic of working for a Native American. At the very least, he seemed to be suggesting that it may not be something I want to announce to the fine folks at the American Legion. Yet, Jo Jo was working *pro bono* for a White homeless man with obvious mental disabilities. Billy was right. This was just like back home. People were probably seeing only the bad. Said another way, they were seeing what was being shown to them on their TV sets, and not thinking about what they could see with their own eyes. The obvious problem with this, was that their reaction to the news further exacerbated the racial problem. The TV teams and the politicians benefited. We out here in the real world, struggled in the trenches.

Jeanie arrived, and pressed a denim-clad, bony hip against my shoulder. She placed a tin bucket filled with ice and brown bottles of beer in the center of the table. "That'll be ten dollars, boys," she said.

I said, "I left my change on the bar, Jeanie. Why don't you take the ten out of that, and keep the rest for yourself?"

That got another little nudge from her hip. It felt like getting prodded by a skeleton. "You need to come around more often," she said. Then she left us alone.

Billy helped himself to a beer.

"What are you trying to tell me, Billy?"

"Just letting you know what the score is up here, Fuzz. I don't want you stumbling blindly into a hornets' nest."

I had little desire for getting into a deep discussion on racism in America, so I changed the subject. "Did you know Katie Couture?"

He nodded his head slowly. "I knew of her." He took a swig of beer. Lightly burped. "I ain't much of a church goer, though. So, we didn't run in the same circles."

"What was your general impression of her?"

"Impression? She was hot." He let out another of his jolly, old' elf laughs. "That I can say for a fact. Everything else is just hearsay."

Hearsay? He was starting to sound like a lawyer. I couldn't have that. "Ok, I've seen the pictures. Agreed, she was hot. What about this hearsay?"

He took another swallow of beer, and wiped his mustache with the back of his hand. "Bad girl, gone good. Is the short version. Depending on who you ask, there might be more to the story."

I took a beer from the bucket. It was so cold that my skin was sticky against the neck of the bottle. "Ok, who's telling more of the story? Natives or whites?"

"Now you're jumping to conclusions," he said. "It ain't

based on skin color. This is a small town. It's filled with gossips. Sit at any dinner table and you'll hear enough stories to fill a season of soap operas. Most of the town, either Native or White, thought highly of Sister. But there were some, who could not look beyond her past. All that three babies out of wedlock stuff." He shook his head. "Now them kids are without a mama. I wonder how those folks feel about it now?"

Most of those people would never think of taking things so far as murder. Hell, most of them wouldn't have the courage to voice their opinions to Katie's face or in mixed company. But I'd need to know, which of them did have the courage to bring their opinions out away from the dinner table. One of them could be the answer to freeing Gary Pressley. "Yeah, so you got any names of those people who couldn't let go of Katie's past?"

Billy nodded in the direction of the bar. "Mr. Trong over there would be one of them. Hell, he got pretty publicly ugly about Katie, when she threw her hat into the ring for a spot on the school board."

I tried to imagine anyone in Myrtle Beach getting ugly with someone for trying to get in on the school board. For all I knew it was made up of volunteers, but I reminded myself Fort Covington was a small town. And small-town politics was probably ripe fodder for the small-town gossip. "You said he got ugly? In what way?"

"Oh, not ugly in a threatening way. It ain't like I think he had anything to do with her murder. He just wrote into the Telegram, that's the Malone newspaper, and said a lot of nasty things. Promiscuous behavior. Not suitable for a position that was all about kids. That kind of stuff."

"And no one defended Katie based on all she's done for kids and others since she turned her life around?"

"Oh sure," he shook his head laughing. "Hell, the Telegram's web forums turned into a civil war. Mostly, Mr.

Trong versus the rest of Franklin County. But I guess he had a handful of folks in his corner."

"So, did she win?"

"The election? They ain't even voted yet. She got herself killed before the election. I think it's sometime next month."

That got my attention. Politics was up there with love and money as a prime motive for murder. "You don't think she was killed for political reasons, do you?"

He stared at me for a few seconds, as if I could read the answer on his face.

I grew impatient. "What?"

"I don't think that homeless kid had any political motivations," he said.

I drank some beer, because I had to have something to do while I figured my next line of questioning. "What about Pressley? Did you know him?"

"Sure," he said. "Everyone knows poor Gary. He's even stayed at my place a night or two."

"And you think he's capable of killing Katie Couture."

Billy raised his bottle. Only a quarter of an inch of liquid resided in the bottom of it. He swirled it around. "You see this stuff? God's honest truth? You put enough of this stuff in anyone, or God forbid the hard stuff... anyone's capable of murder."

I remembered a verse from a Drive-by Truckers' song that preached it is never the bottle's fault. It simply removed barriers from doing what's truly in your heart. If Billy Howe was right, what did that say about the average man's heart?

"When you heard he was being charged were you surprised?"

He nodded. "Never would have thought of it, until it came over the scanner. Gary was about the sweetest boy I've ever met. And he was sweet on Katie."

"Like he had a crush or something?"

"I don't know about all that," he said. He cashed the last swallow of his beer, and reached into the bucket, and grabbed a handful of ice. He tossed the ice in his mouth, and began crunching the ice between his teeth. Between bites he said, "I'm not sure a crush is the same thing for Gary, as it is for you and me. Katie took care of Gary, almost like a little brother. Gary looked up to her like she was a big sister. That kind of thing."

"You said it came over the scanner. What did you mean by that?" I said.

"Police scanner. Every house in Franklin County has one."

They were nosy gossips, at that. "So, everyone knew Gary Pressley found the body and was arrested, before it even hit the news."

His mustache rose up his cheeks again. "Or Facebook."

Billy's eyes followed something over my shoulder.

I turned to see Trong walking past the bar with Patty Pill-popper obediently following behind. He could have easily ducked into the hallway where the restrooms were and exited more quickly. I suspected he wanted us, more precisely me, to see him leave.

"I probably need to talk to him," I said.

Billy nodded, but said, "Not tonight."

I wasn't sure why he said that, but for some reason I agreed with him. It may have had something to do with the bucket of watery beer that still had to be attended to.

As Trong exited, Stefanie Charles replaced him in the entryway. I turned to grab a beer in hopes that maybe she wouldn't recognize me from behind, but I caught her smile of recognition in my peripheral vision as I was turning my back to her.

Seconds later, her icy, wrinkled hands were over my eyes. The smell of nicotine on them was nauseating. "Guess who?"

"Oh, I don't know. The Matron Saint of the Traveler's Rest."

She removed her hands, and play-smacked my shoulder. "Matron Saint, I'll have to remember that!"

I kept my eyes on Billy, as I took a pull from my beer.

His eyes were lit with mischief. "Hey Stefanie, long time, no see. Why don't you join us?"

It was the kind of crap my best friend, Jimmy Alou, would pull.

She slid into a chair beside me. It felt like she ran her entire body down me in order to do so. She draped an arm over my shoulder. "What wrong with this one?" She asked Billy.

"Oh, he's all right. Probably just the end of a long day. Huh, Fuzzy."

All of her touching was making my skin crawl.

I leaned away from her. "I just need a little personal space," I said.

"Whoa, excuse me."

But her arm remained hanging from my shoulder.

Billy stood up, "Y'all obviously have some catching up to do. So, I'm gonna use the little boys' room."

I stared at him in such a way that I hope he felt the stab of it in his own eyes. "Thanks, Billy," I said dripping with sarcasm.

When he stepped away, Stefanie tapped me on my shoulder. With the wide smile, and the heavy make-up she looked like a side show from the circus. "Why don't you feed some coins in the jukebox. There's some space over there. I feel like dancing."

"I don't dance," I said.

"Boy, you really know how to show a girl a good time," she said. "Why'd you invite me out, if you didn't want the company?"

I marveled at the fantasy world in which she lived. I invited her? That was rich.

Still she was draped over me like one of the girls at the club where Veronica worked. It was acceptable, even desired, behavior there. Here? It was borderline sexual assault. I decided to focus on my work. I pulled two beers out of the bucket. Twisted the tops off both of them, handed one to Stefanie, and took a drink from the other.

"Now we're talkin'" she said. "But I hope there's more than the one bucket in our future."

"Yeah, well we'll see," I said.

And with that, her arm dropped from me.

She looked like she was giving up on me, but before she could do that, I asked, "Stefanie, you know why Jo Jo brought me up here, right?"

She nodded, "Sure." The dumb look was replaced with, well, another dumb look. This one included a smile. "But that doesn't mean we can't have some fun after hours. Does it?"

I tried to keep her on point, "What did you know about Katie Couture?"

She leaned back in her chair, crossed her arms under her gravity defying breasts, and allowed the corners of her mouth to drop. The frown etched deep, parenthetic burrows on either side of her mouth. It occurred to me that she had taken on the look of a chimpanzee. I would never be able to get that thought out of my head now. Whatever chances Stefanie Charles had thought she had with me disappeared. There was no way I was ending up in bed with someone that looked like an extra from Planet of the Apes. Not even for the job.

"She was a bitch."

That brought me out of it like the smack of a cold, wet towel to the face. It seemed I was finding as many people who disliked the good Sister, as who liked her. That was a good thing for the purposes of my case. "In what way?" I said. "I thought she was pretty well thought of?"

"Oh, she was by the idiots who live around here. But a leopard never really changes its spots. Once a whore, always a whore."

I had to keep her talking, so I decided not to argue that bitch and whore were not necessarily synonymous.

"I assume you don't mean 'whore' literally."

Her arms seemed to tighten their hold on her chest. "I don't know that she ever took money for it, but she should have. She would have made a fortune with all the sleeping around she did."

It wasn't really any new information. The only thing new was I was getting the picture of a small town that didn't have as short of a memory as I had been led to believe by my client. "But that was in the past," I said. "All the sleeping around, she put that behind her. Right?"

She scoffed. She held out one hand palm open. "Leopard." Held out the other. "Spots."

"I think she cleaned up her act for a while. And she never got to fuckin' around as much as she had before, but there were rumors that she kind of slid back into her old ways after Beau died."

"Who was Beau," I asked.

Her eyes dilated, and the whites set against her jet-black mascara were frightening. This was one ape you didn't want to catch in a dark alley. "Her son. The middle kid. I can't believe Jo Jo didn't fill you in on this."

Neither could I. "How did he die?"

"Kidney failure," she said. "I guess he was born with some issue they never detected. I didn't like the bitch, but I'd never wish something like that on any mother. I could almost understand her going back to her old ways."

I remembered what Jo Jo said about the possible drug

use and the sleeping around in Katie's past. I couldn't imagine her returning to the weed, but I figured it best to ask. "You keep mentioning her old ways. What do you mean?"

"The philandering," she said.

"Philandering? That's a might fancy word for a country girl like you."

That got a sticky, mascara wink from her, and a little chuckle. "That it is."

"So, any idea, who she was doing all of this philandering with?"

"Not a one," she said.

She said it with confidence, and no shifty eyes. I had to believe she was telling the truth. "Seems in a town like this word would get out on something like that."

"Yep, and that's why she was making all of those trips across the border."

"You think she was having a fling with a Canadian?"

She flashed her Simian smile. "Maybe not just one." She took a baby sip of beer, crinkled her nose, and wagged the neck of the bottle at me. "That's the thing. Why else would a holy roller like her be making all of those trips to Canada all of a sudden? She thought she was keeping her slutty ways hidden from us, but some of us, who aren't idiots, saw right through it."

If I spent even a few minutes on it, I could probably come up with half a dozen reasons Katie Couture may have been traveling to Canada, but I didn't argue the point. Stefanie's tongue had loosened, and I didn't want to risk her tying it up in a knot.

"What about Gary Pressley? Do you know him?"

Her chin bobbed sporadically in the affirmative. "I think she was fuckin' around with him, too."

That seemed like more predatory behavior than anyone

had led me to believe about Sister Katie. "You think Gary and Sister were having an affair?"

"Stop with the Sister shit, will you? She wasn't no real nun. No, I don't think they were fuckin'. But I think she was toying' with him. So as maybe he thought there might be a possibility, eh?"

"Why do you say that?"

She placed her bottle down on the table with such authority, that the tabletop rattled. As she leaned into me, I could smell the stale cigarette smoke in her hair, and in her breath, as she spoke. "That's a sweet boy, but he's got a weak mind. About the same time, she started making' them trips to Canada, she also took up with the kid."

"She took no interest in him before that?"

"I didn't say that. I didn't like the bitch. I think she was fake, but I ain't denying she helped people, and Gary was no different. But you really started seeing them together, after she started tramping again."

I could see anger pooling in her eyes. I took the time, and drank down half a bottle of beer. I kept my eyes on hers feigning interest. When I saw the fury subside, I continued, "What did you think, when you heard that she'd been killed, and they had taken Gary in for it?"

She tilted back again. "I didn't believe it at first. Don't get me wrong, I could see someone killing Katie. I just couldn't see Gary doing it. I know the homeless have got a lot of problems, but Gary is just such a sweet soul." She took a swallow of beer. Her cheeks puckered, as if she was holding the beer in her mouth until she could work out whatever thought she held in her mind.

I nudged her along. "So, you don't think Gary had anything to do with Katie's death."

Her throat swelled and contracted, as she swallowed the

beer. "That was my first thought, but I tell you, if that snake got her fangs into him, I think it's possible."

I decided I had subjected Stefanie to enough interrogation. I shifted the discussion to a more interesting topic for her. Herself.

She'd lived in Fort Covington all her life, and she had some years in High School that could have come right out of Katie Couture's biography, though she'd never gotten pregnant. Or never had a kid, there was a pause and some inward looking when she was sharing this.

I suspected there may have been a terminated pregnancy somewhere in her past. That wasn't the kind of light discussion I was aiming for, so I quickly moved us along to breezier topics, like how things were going really well for Stefanie when she worked at the slipper factory and earned twelve dollars per hour.

"That was good money back then, eh?" But about fifteen years ago, all of the industry shut down, including the slipper factory. All that was left were government jobs or government assistance. She felt really lucky to have landed the job at the Traveler's Rest two years ago, because it got her "off the government's tit."

Sometime during the life story of Stefanie Charles, I realized that Billy had never come back from his trip to the men's room. I looked over my shoulder and I saw him sitting at the spot we had abandoned at the bar.

The bastard had stranded me.

12

Around midnight, I prized myself away from Stefanie Charles. It took the purchase of another bucket of beer, and the promise that some other night, when I wasn't so tired from travel, I would take her up on her offer of heading back to her place. When I stepped out of the Legion, a fresh blast of icy cold air greeted me. The night air was actually calm and silent. The sting of the cold felt like a blast. Steam formed from my breath, and it felt as if the tears in my eyes were freezing solid.

The parking lot was half as full as it had been when I arrived.

I made my way quickly to the Nova. As I fished in my pockets for the keys, the door to the Legion slammed shut behind me. Almost on cue, tires crushed the gravel and high beam headlight poured over me, blinding me. Footsteps of more than one person, hurried towards me from behind.

I heard the swish of something slicing through the cold air, and what felt like a 2x4 slammed into the back of my knees. My legs fell out from under me, and I collapsed face first into the crushed stone of the parking lot. Shards of stone gouged my cheek. My hand went to my face and came away wet with sticky blood.

Car doors slammed.

If I wasn't so scared, I'd be pissed off. I pulled myself up to my knees and looked into the blinding light.

It silhouetted two well-built figures in the light. They swaggered like the cowboys in the old spaghetti Westerns.

I did the math. The two of them put the odds at four to one, at least. Those weren't fighting odds, but my anger was replacing my fear. I tried the extra push to climb to my feet.

Again, with the swish.

Again, with the crack of the cudgel. This time hitting me between the shoulder blades.

Again, with me face down in the gravel.

"City boy, you will have to learn to watch your back," a voice said from in front of me.

A leather cowboy boot with a steel-capped toe, which captured the moonlight, stopped inches from my face. The voice came from above me now, "And you need to take to mind who you associate with. Bigtree, ain't the kind of guy, that a guy like you need to be working with. I suggest you head on back to the city."

I didn't know what he was talking about with the city comments. My head was swimming with the beating I was taking. All I could think to do was fight back. I gathered up some stones in my hand and wrapped my fist around them.

The man with the cowboy boots squatted down in front of me.

I tried to look up into his face, but the piercing light made identifying any features impossible.

"Boy..."

I hurled the punch from way down at my hip as hard as I could toward his face. The stones in my hand delivered the blow with such force that when I connected with the side of his jaw, it sounded like a hammer driving home the nail.

I heard something land in the lot in front of me. "Stop calling me 'boy' and stop trying to order me around!"

The sound of my voice blocked the swish sound this time. I only heard a crack like the ball on the bat, and my universe went black, like a dreamless sleep.

13

The smell of cigarette smoke and bargain brand perfume brought me back to consciousness. The concerned look on Stefanie Charles's monkey face almost dropped me back into a coma.

The deep, calming voice of Jo Jo Bigtree kept me comfortably conscious in this world. "Fuzzy, just stay right there. Give yourself a minute to get your bearings. There is no telling how long you have been out like that."

Stefanie's meek voice seemed to come from a football field away, "He left around midnight, I found him at closing time. So, it's been a little over two hours. I'd say."

Her face was splitting in two now, and I felt as if I was trying to get to sleep after a night of heavy drinking. The entire world was spinning out of control around me. I closed my eyes to keep myself steady in the vortex.

"Whoa, Whoa, Whoa," his voice wasn't as calming now. "Stay with us Fuzzy. Do not close your eyes."

I opened my eyes, and shifted my look to Jo Jo. He crouched like my assailant, and even wore boots like his, only half again the size. I had half a mind to punch him, too. But

Jo Jo's image blurred, and I snapped, "I'm not going' anywhere, Jo Jo, I'm trying to clear my mind and figure out what the fuck you have gotten me into." The act of speaking agitated a flap of tongue flesh. A product of my beating, no doubt.

"Fuzzy, my man, what are you talking about? I am here to help."

"What am I talking about?" I shouted. "I'm talking about coming up here to help you ask questions. That's it. That's all it was supposed to be. First night in town, I'm assaulted like I've gotten myself into some deep shit."

Even in my foggy double vision, I saw Jo Jo's lips purse and deep burrows form in his forehead. Little pearls of fatty flesh formed in the creases. The little balls started to bounce around, and I had to look away to steady myself. I focused on the pale, yellow light of a street lamp in the distance.

Jo Jo's voice came like voice-over in a film. It sounded like James Earl Jones providing narration.

"This was not a run of the mill bar fight?"

I maintained eye contact with the streetlight, and opened my mouth to answer, but a wave a nausea hit me, and I clamped shut to keep from spilling my guts. I simply shook my head.

"Did you see anyone follow Fuzzy out of the bar, Stefanie?"

Her far away voice answered, "I'm a little shit-faced, Jo."

"So that is a no," he said.

"They called me a city boy, and told me to head out, and back to the city. Where did they get I was a city boy? I'm from freakin' Myrtle Beach."

"Fuzzy. This town is lucky if it has one thousand folks living here. Plattsburgh is the big city to these people."

"Where's Plattsburgh," I asked.

He laughed. "Exactly."

"So, you don't think you just pissed off someone in the bar?"

My vision steadied. The compulsion to vomit disappeared. I risked looking up into Jo Jo's face.

He had the emotionless face I expected.

I found it comforting. "I didn't piss off anyone in there, Jo Jo. Somebody was trying to send a message. I don't think they want me," I corrected myself. "I don't think they want us working together on this Katie Couture thing."

Jo Jo's hand went to his chin, as he mulled that over. While he did that, I risked a look around to take in the surroundings. The Nova, Jo Jo's truck, and a beat-up Volkswagen Jetta were all that was left in the parking lot. I'm a private investigator. So even in my beat-up state, I deduced that the Jetta was Stefanie Charles's car. I settled on a shadow mass that rested underneath my car. I crawled on all fours, against Jo Jo's protest, and reached below the Nova. My hand settled on smooth, polished wood. I withdrew it from its hiding place and brought it up for closer inspection.

I held a curved piece of dark wood about the thickness of a baseball bat handle. One end of it was splintered. The other side ended in a spherical knob of the same carved dark timber.

"Traditional Mohawk war club," Jo Jo said with wonder in his voice.

14

Before sunrise I awoke in the nasty bed at the Traveler's Rest from a terrible nightmare in which I was being chased by Sister Katie Couture, wearing nothing but her slip and a nun's habit. She waved a Mohawk war club, like the one they had beaten me with, through a labyrinthine basement. I stayed just ahead of her until Gary Pressley stepped out into my path. Then I awakened.

My face dripped sweat, and when I wiped it away the stubble on my face was coarse like sandpaper.

I stepped to the vanity which stood on steel legs in front of a mirror that had a crack that ran from the top right corner all the way across to the bottom left corner. The thought of the mirror folding in half and falling on top of me as I leaned over the sink to wash my face was discomforting. I turned on the faucet to get some hot water running for my shave. It spat brown rusty water for half a minute, but once it was through coughing out globs of the silty stuff, the water that followed seemed to be clear. I built up a good lather with a bar of soap and coated my face. As I did that, I had a vision of the crime scene. In it, Sister Katie Couture slouched in the chair, dead. Behind her, leaning against the wall was what looked like half of a wooden broom handle. Katie's ankle obscured the end of the stick, where it met the floor.

I quickly finished my shave and called Jo Jo.

He answered after five rings.

"Jo Jo, meet at your office in the thirty minutes. We need to look at those crime scene photos and maybe any evidence logs from the County."

"Hey, slow down there, partner. What time is it?"

The old digital clock on the bedside table was flashing 12:00 in bright red letters. I took a peek at the time on my phone. It was 6:15.

"Fuzzy, it has been less than four hours since I dropped you off. I have had less than three hours' sleep, and after the night you had you could sure use the rest. And remember, we are supposed to take you to the hospital this morning to have that gash on your tongue looked at."

The reminder put a fresh metallic taste in my mouth and made me painfully aware of the flap of flesh where I had nearly bitten through my tongue.

"Jo Jo, I remembered something that could be important. I need to see the pictures or this will drive me crazy. Trust me, I won't be getting any rest until I put this out of my head."

"What is it?"

"Just meet me at your office. If I see what I think I'm going to see in the pictures, it could be important. If I don't, we'll just forget about it, so you won't question my sanity."

There was a prolonged silence from his side of the line.

I could feel blood rushing through the veins and arteries near my temples. My breath was coming fast as if I'd just completed running a wind sprint. "Jo Jo, just meet me there. We'll look, then I'll buy you breakfast at the Howlin' Wolf."

"You can buy yourself breakfast there. I will not eat that shit," he said, but added, "Make it forty-five minutes, I need to take a shower."

15

—————

Forty minutes later, layered in long underwear, flannel shirt, jeans, and my too light coat, I sat in the Nova in the unlit lot behind the Howlin' Wolf. It was the only car among the imposing shadows cast by three tractor trailers. Upfront the restaurant had a few snow-capped cars parked for an early morning breakfast. Despite the cold, I had the window down for the fresh air. The chill against my face helped keep me awake. Despite the initial adrenaline rush caused by my vision of the crime scene, staying awake was becoming more difficult with each passing minute.

Just as I nodded off, I jolted awake to the rumbling engine of Jo Jo's truck. He pulled in right beside me. It was 7 a.m. He was right on time.

He hopped out of the cab, and was at my door, while I was still rubbing sleep out of my eyes. He wore a heavy, black coat with a fur fringed hood pulled over his head cloaking most of his face in shadow. His dark eyes peered out like a possum's. "Fuzzy, you look like shit. I told you to get some rest."

"Yeah, Yeah, Yeah, just help me out of here. Will you?"

Jo Jo wore jeans so tight they looked stitched in place around his thighs. His coat looked on the verge of popping buttons. It occurred to me that it may be difficult for him to find a good fit. He grunted for effect as he yanked me by the arm up out of the car seat. "I am getting too old for this shit, Fuzz."

Yeah. Yeah. Yeah. I got beaten by a club a few hours ago. Tell me about too old. I gripped his forearm and let him do all the work of hoisting me to my feet.

He escorted me up the stairs into his office, and we took our spots at his desk again. He reached into a drawer in his desk. "So, what is this about wanting to look at the pictures again."

"I might be imagining things. I probably have a concussion, but I think there's something I missed in those crime scene photos. That club reminded me of it."

He looked at me cross-eyed, as if I were speaking a foreign language. He withdrew the manila envelope from the drawer and tossed it across the desk. He removed his coat, and rubbed warmth into his hands, and waited for me to do my search.

Inside the envelope, the sheaf of photos was about half an inch thick. I removed them and fanned through them looking for the shot I'd seen in my vision. I found three shots that would work, all of them showed the stick leaning up against the wall. One of them was the one Jo Jo shared with me the previous day. In the photo, Katie's ankle hid the end of the rod just like I had seen in my mind's eye. Another one photo was even worse. I could see only the handle of the stick over Katie's shoulder. The third picture showed what I had feared. The carved knob end of the club resting at the wall's baseboard. I couldn't be sure it was the same club used to bludgeon me, but there was no doubting it was a Mohawk club of similar craft.

I slowly slid the glossy across to Jo Jo. "Did you not catch this on the evidence list," I asked.

JoJo frowned. He scanned the photo as if he were skimming the morning paper. Then he abruptly halted. His eyes widened. He started to speak, then stopped to look again. He got up and walked back to his filing cabinets on the back wall of the room. He found a folder he was looking for almost immediately. He stood back there flipping through pages. He extracted a pale green sheet and scanned it like he had the crime scene photo. He didn't screech to a halt like he had with the picture. But he got to the end and shook his head. He silently mouthed, "What the fuck?"

"I take it that war club isn't showing in the evidence log."

He shook his head. "Probably an oversight."

"Maybe not," I said. "How common are those clubs?"

"Not all that common. I can think of only two people, who would have one."

"You didn't think to mention that last night, when we found part of one at the scene of my beating?"

"Fuzzy, you were half out of it. By the time we got you into the car and drove you home, you were knocked out again."

"Right," I said. "And I'm sure you were going to jump right on determining whose club that was first thing this morning."

Jo Jo does not have the most expressive of faces, but I saw hurt register there. "Fuzzy..."

I cut him off, "Jo Jo, you brought me up here. I got the shit kicked out of me last night. I will expect you on my side on this, because we're friends, and because I'm working for you. This isn't the time to protect the tribe."

He strode toward me and dropped in his chair. The floor sagged with the force of him. He splayed his hands across his desk blotter. "Listen Fuzzy. I do not know what poison those numb nuts over at the Legion have been pumping you full of, but I will not turn a blind eye to bad stuff done by Natives. For all I know, a Native may be behind Sister Katie Couture's death. Yet, I am working to free a white man, because I believe he is wrongfully charged. Those are the facts. Whatever, those folks at the Legion will have you believe. Remember that I am working for free to help a white man."

I remembered making the same observation myself last night. I was ashamed and didn't know how to explain myself out of this one. So, I stuck with, "Sorry, Jo Jo."

The top of his head tilted ever so slightly forward. I took it for forgiveness because that was all I got from him.

"So how did it go with Pressley yesterday," he asked.

"Not so fast," I said. "You mentioned two people that may have one of those clubs."

He tapped his fingers on the ink blotter. "Right, and I'm moving Matteo Garrow to the top of the list I will visit today."

"And I'm going with you," I said.

He frowned at that, or maybe not, it was hard to tell with him. "Garrow is Native, Fuzzy. Remember our plan? I work the Rez, you take the rest."

"Jo Jo, someone who owns one of those clubs knocked me silly last night. I'm coming with you."

"Fuzzy, last night when you were talking salad on the ride home, you said you didn't think the guy you encountered was Native."

"There were at least four of them Jo Jo. Only one spoke, and you're right. I don't think he sounded Native. But you said there were two you could think of that might own one of those clubs. Who is number two?"

Jo Jo's hand went to his chin and scratched at the stubble he hadn't gotten around to scraping off his face yet. I noticed there was some gray there. I also noticed faint wrinkle lines radiating from the corners of his eyes.

We weren't 21-year-old kids anymore.

"Dave Hetfield," he said. "He is not Native."

"Good," I said. "So, you get to come along when I see Hetfield. I come with you to visit Garrow"

"Fuck, Hetfield," he said, as he got to his feet.

I could almost hear his chair breathe a sigh of relief.

"I'll let you buy me that breakfast downstairs, and then we'll go see Matteo."

"I thought you didn't want to eat at the Clan."

He fished his keys out of his pocket and waved me to the door. "It is shit, but it is better than fast food, the only other places open at this hour. We have to wait at least until sunrise until we visit Matteo. We may as well eat because we still have an hour to burn."

16

We sat in a booth with cracked vinyl seats and a Formica table against the windows of the restaurant. I had a heavy breakfast of fried eggs and venison sausage and toast. It helped clear my head of the cobwebs placed there by last night's beating.

Jo Jo had a cup of oatmeal that looked like a pile of bird shit.

We spoke little of the night before, or the weapon missing from the evidence report in the murder of Katie Couture, or what we would ask Matteo Garrow. In fact, we ate in silence, except for an occasional grunt of disgust from Jo Jo when he had another spoonful of his porridge.

The only other patrons were an elderly couple in from Fort Covington or Massena for an early breakfast. He had about 40 years on me, but had less gray in his hair, which was slicked back and held in place by some viscous material like Brylcreem that probably had to be special ordered these days. She was a little younger than him. Her short white hair was stylishly done. She wore a white sweater embroidered with lavender flowers. Three decades ago she had probably won beauty pageants at the local fairs. He was animated in telling some story, punctuating key points with exaggerated gestures. Each one seemed to test the limits of the buttons of the flannel shirt stretched tightly on his enormous girth. I could see him as a young athlete before he went soft. She nodded at each chop of his hand, not really paying any attention to his rant. Instead, she set about stacking the used plates and silverware neatly on one corner of the table. I'm sure the waitress or busboy would appreciate the effort. Watching them I wondered if I glimpsed my distant future with Veronica.

Easy boy. We haven't even talked marriage yet. And I was in no hurry.

Outside, the morning sun painted the gray canvas of the morning sky with its plums and pinks and oranges. Jo Jo stood and nodded his head.

I dropped a twenty on the table for the check and tip and followed Jo Jo to his truck.

I STILL HADN'T ACCUSTOMED myself to the cold, and my fingertips, toes, and cheeks were chilled numb, a few minutes later when Jo Jo pulled us into a gravel lot in front of an A-framed building with white, vinyl siding and a rust-colored, painted metal roof. There was a sign, shaped like some medieval crest, beside a door painted to match the roof. The sign read, "Akwesasne Tribal Police."

Jo Jo must have read surprise on my face. He clapped me on the shoulder. "I did not tell you that Mr. Garrow was Chief of the Mohawk police."

I thought of the Mohawk War Club leaning against the wall less than ten feet from Katie Couture's limp, lifeless body. Muscles in my face tightened, and I could feel blood rush to my forehead. My cheeks were no longer numb. "No, you didn't, Jo Jo. Any reason for that?"

He cracked what passed for a smile for him. "Just never crossed my mind."

"You don't think Matteo had anything to do with keeping that club off the evidence list, do you?"

"Nope," he said.

When he volunteered nothing else I pushed him to continue. "C'mon Jo Jo. Don't leave me in the dark here. Is this Indian corrupt?"

"I do not think this American is any more corrupt than your average policeman, Fuzzy. He is tribal police. He was not there when they worked the scene. He could not be. State Police worked the scene out of Malone."

"Do you think he knows anything about how this club was at the scene of the crime and found lying beside my crushed skull?"

He opened the door to his cab, and jumped down, icy snow crunching under his boots. He looked back in at me. "That is what we will ask him. Come on."

I got out of the truck and followed behind him. "Wait a minute, Jo Jo. How are we going to play this?"

He continued to the front door, when he placed his hand on the ice-glazed knob, he stopped and said, "There is no play. I talk. You listen."

Great.

THE INTERIOR of the tribal offices looked like a large modular home. The faded blue carpet was the indoor/outdoor stuff you'd pick up at one of the big box hardware stores. The walls were trailer grade wood paneling, and the ceilings were cheap lay-in tiles spotted with coffee-colored water stains. There was no receptionist. No lobby. Just an open room, the living room of the modular design, that housed four metal legged desks with vinyl-covered desktops. They reminded me of the fold-out card table my mom and dad would haul out when friends came over to play penny poker. Either side of the main room fed corridors, no doubt ending in bedrooms which served as private offices. The corridor to the left was dark. Flickering fluorescent lights illuminated the one to the right. It brought a twitch to my eye.

As the door settled back in place behind Jo Jo and I, a figure spat out of the flashing corridor. He was the anti-thesis of Jo JoBigtree. If Jo Jo was the FBI, he was the FLI — Fucking Little Indian. He was short, maybe five-four, and built delicately, like a Native American elf. His nose was thin and pointed. His striking green eyes gleamed like peridot gem stones. Eyes like that deserved a smile to match, but a non-expressive face was one thing he shared with Jo Jo. He wore a crisp, dark brown uniform, with a polished black belt, which held a holster like you'd see in an old Western movie. The holster held a six-shooter that was a little more modern than what you'd see in the Old West.

Matteo Garrow appeared to be the only officer inside the offices of the tribal police at that hour.

He eyed Jo Jo with something less than contempt, but greater than uncertainty. I settled on distrust.

He strode to us with military precision. Held out a hand to me, and shook mine with a one up, one down motion. "Matteo Garrow, Chief of Police."

I introduced myself, and he released my hand.

He kept his translucent green eyes on me. I wondered if he was the offspring of a Native and a non-Native. He didn't offer a hand to Jo Jo, and he didn't look to him. "Jo Jo, what brings you here at this hour?"

The floorboards chirped as Jo Jo shifted his feet.

I kept my eyes on Garrow. It was like one of those staring contests you engaged in with your hated enemy in grade school. Minutes dragged on while both of you stared deep into the other's eyes. You blink. You lose.

I'm sure it lasted a lot less time than it seemed. And he never blinked.

Jo Jo answered, "The Pressley case, Matteo."

Something like humor arrived in Garrow's eyes, and he broke the stare to look up at Jo Jo. If it had been the school-yard bully, I would have claimed victory. With Matteo Garrow, I don't think I won anything.

"Very well," he said, and held his hand out, palm up toward the closest desk. "Let's have a seat at Horse's desk."

Jo Jo and I took seats on the public side of a desk with a nameplate for Tony American Horse. Garrow swung around to Tony's side. The desktop was clear of everything except an old putty colored computer monitor and matching, bulky keyboard which looked like the one that came with the Commodore 64 I owned as a kid, the nameplate, a lone plastic white ballpoint pen with a burgundy cap, and a framed 5-x-7 photograph of a teen-aged Native American dressed uncomfortably in a tuxedo, holding a beautiful blonde, white-dressed bride on his arm. I get paid for this, so I arrived at the conclusion the boy in the picture was Tony American Horse.

There was no desk phone. Sign of the times.

Garrow broke my spell of deductive reasoning, when he said, "The Couture case is not mine, Jo Jo. You know that. It happened in the Fort. So, I am not sure how I can help you."

"I know, I know," Jo Jo said. He reached into a pocket inside his coat and removed the folded glossy. His hand trembled as he smoothed it out on the desk before us.

It was the shot that best showed the war club in the background. The crease where Jo Jo had folded the picture bifurcated Katie Couture's image. It seemed like one last indignity.

"So?" Matteo said.

I didn't like him. It was one thing to inherit the stereotype of the unemotional Native American from your ancestors. It was another to show complete indifference to a scene like Katie's. I remembered Jo Jo's insistence that I listen and let him do the talking. So, I bit back sharing my feelings.

"Look closer, Matteo," Jo Jo said.

He took the photo in his hands and studied it. After several seconds, his lips formed the word, "So", again.

But before he could speak, Jo Jo cut in with, "Back wall, Matteo."

Garrow's eyes dilated, and he slowly raised his head to look at us. He chose his words carefully. "Again, this is not my case. I am not working it. I cannot."

I felt a deep desire to reach across the desk, and take Garrow's throat in my hand, and squeeze until he felt empathy for the fate which fell upon Katie Couture. The chair felt hard against the backs of my thighs. I stood abruptly.

Jo Jo grabbed my wrist. "Matteo, the war club. Have you seen one like it before?"

Garrow looked off to his right. "Why do you come here to ask questions to which you already know the answer, Jo Jo Bigtree?"

"Matteo, I mean no disrespect, and please do not think we suggest that you are involved in any foul play. I merely want to know if you have a missing club?"

"I do not," he said, still staring off into the darkened hallway.

I was losing my patience, and stepped back from the desk, breaking free of the grip Jo Jo had on my wrist. I turned my back to the two Native Americans and watched out the window as a lonesome sparrow dug in the snow for buried seed.

I watched it for over a minute. It pecked little holes in the icy surface of the snow, and when it covered the immediate area in front with these tiny punctures, it used the top surface of its beak to push the loose snow forward into a miniature pile of snow. The beak was a poor substitute for a bulldozer, but my little friend stubbornly pushed away enough that I could see a small, lifeless patch of brown earth. The sparrow nosed around in the dead grass and, eventually it came up with something in its beak.

Its survival counted on it finding food, there was no other way. I thought of Jo Jo and Matteo talking circles around the weapon found at the scene of Katie Couture's murder. I tried to imagine this sparrow flying circles around a snow-filled landscape, not willing to drop and do the work for a meal despite its survival depending upon it.

I would survive my visit to the tundra. Of that I was certain. But I realized that if I was to get anywhere in determining who assaulted me, and by extension the case to clear Gary Pressley, I would have to dig my own way. Just like that sparrow because this was personal now.

I turned to face them. Matteo was mumbling something to Jo Jo between clenched teeth. He looked like a bad ventriloquist.

I marched purposefully back to the desk, dropped both fists, knuckles down, on its surface and leaned all my weight forward on them. I could feel the vinyl give under the pressure. "Dave Hetfield," I said as if no further explanation was needed.

Garrow leaned back in his chair. His mouth was still a sharp, non-expressive slit in his face, but his eyes found mine. I saw amusement there.

I felt the floor sag with Jo Jo's shifting weight beside me.

"What about him," Matteo Garrow asked.

My fingernails dug into the heels of my hands, and my knuckles felt as if they were being ground to dust as I pressed harder against the desktop. I breathed in deeply and spoke as calmly as I could muster. "Could he have a war club like this?" The words came out dripping in venom.

Garrow was back to the "don't blink" game. "I would suspect that is a question for Mr. Hetfield."

I concentrated on the in and out of my breath. The way my chest expanded and deflated. It was a trick my Uncle Rod taught me to control my impulses and my anger. Something he was forever trying to get me to control. Plus, I think he liked to share all the Buddhist shit he learned from some meditation sessions he took in the basement of the Catholic Church, of all places. Same place, different night, where they had the Alcoholics Anonymous meetings. The thought of my Uncle Rod's sage advice brought a smile to my face.

And a concerned look to Garrow's face.

It must have been as if looking into the face of the mentally deranged. Batman realizing that the smile forming on the Joker's face was not one to bring reassurance. It was a message. A dangerous one.

I concentrated on keeping that smirk firmly in place. Pushed myself back from his desk. The impression of my fists stamped in relief on the desk's black vinyl upholstery. I could feel the muscles go slack in my shoulders and the base of my neck. I dropped in the chair and slouched back like Garrow. "I'm not talking to Hetfield. I'm here with you, Garrow. So, tell me how well do you know Hetfield?"

This time when Garrow broke his gaze and turned to look at Jo Jo, I felt I had won something. But it was fleeting.

Jo Jo laughed nervously.

Garrow returned his attention to me, but said nothing.

Jo Jo answered, "Fuzzy, Hetfield and Matteo are not exactly friends."

I kept my Joker expression in place. "Well, now that's something."

Garrow got to his feet. "Perhaps you do not know how

this works, Mr. Koella. You are in the offices of the Tribal Police. I am the Chief. You do not interrogate me. Interrogation is my job."

He was right. I hadn't shown his office or position any respect. On the flip side, he had eroded any respect I may have brought with me quickly, when he showed so little concern for Katie's murder. I had no retort.

He turned his attention to Jo Jo. "I do not know why you felt compelled to come here to ask questions about a crime scene out of my jurisdiction. I suggest you speak with the State Police about your concerns regarding the evidence in their case." He looked to the door. "And with that, gentlemen, unless you have a tribal reservation concern you need to report, I will have to take my leave of you."

Jo Jo patted me on the back. "Come on, let us go."

We walked to the door.

I could feel Garrow's serpentine eyes slithering up behind me. I turned, and he still stood behind the desk. Somehow appearing a foot taller than he actually was.

"Thank you for your time, Mr. Garrow."

He nodded.

"I trust that the assault upon me with that club." I pointed to the folded glossy that lay on the desk. "Should be reported to State Police, as well?"

He said nothing.

We stepped out into the morning cold, but the temperature felt not much different from what we had left it inside the office.

17

After we climbed into the cab of Jo Jo's truck and were safely, quietly sealed behind closed doors, Jo Jo said, "Fuzzy, I thought we agree that I would do the talking."

I didn't acknowledge his condemnation. I turned away and looked out the passenger window. The way Jo Jo's hand shook when he handed over the evidence to Matteo Garrow bothered me. When he was around Garrow, he also seemed to get the dancing feet of a fearful quarterback with the pocket closing all around him. And the coward's laugh, when I asked Garrow about his connection to Dave Hetfield? I could not believe my friend, the Fucking Big Indian, could be so afraid of a man less than half his weight, but fear was a funny thing, and it did not always manifest itself from a physical threat. I wondered what Matteo Garrow had on Jo Jo Bigtree, or what power he held in the community to illicit such fear.

Whatever it was, my friend had taken the case of a scared, helpless kid, and was collecting no fee. That trumped any suspicions I may have had.

Still, I kept my gaze on the white shroud outside my

window, as Jo Jo wheeled the truck out onto the empty pavement of State Route 37.

We managed the short drive in silence, only the hiss of the heater trying to make it through one more winter day accompanied us.

As we approached the turnoff to his office, Jo Jo asked, "Did you want to get to the hospital to get that tongue stitched up and get checked for a concussion?"

Only after he had mentioned it did I recall my torn tongue. It was numb, or I had accustomed myself to the pain. I rolled it around against the roof of my mouth. No pain, but the raw hamburger meat texture of it turned my stomach. "Back to the office," I said. "We got work to do."

NORMALLY, I hate a space with no natural light. I get enough of that at home where my only window to the world is a half-moon pane of glass inset eye-level in my door. In the summer, Jo Jo's windowless office would probably bother me to no end. In the current season, I was just fine. I needed no more visions of snow and ice.

Jo Jo continued by his desk and disappeared into the rear quarters.

I sat on my side of his desk, and rubbed my jeans, feverishly trying to coax life back into my hand. The knobby flesh of my tongue would be difficult to ignore now that Jo Jo brought it back to my attention. I scraped it against the bottom of my two front teeth. The sensation curled my toes, but like a mosquito bite you could not keep from scratching, I couldn't stop fooling with the tongue.

Jo Jo returned with two steaming mugs of coffee.

I assured him that black was fine, and we both sat with

our thoughts and sipped piping hot coffee, which I don't recommend pouring over an open wound.

On the paneled wall behind Jo Jo there were two items in cheap plastic picture frames that I had not previously noticed. One was a law degree from SUNY, the state university system of New York. The other was a faded black-and-white image of the FBI wielding a black aluminum Easton baseball bat that looked undersized in his massive hands. He was in Carolina Atlantic practice garb. His present and his past on display. I wondered if he looked upon the baseball picture with pride or sorrow. I kept my eyes on the display because I could feel Jo Jo's dark eyes boring down on me.

The damn Indians with their staring contests.

"You are one stubborn son of a bitch, Fuzzy Koella."

I raised my mug to that and dropped more scalding hot coffee on my raw tongue.

"So how did it go with Gary Pressley yesterday?"

I summarized my brief, fruitless discussion with Gary Pressley, and pointed out how he claimed to have put Katie Couture in that chair.

Jo Jo shook his head. "This is what will make this so difficult. No matter how many times I tell Gary not to talk to anyone, the kid still spouts this kind of nonsense. And the State's prosecutor just smiles and takes that shit for the gospel. Gary is digging his own grave because he knows no better."

"I came away less certain he's innocent than you seem to be," I confessed.

"Did he mention the high truck?"

My confusion must have shown on my face because he quickly explained. "When he was first brought in, he kept mentioning 'high truck'. Over and over again with 'high truck.' With enough questioning, I finally got him to add 'shadows' to 'high truck'. But that was about it. And he has not talked about it since. When I ask him about the 'high truck' I just get a blank stare. Which with Gary, admittedly, could mean nothing."

"What kind of truck? High truck could mean a lot of things."

"Beats me," he said. Jo Jo pursed his lips and clapped his hands, to let me know we were moving onto other subjects.

"Obviously, Hetfield is on the list I need you to talk to. Hell, the whole family, if you can manage it. I also would like you to talk to Sonny LaPage. He's a volunteer firefighter responsible for annual fire inspections."

"The building looks like it's been deserted for years, Jo Jo."

"I know," he said. "But we have a lot of old decrepit buildings around here, and I understand Sonny recently had a look at the library as a public safety measure. Just to be sure there was no fire danger there."

"Okay, whatever you say, Chief."

Something in the way his cheeks dropped at the word 'Chief' told me I had offended him.

Before it became an uncomfortable situation, I said, "Look, I need to get some rest, so I probably won't get around to this questioning until tomorrow…"

"We need to get you into the hospital to get looked at."

I let that pass. Jo Jo had no way of knowing how much time I'd spent in hospitals over the last two years. I was in no rush to compare the medical help in the North Country to the friendly confines of Grand Strand Medical Center.

"Do you have an Asian guy named Trong on your list of people to talk to?" I asked.

Thought lines burrowed across his wide forehead. "I do. Though he is far down the list. Why do you ask?"

"I understand he had an issue with Katie running for the school board."

"A typical internet quarrel, if you ask me." He took a long swallow of his coffee, looked into the empty mug, and set it aside. "But that is why I have him on the list."

"Ok, say, do you have a computer I can use?"

"Sure," he said. "Follow me."

He led me back to the room that had produced the coffee. The door had been removed leaving empty brass hinges. The room was only about ten by ten and was lit by a single forty-watt bulb mounted in the center of a cracked plaster ceiling. A thin, nylon cord hung from the light's ballast. Two five-foot-tall, battleship-gray filing cabinets were pushed against the opposite wall, and a heavy wooden drafting table, like you'd see in a high school drafting class before the advent of computer-aided drafting, lined the wall through which we entered. The floor was covered with linoleum tile. Umber and urine colored streaks radiated from a rusty floor drain centered in the room. But the room did not smell like piss. It smelled like dusty, old paper. Like a used bookstore. It was not an unpleasant odor.

Centered on the drafting table was a black, plastic laptop computer with a bird's nest of cables pouring out of its ass-end. They terminated somewhere underneath the table.

"It's all yours, Fuzz. We should have a good Wi-Fi connection back here. You want some privacy to check email and stuff?"

"Ah, sure."

I slid a backless metal stool out from under the table and went to work on the laptop.

I searched the Malone-Telegram's site for articles on the school board elections. First searching on the election, then on Katie Couture. The amount of coverage a school board election received at the tiny paper surprised me. Over a period of about a month, there were about forty pieces on the election or Katie. Each article had a thread of comments beneath it. Again, I was surprised at the community's activity regarding a simple school board election. Many comment threads continued for multiple pages. All of them, the subject inevitably became Katie Couture, mostly because of the efforts of a troll by the handle of WrathofTrong. Usually, a chorus of Couture supporters diluted his venom, and after about ten attempts at libel, Trong would give up.

However, the Katie hate ratcheted up in the week leading up to her death, as Trong was backed by a triumvirate of anti-Couture posters. Emboldened by his new allies Trong spewed greater and greater on Katie Couture and her promiscuous past. The Telegram deleted many of the posts, leaving only footprints behind, "This post has been removed due to subject matter inconsistent with the standards of the Malone-Telegram." A formal way of saying, removed for obscenity. The poster of these deleted comments wasn't identified, but it was easy to see by the trajectory of Trong's comments, who was the offender.

One Trong comment four days before Katie's death, caught my attention. It read:

"Our children deserved better than a diseased whore."

It caught my attention because all of Trong's posts questioned Katie's past. The language was salty, and what her past may lead to was suggestive, but Trong never seemed to suggest any dirt on her current state. I might have been reaching, but this sounded like slandering the current Couture state. I'm not sure he literally meant whore, but I wondered where he got "diseased."

I took a chance on the laptop being set up for printing and sent a copy off of the thread of comments that culminated in the "diseased whore" declaration.

The hum of a laser printer kicked on from the darkened room across from the doorway of the room I was working. I collected my printout by following the printer's dim green light, bashing my shin against some unseen piece of furniture.

When I turned, Jo Jo's massive silhouette filled the doorway. "What do you have there, Fuzzy?"

He stepped aside to let me squeeze past him. "Probably nothing," I said. "Did you read through all the postings on the Telegram site?"

"There is only so much of that stuff a man can take, Fuzzy. And after a while it is all the same, anyway."

I nodded in the direction of the desk. "I agree," I said. "But let me show you something."

I headed back into the front room. He followed behind me. A wave effect rippled out from his footfalls as the sub-floor boards sagged beneath his weight.

"Is there any other funny evidence regarding Katie Couture that you need to share with me?" I said over my shoulder.

I felt him stop behind me.

It had been a throwaway question. The kind you have to ask but don't expect a helpful answer from. But then maybe I should have expected this reaction. We already had the picture with the war club in it.

Jo Jo continued by me and stood before his chair. "What do you have there?"

I let him have his secret. Walked around the desk and had a seat on my side. Dropped the six-page printout in front of him. "This discussion got a little different," I said.

Jo Jo picked up the sheet and flipped through them, scanning quickly. If anything jumped out at him, he was good at not showing his cards. "So," he said.

Matteo Garrow had used that word when he saw the picture of Katie Couture's crime scene. It disturbed me when used by Jo Jo.

He tossed the stack of printouts back on the desk. "Looks like the same old shit."

I leaned forward and slid loose the last sheet. "Obviously, WrathofTrong is our Asian Mr. Trong."

"Right, Derry Trong. That is why he is on my list. He is obviously a sicker fuck than I have ever given him credit for," Jo Jo said. "But I do not think it makes him a suspect. Or even someone we even need to move to the top of the list for questioning."

"Why does he call Katie Couture a 'diseased whore', Jo Jo?"

I noticed a slight tremble in his hand as he studied the page.

I wondered if he was struggling with high blood pressure, or if he was just an overly anxious person. His hands had shaken at Garrow's place, too. Hopefully, he wasn't on some pharmaceuticals that gave him the shakes. A drug dealer I know said he stayed away from meth because he couldn't handle all the nervous ticks and shakes the customers showed up with.

Jo Jo's hand settled, but he remained silent.

"Jo Jo, did anything come up in Katie's autopsy?" I said.

I could tell by the inward look of his eyes something had.

"Was Katie HIV positive from her promiscuous past?" I asked.

He turned his head to not look me in the eyes, when he answered, "She had chlamydia."

"Chlamydia? After all this time? Doesn't it cause major complications for women if left untreated?"

He stood and spoke to the pictures on the wall. "It was a recent bout of it."

Even I felt let down by the revelation, and I'd never known the woman. "So," I said. "Katie Couture wasn't as lily white as everyone believed her to be."

"It does not appear so," Jo Jo said in a flat, monotonous voice.

"Jo Jo, we need to move Derry Trong to the top of the list."

He stopped himself before saying something, then slid his hands into the back pockets of his jeans and rocked back on his boot heels. "It would appear so."

18

As much as I wanted to have a word with Derry Trong, I decided some rest was in order for the old bear. So, I returned to my dusty room at the Traveler's Rest.

Housekeeping had not been in. Housekeeping probably did not exist.

The bed was unmade. The sheets were kicked off the foot of the bed, and the pillow had a dark brown scab from blood I had spilled the night before. I did a quick appraisal of my scalp. There were a lot of tender spots and lumps, but my attacker had somehow managed to not break skin on my head, and I was reasonably sure I had made it through with no cracks to the melon beneath the skin. A look into the mirror showed some scabbed over minor lacerations, probably from falling face first on the gravel in the lot at the Legion. Neither Jo Jo nor Garrow had commented on my appearance or displayed any real concern. Then again, concern rarely registered on their faces. My head ached, and if I stood in the same place for too long, the world tilted on its axis. But I think I would live. I scraped my wounded tongue across my teeth. Blood from my mouth was probably what left the scab on my pillow.

Eventually, I called Veronica to let her know I had arrived safely. She was her normal inquisitive self. I didn't mention my assault. I hated the idea of her worrying about me when I was over a thousand miles away. When she asked about the case, I evaded further questions by saying it was too early to say. I redirected the discussion to how she was doing, and she treated me to a long diatribe about how much the Christmas season sucked for strippers. It forced the DOWDs, that would be stripper code for, "dirty, old, white dudes," to spend the holidays with their wives and kids. So, the clubs were dead. And the poor losers that sneaked away for a few hours at the club, had had their cash flow drained by all the gift buying. For Veronica, it was hardly even worth showing up for work. I'd heard the rant countless times over the three Christmas seasons I'd known Veronica. It was cute to hear her get worked up about something. Especially, when I wasn't the target of her anger. I begged off, when she started in on sexy talk about how much she missed me and what she would do to me when I returned, explaining that I had gotten little sleep since landing yesterday. I needed a nap.

And that's what I set in to do, when we said our goodbyes.

Except sleep was hard to come by. I kept thinking about Katie Couture, and I had to admit some of those thoughts weren't pure. I imagined what she looked like in life, wearing only that slip from the crime scene photos. I could picture her as a sensual woman. What I couldn't imagine was Katie Couture and Derry Trong. But the "diseased whore" comment reeked of someone who had caught the disease from the "whore".

How else would he know about Katie's sexually transmitted disease?

Could it be a random coincidence?

I thought not.

Trong seemed married or in a relationship with Patty Pill-popper, the blonde from last night. Patty was far from an ugly woman, but I could see Trong with her. Katie seemed far out of his league though. But maybe that was the point. Maybe she had the urges, and she latched on to a convenient solution. That nobody would expect.

Then I remembered Stefanie Charles's assertion that Katie was getting her taste north of the border. I couldn't see Trong and Katie traveling across the border for a tryst. Maybe she brought something back, and she shared it with Trong?

I fell asleep, and immediately returned to the image of Katie in the silky, white slip. And then she was out of the slip. "Run Around Sue" piped in from the heavens. It was the same song that played on an old clock radio on my dorm nightstand, the first time I had made love to my deceased fiancée.

My bed sheets stunk of stale sweat and testosterone.

I AWOKE DISORIENTED and short of breath in the jet-black darkness of the room. It was the dull pain and nasty feel of the loose flap of flesh in my mouth, of all things, that brought me back to the present.

I was still fully clothed. My phone was still in the pocket of my jeans. It was just before midnight. I grabbed my keys and headed back to the American Legion. I'd like to say it was against my better instincts, but it was instinct that led me there.

THE SCENE at the Legion was much like the night before with

everyone sidled up to the bar. Some faces were familiar. Some were not. I did not see Derry Trong.

It was a little later in the night, so the eyelids were heavier, heads hung on some patrons, and the collective chatter seemed to slur. The jukebox poured *"The Dance"* by Garth Brooks over the small crowd. It's the only Brooks song I have ever liked, and I caught myself humming along.

I saw my friend, Billy Howe, seated at the same stool I had found him the night before. When he saw me, his eyes sparkled with good cheer, gin blossoms flushed the small patch of exposed skin on his cheeks and nose which peered over his bushy beard. "Well, lookie here, if it ain't Jim Rockford," he called out for the whole bar to hear.

Only he laughed at his joke, but he got a good one out of it and nearly choked himself to death on a popcorn kernel.

I hurried over to him, as he bent over gasping, and smacked him on the back with as much force as I could manage without knocking him off his feet.

Billy steadied himself with one hand on the bar rail. And hacked up the offending kernel. He held up the other hand to call off the beating on his back.

He kept his head down while he gobbled up oxygen in short, gasping breaths.

Two knuckles on the hand holding onto the bar were freshly scabbed.

I remember how much I had shared with him the night before, and how he had disappeared when Stefanie Charles had arrived. I ran the flap of skin on my tongue back and forth over the roof of my mouth. A bitter taste formed there. I stepped back from him and looked for another empty stool. *The Dance* concluded, and the house system faded to silence.

I should have let him choke on that fucking popcorn.

Billy reached out and clasped my wrist before I could

walk away. "Where are you headed, Rockford? I owe you a beer for saving me from death by popcorn."

I snatched my hand out of his grip and fought back the urge to bury my fist six inches deep in his pillow-like stomach. I slid onto the stool beside him.

Howe waved Jeanie over and ordered a Bud for me.

"What happened to your face, Fuzzy?" Billy asked.

I searched his eyes to see if there was any deceit there. I saw genuine concern. However, if I was any good in registering deceit in the eyes of my foes, I probably wouldn't have spent so much time in the hospital over the last couple of years. Maybe Billie Howe had wielded that war club. Maybe Matteo Garrow was a sweetheart. I rubbed my palm across my forehead to clear my thoughts.

"Had a tough time keeping the hand steady when shaving this morning," I said.

His eyebrows pinched to the bridge of his nose. "Whatever you say, partner."

My beer magically appeared at my elbow. Tendrils of steam danced from the thin film of frosted condensation that coated the surface of the bottle. Half the label had peeled away, and when I took the beer in my hand, the bottle and frost were ice cold and sticky against the palm of my hand. But the contents had not frozen, and the beer was crispy and about as cold as I had ever tasted. It may have been the best Budweiser I had ever experienced.

I finished it with one long, deep pour down my hungry throat.

"Damn, son, take it easy. I got four hours on you, ain't no way you're catching up to me," Billy said, in a voice doused with those four hours of drinking.

"So, you have been here all night?"

"Boy, you are a smart detective." I noticed his voice went further south into the trailer parks with the more he drank.

"Did you see Derry Trong come in tonight?"

He was amid another swallow of beer. Removed the bottle from his lips. Swished the suds around in his mouth. Quick nod of the head. Down the throat. "Sure, he's in most nights. Though, Lord knows why? I don't think that crazy gook has ever had more than two a night. Poor Jeanie, here, entertains and serves him bowls of popcorn all night for maybe a fifty-cent tip." He took another swallow of beer. "And don't get me going on that crazy bitch of his."

Patty with the pills. She had a wild-eyed look that led me to believe she was on those pills for all the wrong reasons. I'd seen the same look in the eyes of some of Veronica's coworkers. An unfortunate byproduct of the profession which fortunately Veronica had side-stepped. "Since you brought her up," I said. "What did she think of Katie Couture?"

Billy leaned away from me and rotated his head to look up at me the way a golfer follows his putt as it makes its way to the cup. He laughed. "You ever stop working, Rockford?"

I shrugged. "I didn't come up here to enjoy the weather."

"Ain't that the truth," he said. He pronounced 'truth' 'troof'. "That I know of, Claire ain't had no beef with Katie. Usually, you know the ones that had a problem with her, because it kind of sticks out like a sore thumb on account of how sweet Katie was."

"What about if Derry and Katie had a thing?"

"A thing? What, like in high school or something? I ain't sure Trong has been around here that long."

"I meant as of late," I said.

"Son, have you been in Claire's stash of pills? Katie ain't had a 'thing' in over ten years."

It was interesting how aware he was of Claire's pill problem.

"But what if she had, and it was with Trong? And with

Claire's pills entered into the equation, do you think Claire might have a problem?"

"Equation? What the fuck are you, Einstein? Look, you and I know, a woman finds out her man is stickin' it somewhere else, there's a problem. What you're failing to understand is there ain't no way Trong was stickin' it to Katie Couture. You seen pictures of Sister, ain't you?"

I grabbed a handful of popcorn from the bowl in front of us, and tossed it into my mouth. It was just as stale as last night's. Hell, it probably was last night's. Mouth full, I mumbled, "You have a point."

"Damn straight, I gotta point," he said. "Ain't no way Sister is getting with Derry Trong, any more than she's getting with my pencil dick."

A piece of popcorn lodged in my throat, and I coughed to try to clear it free.

"What?" Billy said. "It's a certifiable fact that I have the smallest penis in America, but it's okay. I get my shoulders into it." He rolled his shoulders like a boxer entering the ring.

He had spoken loud enough for most of the bar to hear his confession. And there was good-hearted laughter. A woman a few seats down from us, with a bad pinkish dye job and tattoos on her exposed neck shouted, "Good Lord, is he talking about his dick again?"

I worked the kernel loose and swallowed it, but it left the feel of sandpaper in my throat.

"Bring this man another beer," Billy directed Jeanie.

She took my dead soldier. A smile on her face, she whispered, "It really isn't that small."

The thought of 300-pound Billy mounting 90-pound Jeanie was almost as hard to imagine as Derry Trong getting it on with Katie Couture. And it was probably more disturbing.

Jeanie winked and reached to the cooler and produced another frosty Bud.

What the hell do they cool these with, dry ice? I took another long pull of beer, and it helped relieve the dryness in my throat. It felt good on the tongue, too.

"Can we change the subject?" I said.

Billy's attention had shifted to where Derry Trong had sat last night, "Well, today must be your lucky day, Rockford. Look what the cat dragged in?"

Derry Trong was searching the bar stool, and floor of the area where he had sat the night before. He scanned the bar, his head pivoting like a tennis spectator. Craned his neck to look over the bar to the cooler top and floor on Jeanie's side. Stepped back and examined his barstool. Patted it down as if something might be there that was not visible. Then his head and torso disappeared, as he crouched down out of sight, presumably to search the floor around his stool. Then his head popped up again, like a whack-a-mole. The whole process happened in a manner of seconds. Then he would repeat it.

Half a dozen times through, Jeanie approached him, and asked him something.

He nodded his head frantically.

She smiled.

His shoulders sagged in relief.

Jeanie pulled out an amber prescription pill container from beneath the bar and handed it to him.

He thanked her and disappeared into the corridor behind the bar.

I hurried over to the other side of the hall where it ended in the Legion's exit and caught Derry Trong just before he reached the door.

"Mr. Trong? May I have a minute of your time?"

He still had the pillbox in his hands, and he quickly slid it into his coat pocket. He reached for the door lever with his other hand.

I reached across the door and placed my hand on the doorjamb. My arm barred his passageway.

Trong was an average-sized man, but I must have been an imposing figure to him. His cheeks were sprayed with black-heads, his hair dank with grease, and his teeth were an unhealthy yellow. There was a strong odor of beer-soaked sweat emanating from the pores of his skin.

"It is nearly one in the morning," he said. "I don't know who you are, but surely this can wait until tomorrow."

I had figured him for an immigrant, but he spoke the clear English of someone who had been born here or had lived here since early childhood.

He looked like a loser, and at this distance, I had a hard time seeing what Patty of the Pills saw in him, let alone what Sister Katie would see in him. I was less certain of my hunch about the two of them.

I pulled out my wallet, and flashed the little, laminated card that served as my private investigator's license.

Trong leaned closer trying to get a closer look. "Francois Koella?"

I snapped the wallet shut against further inspection. "I'm a private investigator, Mr. Trong. And I'd like to talk to you about Katie Couture, who, I'm sure you are aware, was murdered. This will be a lot easier, Mr. Trong, if you cooperate."

I am always amazed at how making it appear official works with my subjects.

Derry Trong was no exception. He released his hand on the lever. "You can't think I had anything to do with that."

"That is what we are trying to clear up, Mr. Trong," I said. The 'we' in this case were Jo Jo Bigtree and myself, but I'm sure he heard the police, the media, and the District Attorney.

I gestured to the empty tables in the dining area. "We can just take a seat over there. We'll have some privacy. Get this cleared up, and then you can go home and forget about it."

That last part was a lie. I was sure this would not be the last time I talked to Derry Trong.

This time his shoulder sag was not from relief, but resignation.

"Ok, but I hope this won't take too long. I have to work in the morning."

I flashed my best reassuring officer of the law smile. I stepped aside and let him pass.

As we trotted over to the tables, I patted Trong on the back. "So where do you work?"

"Huh?"

"Your job," I said. "You said you have to work in the morning."

"Oh," he said. "I write."

We reached the tables, and I swung around to the other side of one. "Really? Very cool. What do you write? Anything I may have read?" I turned the smile up a few watts. "I'm a book lover."

"Mostly, Star Trek stuff," he said.

Wrath of Trong.

"Nice," I said. "That must be lucrative. Licensed stuff like that. Especially with a brand like Star Trek."

We hadn't seated yet, and Trong studied his shoes, as if he were ashamed of something.

Thing is, even though I'm not a Trek fan, at all, it impressed me that he was a writer of the material.

I tried to make that come across, "Do you write books on the originals, next generation, deep space, what?"

"Most all of them, but I prefer the Next Gen."

All of his answers were coming short and clipped. I knew I needed to get him to open up, if I was to get anywhere with him. "Cool, if you're contracted for all of them, it must be a great gig."

He kept his eyes on his feet and mumbled something. I couldn't hear it.

"What's that?"

He looked up, his shoulders pulled back and chin jutted out, like an assured cock. "I said, it's not contracted. I write for the fans, not for some corporation."

Fan fiction. He was trying to use the excuse he had to get up in the morning to write fan fiction. Really?

He remained standing. Motionless, except his nostrils flared.

I was getting nowhere with opening him up. I gave him an easy does it gesture with my palms held out in surrender. "Hey, I haven't written a word since they made me in school. So, I think it's impressive that you get up in the morning and write for the fans."

His facial expression didn't change, but he pulled a chair back from the table, and dropped into it.

I did the same and made a steeple of my hands in front of me. Time to cut to the chase. "What did you have against Katie Couture, Mr. Trong?"

"Nothing at all. Katie was a flawed human being like the rest of us. But as far as human beings go, she wasn't so bad."

I broke the steeple and dropped my hands flat on the table, just forcefully enough that there was a light thud. "So, are you telling me you are not 'Wrath of Trong'?"

He tilted his head to the right and searched my face. I had a black Lab as a boy that would do that when I spoke to her. She, like Derry Trong, was trying to find understanding in what I had said. Unlike my dog, Trong spoke the language and eventually recognition appeared in his eyes.

"You speak of my campaign against her in the Malone-Telegram?"

I stared back at him. "Is that what they call internet trolling now?"

He smirked. "Mr. Koella, as I said. I had nothing against Ms. Couture as a citizen. I took an issue, however, with her running for an office that involved the education of our children."

"Do you have children of your own?"

"What does that have to do with anything?"

"So, I take that as a no," I said.

He slid his hands back from the table where they had been folded comfortably and drew his arms in and crossed them at his chest.

Yeah, not good 'opening up' body language.

But I pushed forward. "What issue did you take with her run for a post on the School Board?"

"Surely, you know her checkered past, Mr. Koella."

"Call me Fuzzy," I said. "I do know that Ms. Couture had a bit of a wild youth. Like most of us. But I also know she had an exemplary present. I would think she could make a good example."

"Yes, well sometimes legends are not as accurate as they are told," he said. "The martyr is always much more honorable, than those of us who remain. Don't you think?"

When I didn't answer he continued. Apparently, Derry Trong was a man who liked to hear himself talk. "Changing ourselves is difficult. We have a whole industry in this country. We spend billions of dollars every year on addiction recovery. Yet, even these institutions admit that the addict never truly recovers." He smiled. I almost expected him to pat himself on the back.

The yellow teeth exposed by his smile looked like they could use some rearranging. I kept my hands firmly in place on the table.

He continued, "Wouldn't you think this could apply to

Ms. Couture? Sex addiction, after all, is a recognized disease. Could anyone ever truly rehabilitate enough that the risk of relapse was so little we should accept them in a position which is partially about protecting our children?"

"Are you religious, Mr. Trong?"

He sighed. "Again, what does that have to do with anything?"

I was asking the questions. So, again, I left his go unanswered.

He continued, "Religion can be a positive influence on many individuals suffering from an addiction. Many of them make strides in correcting their lives' paths. Yet again, all the experts agree, the individual is never truly recovered. They are all one taste away from the drunk tank. One plunge of the needle away from the downward spiral of overdose. One lay away from a return to uncontrollable sexual compulsion."

"You sound like quite the expert on the subject, Mr. Trong. Do you have a background in clinical rehabilitation or psychiatry?"

"I have lived with an addict for five years," he answered in a tone reflective of reporting yesterday's weather.

I recalled the pills in his pocket, and his frantic search for them. Was he referring to Patty Pill-popper when he said he had lived with an addict? Or was he referring to himself?

"So, you think Katie may have slipped back into her old ways?"

He shrugged indifference. "I do not know. I never have suggested that. I simply recognize that the risk was there. Katie could truly have been celibate these last ten years, but the demon was always sitting on her shoulder."

"But how dangerous could she be as a member of the school board?"

"That is a typical response of a citizen who has become de-sensitized by the behavior of our country's politicians."

He had me there.

"But…"

"There is no but, Mr. Koella. Placing Katie Couture, a woman who bore three children out of wedlock, and aborted who knows how many others, on the school board would have sent the wrong message to our kids."

I wasn't going down the abortion rabbit-hole, but if that was conjecture it brought me back to the legitimacy of his 'diseased whore' comment.

"You said you've never suggested that Katie had returned to the promiscuous behavior of her past," I said. "But on the Telegram site you called her a 'diseased whore.' Which sounded like you stepped away from her controversial past and were commenting on a present condition."

His lips parted to answer, but he bit back his response. Paused. When he continued, his eyes shifted from me to his crossed arms and settled there. "That, I admit, was a little hyperbole," he said. "Things escalated in that thread and I responded from an emotional position, rather than one of logic. But, even though I cannot say for a fact she was carrying a disease. Does it not stand to reason that the possibility she was carrying the disease exists?"

Again, I let his question go unanswered. I also didn't point out that the 'whore' piece of that comment wasn't based in fact, either. "So, you weren't aware of Katie having a disease?"

"I was speaking metaphorically," he said.

"Mr. Trong, what was your relationship with Katie Couture at the time of her death?"

He flashed his buttery smile and shook his head. "I am in a long-term relationship, Mr. Koella."

"I make a good portion of my income from people in long-term relationships, Mr. Trong. They do terrible things to each other, and then they hire me to prove it. Please answer the question?"

"I knew her enough to say 'Hello' when we passed each other at the supermarket. Once the campaign started in the Telegram, those instances passed in silence."

"What is the name of your significant other, Mr. Trong?"

He stood. "You'll have to excuse me if I don't answer that question." He looked at a black vinyl, digital watch on his wrist. "It is getting close to closing time, Mr. Koella. I hope I was of some help, but now I must take my leave."

The only thing I knew for certain out of the whole conversation was that there was more of a story to his 'diseased whore' comment. Unfortunately, I knew no more of that story than I had when I walked into the Legion.

19

The next morning, the sky was the pale, flat blue of a robin's egg. The sun hung over the trees, a pure gold like the color of a farm-fresh egg yolk. U2 sang about it being a beautiful day on the public radio station. If I had not felt the sting of the cold against my nose and cheeks, when I had walked from my room to the car, it would have seduced me into believing that.

I pulled into a narrow strip of pavement in front of a turquoise metal building with large white overhead doors fronting Highway 37. A sign above the doors with red letters offset against a white background read, "Fort Covington Fire Department."

I got out of the car and made my way to a set of wooden stairs off the side of the building that climbed about six feet to a landing that fronted on a white door.

I walked up the stairs. They were surprisingly sturdy. Tried the door. Locked. I knocked. There was no answer.

I stepped back down and circled around the back of the building. The turquoise siding ended on the side of the building. The back was all white siding and dappled with algae and rust stains. There were three darkened punch windows, but they were all at an elevation out of reach, even for my 6'-5" frame.

Around to the other side, and more turquoise siding but no door.

Shouldn't there at least be someone at the Fire Department?

I had scheduled to meet Sonny LaPage here, at 9 a.m. I was late, and it was ten after now. But no Sonny. No anyone.

I walked around the front and peered into the darkened windows found in the overhead doors. The station was cloaked in darkness. I saw only the shadowy bulk of an under-sized fire truck.

Nobody.

I got back in the Nova and scrolled through my recent calls for Sonny LaPage's number.

As I did that, I heard the crunch of tires on the loose pavement behind me. In the rear-view mirror, I saw a black and gold full-sized truck wheel to a stop just behind my bumper.

The door swung open and a short, elderly man with black greased-back hair, and an enormous girth balanced atop short stumpy, Popeye legs hopped down to the pavement. He grimaced at the shock of his feet hitting the pavement. Shook his head and headed in my direction.

Sonny LaPage was the old man I'd seen with his wife at the Howlin' Wolf Restaurant for breakfast yesterday.

I got out to greet him.

"Sorry I'm late, Fuzzy. I take some time to get going in the morning these days." He had a squawking voice that reminded me of the Penguin from the old, campy Batman television show. The Adam West - Burt Ward vehicle, not the animated stuff they showed these days.

He smiled a toothless grin and offered his hand. "Bob LaPage."

His hand was crusty with callouses like a common day laborer's. He had to be in his early 70s, yet he still worked with his hands. I had a feeling I would like Sonny LaPage. "Thanks for making the time for me this morning, Mr. LaPage," I said.

He waved that off. "Have you had any breakfast yet?"

My stomach came to attention at the mention of breakfast and responded in the affirmative in its own guttural dialect. I translated, "Not yet."

"Come on then, we'll head over to the Willow Creek, and we can talk over the meal."

I went to get back in the Nova.

"Leave it, Fuzzy. We'll take my truck, and I'll drop you back here after we're done."

"You sure it's not a problem for you to drive back by?"

He laughed. It came out the same way as his Penguin voice. "Not at all, let's go."

I took two tries at hauling myself up into his truck. And it finally took him reaching over and giving me a hand to grip for leverage. "It's only taken me ten years to master swinging up into this thing." He patted his enormous belly, squeezed beneath the steering wheel. "This doesn't help much, either."

He pulled us across the highway. Into the parking lot of the gas station & restaurant with the abandoned ice cream stand in the parking lot. Hung in the storefront window, a small white sign with green cursive lettering read, "The Willow Creek."

I guess it wouldn't be a problem to drop me back at my car after all.

THEY SEATED us at a booth beneath a cork bulletin board where the Salmon River Central High School Shamrock's hockey schedule was posted. "Home of the 2017 New York State Champions" was emblazoned beneath the schedule on the poster. They were playing at home tonight against some school called Governeur. I'd never been to a high school hockey game, and I was intrigued at the possibility of seeing a team at the top of the food chain. There was also a black-and-white photo on the poster of an athletic man in his forties, with a mop of what appeared to be blond hair. He had the smile of a car salesman. The poster identified him as Coach Dave Hetfield.

The dining room was almost full and there was the singsong of friendly voices all talking at once. Everybody seemed to know everyone, except me. And I caught imploring looks. Sizing me up. Sonny was popular with the crowd. Half the men, and nearly as many women, stopped by for "How you doings".

I left him to his socializing and contemplated my plans for the night. I wouldn't get a word with Hetfield at the game, but it might be a good idea to get a look at him. How a man coaches kids says a lot about what he's made of. And I really was interested in taking in my first high school hockey game.

A middle-aged waitress interrupted my thoughts. She wore a flour-doused, black t-shirt and baggy blue jeans and rose-tinted glasses perched on her beak nose. Visible gobs of hair product held her red hair in its place like the end of a Q-tip with visible gobs of hair product. Her smile put her last dental work at some time in the last century.

She laid a hand on the back of Sonny's seat. "Now, Sonny, who's this tall drink of water you've brought in to see me, eh?"

Sonny studied a laminated menu, which also served as a place mat. Without raising his head, he said, "Fuzzy Koella, meet Tara Latulieppe."

She leaned a hip against Sonny's shoulder.

His eyes shifted, and his mouth turned down at the corners. Then he went back to the menu.

"So, Fuzzy, I haven't seen you around these parts. Where are you from?"

"South Carolina, ma'am."

She play-swatted my shoulder. "What's this ma'am stuff? I'm not old enough for you to be calling me ma'am. Isn't that right, Sonny?"

Sonny grunted something and continued ignoring her. There was something between Mr. LaPage and Tara Latulieppe that he didn't want coming to light. I'd seen his wife, and the only thing Tara had on Mrs. LaPage was age. I suspected in a weak moment, Sonny LaPage took a taste of the younger fruit, and forever regretted it.

The silence hung from the smell of bacon grease in the air.

"So, what can I get started for you'se?"

Did y'all sound as excruciating to Northerners as you'se did to me?

Sonny said, "Coffee, black."

I ordered grapefruit juice, which they didn't have, and settled on orange juice.

Tara walked off. When she was out of earshot, I said, "History, there?"

The frown remained on his face. "Just a goddamn idiot is all." And almost as if a switch was flipped he went back to his amiable self. "So, South Carolina, eh? I bet it is nicer down there than this shit."

I winked, "I hadn't noticed."

Tara dropped off our drinks and took our orders. Eggs in a nest with home fries for me. Three scrambled eggs, a double order of bacon, and a double order of buttered toast for him.

She smacked him with her checkbook, "You're gonna end up in Alice Hyde, you keep eating like that."

I assumed Alice Hyde was the hospital, and I had a

similar thought, but it was pushed aside by my admiration and secret hope that when I reached my 70's I could still put away such a meal.

After Tara left us again, he asked, "So, Jo Jo said you're helping him with the Pressley kid case?"

I nodded and took a sip of my juice. As Gary Pressley had noted, I don't use a notebook, and I seldom plan how these interrogations go. "That's right. Obviously, we're looking for anything that can help with casting some shadow of doubt on the prosecution's case against Gary."

He held his mug of coffee between his hands. He hadn't taken a drink from it yet. "Right, right," he said. "It's funny. When I heard it come over the scanner, I was in disbelief. I thought there was no way Gary could do such a thing. And especially not to Sister. But as the days passed, and it took over the local news, you start coming around to the idea that maybe he did."

"You think maybe Gary killed Katie?"

"In my heart, I know he didn't." He took a kitten sip of his coffee and quickly put it back down. "In my mind? I don't know enough to say. Hell, I'm sure you know more about what happened than I do, and you aren't even from around here. What do you think?"

Unlike Trong last night, I answered Sonny LaPage's question. "I don't know, either. Jo Jo seems to be certain he's innocent. So sure, that he's working for no fee. I'm not so sure, myself. I've only talked to Gary Pressley once, and I don't have the benefit of knowing him for years like the rest of you. As you know, he can be a little…," I searched for the right word. "Incoherent."

"Right, right," he said. "But a good kid, eh?"

I wasn't sure if that was a question or not. And if it was whether it was rhetorical.

I changed the subject. "How well did you know Katie Couture?"

"Sweetest girl you could ever know," he said, and backed it up with a smile and a gleam in his eye that left nothing to doubt in his opinion of the Sister. "Heart of gold on that one. And she doted on Gary Pressley, like he was a little brother. In fact, I always felt that after Beau died, Gary Pressley kind of took his place in her heart."

"Beau?" I said. "That was her son?"

"Terrible thing I tell you," he said. "To go so young, and not ever really know anything was wrong until it was too late."

He took a sip of coffee and wrinkled his nose when it hit his palate. "Damn, if they don't serve it too hot to drink, and then when it cools down enough so you can taste it? It's shit."

He had a good laugh at that, and maybe with the talk of Katie's son, he needed it.

"So, there was a special connection between Katie and Gary, even beyond how Katie treated others in town?"

He thought on that for a second while he tried to stomach more "shit" coffee. "Yeah, I guess there was."

I didn't share my thought, which was that the connection actually may have made Gary a more likely suspect. Most violent crimes are crimes of passion. I didn't think there was an affair between them, but it was becoming clearer that there was love. Be it sisterly or motherly. It was there.

And it made Gary Pressley a strong suspect.

But that wasn't what I was here for. "I understand you did an inspection of the old public library recently."

He looked past me, and I thought he was dodging the question until Tara showed up at my shoulder and served us heaping plates of food. Sonny's more heaping than mine.

Tara slid in beside Sonny.

The sour look returned to his face.

I could understand why. I didn't like when waitstaff sat down to chat while you ate.

She put both elbows on the table and rested her chin on a cup formed by both of her palms. "So, what brings you to the North Country, Fuzzy?"

"Jo."

"Oh. My. God. You're the private investigator?"

I felt like I was in high school again. "That would be me," I said.

"You don't think Gary did it, do you?"

Sonny LaPage looked at her sideways, rolled his eyes, and shook his head.

"I hope not," I said. "Otherwise, I'm going to be a big waste of money."

She continued on as if I hadn't spoken. "And poor Katie. And the girls."

She reached across the table and placed one hand on my wrist. It was as if I was a grieving widower. I slid my hand clear and took a sip of orange juice. "How well did you know Katie?"

More eye rolling from Sonny.

"Oh, we go way back. We went to high school together. And you know people talk about her past, which they shouldn't, but they do. And it's like she was some horrible person. And she wasn't. She was just as sweet back then as she was the day she was killed. She just liked to have a little fun, back then." She smiled at the memory.

"And she kept all that fun-loving under wraps all these years," I asked.

"I think she learned a different sort of fun," she said. "One that hurt a little less the next day. I think she really enjoyed helping people. And she doted on those kids of hers. And Gary. And all of us, really. Ain't that right, Sonny?"

"That's right," he said.

"But she left the wild days behind her?"

"Honey, she buried the wild days."

I wasn't sure if there was more to that comment than just an odd turn of phrase, but she got up and left to wait on another customer.

Sonny spooned a forkful of scrambled eggs into his gummy mouth.

I cut into my toast.

He threw his fork down. "Fuckin' cold," he said.

He watched patiently as I took a bite of my meal.

The toast was room temperature and the bit of egg tasted like it had come out of the icebox. I nodded my head.

He squawked, "Crazy bitch does this whenever I come in here without Audrey. Sits down and chats, so I can't get to my meal, and the food gets cold."

I laughed. He laughed. And we ate our cold eggs.

"So, back to the inspection," I said.

"Right, right. I completed it oh," his irises bounced up and down, as he counted back in his mind. "I'd say three months ago."

"And?"

"And what," he said. "The emergency generator had never been de-commissioned, so things could still power up. I recommended that it be shut-down. All that diesel sitting there in a tank, beside a wood-framed building built in the 1800s, and unattended?" He shook his head. "It was an accident just waiting to happen. Though, I never would have imagined the accident we ended up having."

"Other utilities?"

"It was still tapped to the well, and there was plenty of heating oil in the tank."

None of that meant anything to me, but I nodded to show my understanding.

"So, you weren't surprised to find out someone had that boiler room cooking, while Katie suffered in there."

"The hell I wasn't," he said. "But, what you're really asking is if I understood this was possible based on the inspection. And the answer to that is yes, I knew it was possible."

"So, what came of the inspection?"

"I sent it off," he said. "I suspect it's sitting on someone's desk at the State."

"But you don't think someone is purposefully dragging their feet?"

"No more than they ever do it on purpose," he said.

I remembered what Jo Jo said about 'high truck'. "Do you think it's possible a utility company came by on the day Gary found Katie?"

He shrugged. "Anything's possible," he said. "How would I know?"

We left half of our breakfast. I made an attempt on the check, but Sonny LaPage insisted on treating. We got out of there before Tara could ensnare us in a web of local gossip. I could probably use some local gossip, but I was afraid Sonny's eyes would roll right out of his head.

He pulled me across the street to my car. As we shook hands he said, "Fuzzy, I hope you find what you're looking for, and I hope Gary gets out because of it."

I hoped so, too. But I wasn't sure Gary, or I, would be so lucky.

20

I called Hetfield. As expected, he wasn't available to talk today due to the night's game. He seemed disturbed because I wanted to talk to him about the case. I tried not to make much of it. If someone called me out of the blue, and wanted to talk about a murder, I probably wouldn't appreciate it.

I also called Jo Jo to check-in. He had just finished questioning Dobie Cooke, a teen-aged Native that Katie Couture had been tutoring in math. Jo Jo said Cooke was certain to receive a full scholarship to the University of Vermont in hockey if he could keep his grades up. With Katie out of the picture, Jo Jo seemed to think it was a fool's errand. His questioning went nowhere, either.

It seemed Jo Jo was grasping at low hanging fruit. Sonny LaPage and Dobie Cooke didn't seem the kind of folks that would break this case.

I was eager to talk to Hetfield, especially after our brief phone conversation. But that would have to wait until tomorrow.

I told Jo Jo I would be by the office in the early afternoon if he wanted to compare notes. He told me to use the key he had given me, and that he would see me sometime.

I didn't ask what his plans were now.

And I didn't share mine. I was going to church.

THE SUN HAD CLIMBED to its apex, and its glare reflected off the snow and icicles draping the roofs and eaves at St. Mary's of the Fort Catholic Church.

I didn't call ahead, but I didn't figure I needed to, it was a church. You shouldn't have to schedule an appointment.

The church was a structure built of enormous slabs of carved stone. It was narrow and tall with a steep, peaked roof. Atop the roof above bright red entry doors sat a bell tower cupola.

Despite the brilliant red doors, I felt like I had stepped into the composition of an old black-and-white photograph from a long-gone generation. A long-gone America.

But I didn't put those times on a pedestal. So, I will not wax poetic of a better time. Nostalgia paints the past in brighter colors than ever existed. Go back and read articles, letters to the editors, and stories from generations past. You'll see the history repeats itself. Every generation wantonly looks back to their youth as some idealistic vision of how things could be if just…. They complain about the new generation. The youth of America. When I catch myself commenting on the ear gauges and the body piercings and all the tattoo ink, I realize I have become the old bear that Veronica calls me. Besides all that, I also understand that the better America of the black-and-white vision I saw as I stood before St. Mary's Church, could only possibly be better for a portion of America's population. It was definitively worse for others not fortunate enough to be born into that segment of America.

I stepped to the doors and sidestepped a dagger of ice which fell from the roof eave. That seemed awfully ominous for my first trip to a church since I went to one back home when I was struggling with the decision of turning my mother in for manslaughter.

I continued through the doors into a nave not much larger in area than my room at the Traveler's Rest. A Holy Water urn the size of a small hot-tub sat in the center of the space. I could barely squeeze past it without turning sideways. The nave emptied into a full-height sanctuary with a peach-colored, barrel vault ceiling. Half a dozen Renaissance-style frescoes were on the ceiling, illustrating the story of Mary, the mother of Christ. They were impressive, and I stared at them like an art history student getting to see painting previously studied only in books.

There was a faint smell of burning candles. They were on the back wall on either side of the entry I had just come through. Only a couple of candles were lit on either side. I wondered if any of them had been lit for Sister Katie Couture. Rather than rack myself with worry over that question, I slid a five-dollar bill in the poor box, and lit a candle. Prayer was something that didn't come easy for me. I only seemed to send them up when my situation was truly dire. But lighting the candle seemed to do the trick. I felt better.

Hopefully, it did something for Katie's soul, too.

The sound of scraping feet interrupted my meditative state.

His hair was so white that my first thought was that the snow must have started outside again. He was only an inch or two short of my height, but I had close to fifty pounds on him. And I'm not a heavy guy. He dressed all in black, except for his Roman collar.

Starting in perfect upright posture, he stepped forward with his left foot. Leaning forward at the hip, his back still flat, he then dragged his lame right leg. The foot flared, ninety degrees, and provided the scraping sound which had awakened me.

After two steps, he caught me in his peripheral vision. I still held the burning punk I had used to light the candle. His nose was razor thin and pointed at the end. Standing there upright, like a cadet at a line-up at boot-camp, I caught an image in his demeanor and facial expression of the Eagle character from the Muppets.

"Well, hello," he said. "Have you come for confession?"

What passed for a smile crawled up his face, but it popped goose bumps on my arms. It reminded me of the fake smiles on the faces of the morticians when they had greeted my mother and I at my father's funeral.

"No, Father. I'm not here for confession, but if you have some time I would like to talk to you."

His lips were so thin as to be almost imperceptible from the rest of the skin surrounding his mouth. It added to the creepiness of his smile. "Talk is one of my key job descriptions," he said. "Come, let's have a seat down by the altar."

Heat arrived on the edges of my finger and thumb where I held the punk. The flame had crawled down the stick to about a quarter of an inch from my fingers. I shook it frantically to extinguish the flame and dropped a four-inch column of ash on the carpet.

"Don't worry about that," the priest said. "the janitor will take care of it." His voice was an octave too high for his imposing presence.

There was a center aisle with scarred, wooden pews on either side.

I followed him down it at about half my normal gait as he stepped and dragged his way down to a pulpit that was just two steps up from the sanctuary floor.

When we reached the pulpit, he turned and exhaled. "There now. Shall we pray?"

Without waiting for my answer, he lowered himself to the one tread leading up to the platform. His face contorted and then slackened as he situated himself in a proper kneel.

It wasn't any joyride for me, either. When I got into the kneeling position, I could feel jabs of pain in my knees and beads of sweat forming on my forehead.

He did the sign of the cross.

I closed my eyes, and cleared my thoughts of everything, including whatever the good father was mumbling about.

He brought me back, again. This time with his hand upon my shoulder.

His smile would take getting used to. I almost wanted to sin right there in his presence to wipe it from his face.

"I don't think we have ever met." He held his hand out. "Father Wiley Cooper."

Shaking his hand was like grasping a bag of chicken bones. "Fuzzy Koella," I said. "Up from South Carolina."

He dragged himself over to the front pew and eased himself down. "South Carolina, eh? I bet the weather's a little different there."

The way these Northerners seemed to envy our weather, I wondered why any of them remained. But they probably didn't have a good feel for what two weeks in a row of a hundred degrees felt like. I tried on my smile. "I've never seen this much snow."

"I bet."

He patted the pew beside him.

I took a seat a few feet away.

"So, what can I help you with?" he said.

"It's about Katie Couture, Father."

Still, he fucking smiled! How could he smile? Just like the

damn morticians. Don't they know that we can see through the charade? See how fake it all really is. I rambled on if for no other reason than to keep from dwelling on his Angel of Death smile. "I'm investigating her…" How to say this? Technically, it wasn't the murder I was working. Why did I care? I was perfectly fine obfuscating with Derry Trong. Never underestimate the power of the Roman collar. "Well, I guess what I'm saying is, Jo has hired me to ask around, and see if there was anything that might suggest that it wasn't Gary Pressley."

He took a deep breath and closed his eyes.

I continued, "Obviously, we're not looking to fabricate anything. Jo Jo loved Katie just as much as everyone, and I'm sure Jo Jo won't push far on this, if it turns out Gary really was behind it."

His eyes were still closed, and the smile had disappeared. A tremble in his lower lip replaced it.

I almost wished I could have the smile back. "I understand Katie lived here at the rectory."

"I don't think he did," Cooper said. "Kill her, that is." He opened his eyes. They were pools of black, like India Ink. "And no, Katie did not live here at the rectory. That would be against Church policy. We set up a convent for her, two blocks down the road in a small, mobile home."

"So, she was a nun?"

"We refer to persons like Katie as religious sisters. I guess it wasn't truly a convent she lived in, but the Church provided for her living expenses."

"Was it only Katie? Or were there other sisters?"

"When you read reports of the Church's struggles, inevitably you read about the shrinking clergy. It always focuses on the Priesthood. And I will not argue that this is not an issue. But what these reporters always fail to mention is the lack of new sisters. Nuns or lay sisters, like Katie. The erosion of young women committing themselves to the

Church is a wasting disease, like leprosy, on the heart of the Church." Again, his thin lip curled into that decrepit shape. "Sorry, that was a long way of saying, no. Katie was the only sister we had in the Parish."

"How long had you known her?"

"Sister was here when I came to the Parish in 2014."

"Were you here when Katie lost her son?"

"No, I think that happened at least two years before my arrival, but I know that it still weighed heavily on her soul."

Of course, it did, and stop smiling about it. "Did she confide in you about it?"

The smile dropped. "You know I can't discuss things shared in confession."

And with that I realized I had a clue. "That's not what I asked, Father. I meant any discussion outside the confessional. But, would you really not share information from the confession of a dead person, if it could help bring the killer to justice?"

"To answer your first question, most anything she or anyone would share with me, I would consider protected, whether or not it occurred in the confessional. People come to their priest believing they can confide in them. If I break that trust, the Church and I lose them forever. As for your second question, the seal of confession remains even after the sinner's death. So, no, I would not feel compelled to reveal details discussed in confession."

"Ok," I said. "You said Katie still carried the weight of Beau's death. And you shared that, so I assume you can talk about it."

"I think I'm safe in saying she still struggled with it. Sometimes when we face a tragedy that seems to have no explanation, it leads to a spiritual crisis. The age-old question of why do bad things happen to good people."

"Katie questioned her faith?"

"We all do from time to time, Mr. Koella. It is healthy for the faithful to look closely at their faith. The answer comes with regular prayer. Something that Katie was religious about." The smile somehow reached his eyes this time. "No pun intended."

"And you noticed this without her speaking about it?"

"We spoke about a lot of things, and this came up. As it's not really a sin confessed, I feel comfortable sharing."

This guy was hard to pin down. "Anything else about Katie and her son's death?"

"She still felt his presence."

"His presence?"

He rubbed his hands together. I wasn't sure if it was because he was an old, skinny man, and it was a little cold, or because he was nervous.

"Yes. Katie would see and hear her son in the actions of others. It could be a facial expression, or turn of phrase that reminded her of something her boy would say."

"I'd guess those type of memories is hard to shake, Father."

He kept at it with the hands. It was creeping me out almost as much as the smile. If he ever put the two together, I was out of there. "It was more than memories, Mr. Koella. Sister was very much convinced that she was in the presence of her deceased son. Or at least his soul. It is common in deeply spiritual persons."

"Seems kind of spooky."

Oh shit, there was the smile. "Not really for the spiritual. And there is really no harm in it. Unless the individual seeks answers outside the Church."

"And was Katie seeking answers out of the Church?"

He turned his head to look at the figure of Christ staked to the cross above the altar. "That is something I cannot discuss," he said.

So, that's a yes. But I pushed no further. "Okay," I said. "When was the last time you saw Katie?"

The tremble had returned to his lower lip. He continued to watch Christ. "That I can discuss, and I already have with several detectives. I last saw her a few days before they found her body."

"Were you concerned about not seeing her for a few days?"

"Initially, no, I was not. It wasn't common for us to go a couple days without seeing each other, but it also was not rare. However, the night before they found her she missed her RCIA class."

"RCIA?"

"Yes, it is a class for adults who wish to become Catholic, either by baptism or conversion. Adult Catholics who simply want a better understanding of their religion, may also take it. Though, sadly, very few of them do. As a result, many people of other religions have a better understanding of Catholicism than the average adult Catholic."

I had to stop him before he taught the class to me. "Ok, and Katie missed a class. That was rare?"

"Katie taught the class. It wasn't rare. It simply did not happen. Even with a horrific case of bronchitis last winter, Katie taught her class. She sounded like a throat cancer survivor, but she taught the class."

"Did you call the authorities?"

I got the answer in the way he hung his head. He no longer watched the Christ. It was as if he could not look him in the eyes.

"I did not hear about the missed class until the morning of her death. At first, it disappointed me, then it worried me. In the end, I decided to give it a day before I contacted the authorities out of deference and respect for Katie's privacy."

"Privacy? Was there something you thought Katie wanted

to keep private? That seems quite a decision to make when you're worried about her being missing."

He continued to study the concrete floor six inches in front of his toes. "I am sorry but I cannot discuss that."

"So, Katie had skeletons in her closet, then?"

His head snapped to me. His brows pinched over his eyes. The smile disappeared, replaced by a hateful frown. "I did not say that."

I tried on my version of the frown and leaned forward. "You answered 'yes' when you said you could not discuss it."

He shook his head. "I will not sit here and let you drag Katie's name through the mud."

I held my breath, allowing it to expand my chest, before exhaling and slouching back in the pew. "How well did you know Gary Pressley?"

He paused. Either due to the change of the topic or to gather his thoughts before answering. "I feel like I was beginning to know him well. He was taking Katie's RCIA class. She was trying to prepare him for full Confirmation during the Easter season."

"So, you knew him well enough and knew his relationship to Katie well enough. Now understand, I am not asking you to share anything told to you in confidence. If you could just ignore anything like that, could you tell me what you thought about Gary, and about his relationship with Katie, and what that means about the current situation. For example, you've already said you don't think Gary did it. Can you explain?"

"Gary is a lost child. He's a young adult who lost both of his parents right around the time he turned eighteen. A child with his mental incapacities, is understandably more reliant on his parents. Independence comes more slowly if at all. His parents were poor and got by mainly on government assistance. They moved from one rental trailer to another as they became unable to meet rent, but they almost always kept a roof over Gary's head. When they died, however, there was nothing left for Gary."

Homelessness, is literally, my greatest fear. I know it's odd for someone who essentially lives in a storage closet, but the thought of living hand to mouth on the streets horrifies me. I didn't want to dwell on how Gary lived after his parents' deaths. "How did they die?"

"The cancer got his father. One month later, his mother was returning from a night of drinking at the Legion. A deer crossed her path, she swerved to miss it. She missed the deer all right, but she hit an eighteen-wheeler on Highway 37 head-on."

There was the slightest chuckle. The smile that formed with it was probably the sincerest facial expression I had seen from Father Cooper. Again, it was a strange response to what he had just communicated, but it, at least, seemed authentic.

He continued, "All of this happened before I arrived in the Fort." He shook his head at that thought, the warm smile still residing on his face. "I've heard the story about it from just about every parishioner that has walked through those doors." He gave the thumb to the front doors. "I have my fair share of problems with our parish. The backbiting, the gossip, those God-forsaken scanners." He watched for some reaction from me.

"You're not from around here," I asked.

He turned his attention back to Christ.

I guess we were on safe ground, again.

"Buffalo," he said. "We have a different set of problems there. I try to remind myself of that. Especially, when our folks start in on the gossip. But even with these failings, the way this community has cared for Gary is remarkable. Gary is too proud to just let anyone take him in for good. But he's probably had dinner at every dining room table in town at least once. And I'd guess that's how it would have continued for pretty much his entire life, if he hadn't been arrested."

No matter the result of the case, it would be hard to go back to that reality. Gary would find that much harder whether or not he was convicted.

I suspected the Father and I were arriving at the same conclusion.

A prolonged silence enveloped us.

It was broken by the sound of the front door closing.

The attractive older woman from the Howlin' Wolf, Sonny LaPage's wife, stood in the nave just in front of the baptismal font.

Father Cooper called to her, "Just a moment, Audrey, I will be with you shortly."

Her eyes weren't on the priest. They watched me.

I turned back to Father Cooper, but I could still feel her penetrating stare.

"We should probably wrap this up," Cooper said. "But my door is always open. I want to help Gary." He clapped his hands together as he struggled to get to his feet. "And Katie."

He slowly led the way back up the aisle.

I tried not to watch the effort it took for him to walk. It was uncomfortable for me, and I'm sure if he caught me it would be uncomfortable for him.

Halfway up the aisle, he looked over his shoulder, "Tell me, Mr. Koella. Do you have a passport?"

That wasn't just out of left field. That came from the bleachers built atop the Green Monster in Fenway Park. "I don't have it with me," I said. "Why do you ask?"

The deathly smile returned. "Maybe you should have it sent to you. I don't think you will find the answers you seek about Katie on this side of the border."

I knew better than to probe any further. He would simply hide behind the confessional seal.

We continued up the aisle.

He stopped before Audrey LaPage. He introduced me to her.

I took her hand. "It's a pleasure to meet you, Mrs. LaPage. I had breakfast with your husband this morning."

Her eyes dilated. "I'm going to kill him. He is supposed to lose weight and here he is eating breakfast twice!"

Father Cooper cackled. It lacked the warmth of the chuckle he had shared before explaining the community's outreach in supporting Gary Pressley. "I guess this is what we pray for today, Mrs. LaPage."

Her eyes remained wide and focused on me. "We should pray that I don't wring his neck when I get home."

I took my hand back from Audrey LaPage, and turned to Father Cooper. "Thank you for taking the time to speak with me, Father."

"The pleasure was mine," he said, and offered his hand.

I ignored it, wanting to avoid feeling I would grind his finger bones to dust.

As I walked away, I heard Audrey mumble, "Who is this Fuzzy character, Father?"

I opened the door to leave before hearing Father Cooper's opinion of me, but a thought occurred to me. "Father, you said Gary was a student in Katie's RCIA class?"

He waited on me to continue. When his smile evaporated, I realized he understood where my question was leading.

I teed it up for him. "Was he there the night Katie did not show up to teach?"

Audrey LaPage's glare returned.

Father Cooper said, "Interesting that nobody has asked that question yet." He shrugged. "Though I didn't think to ask it, either." He looked to Mrs. LaPage. "You were there, weren't you, Audrey?"

She said, "He was there. What of it?"

Father Cooper and I shared a smile.

I had what I needed to believe Gary did not do this.

Father had what he needed to continue believing it.

And why was Audrey LaPage taking RCIA classes at her age?

21

I sat in the car for several minutes and contemplated all that I had learned and not learned from my discussion with Father Cooper.

He seemed convinced that Gary Pressley had nothing to do with Katie Couture's death. Though that conclusion came from no facts, at least until we determined that Gary had attended the RCIA class that Katie missed. I suppose that did not prove that Gary was innocent of Katie's abduction and murder, but it was compelling circumstantial evidence. Gary Pressley was not a criminal mastermind. I felt he could commit a crime of passion, but I did not feel he would then arrive at a cover-up solution that included ensuring he would attend Katie's class to establish an alibi. I was certain he fully expected to see Katie that night at RCIA class.

Back to what I had learned; Father's evasiveness on keeping Katie's privacy led me to believe there had been substantial skeletons in her closet, that she had revealed to him in confession. He had nudged me toward Canada, which further led me to believe there was more to be found about

Katie. Unfortunately, Canada is an enormous country. He hadn't given me much to go on.

Katie had some demons regarding her son's death. She had been seeing and hearing things. She'd taken to Gary like he was a son. I believed, even with her Good Samaritan ways, that Gary had become a surrogate Beau. There was something there more than just being the good Sister. Father had warned of the danger of seeking answers outside the Church. He hadn't said Katie had done this, but it seemed obvious she had.

Where would a 'religious sister' look for spiritual answers, if not the Church?

I didn't have an answer for that.

And I had no clue why Father Cooper was sending me across the border.

I put a call in to Veronica. It went something like this:

"What do you need your passport for?"

"I don't know," I said. "And I may not need it, but I'm feeling a pull to Canada, and if it comes to that I want to be ready."

"A 'pull'? What is this woo-woo shit, Fuzzy? Are you on drugs?"

I loved her for her refusal to beat around the bush, but sometimes I wished she would just leave well enough alone instead of challenging everything I said and did. Still, she'd probably end up saving my life one day because of it.

I explained, "It's not woo-woo shit, dear. I've received some new info today. It's possible I'll need to run up to Canada to track it down."

Please don't dig deeper, V.

She did.

"I thought you were supposed to take your cues from this Jo Jo."

I felt my fingers cross in my lap. Funny how the little quirks you had as a kid followed you into adulthood. "Given this new information, he may want me to head up there."

I heard her exhale. "Where do I send it?"

I gave her the address at the Traveler's Rest and told her I loved her.

The snow began to fall, again, after I signed off with Veronica. I didn't know what the roads would be like or how bad the storm would be. Even listening to the radio would be of little help, what they would call dusting could be treacherous to a southern boy like me.

I wanted to see Gary Pressley again, and I definitely wanted to go see the Shamrocks play that night. It was early afternoon.

I decided Gary could wait another day, and headed over to Jo Jo's place to gather my thoughts, share notes, and maybe look over some evidence.

***

IN THE FIFTEEN minutes it took to drive to Jo Jo's office, the snow increased to a blurry visibility, like a Photoshop filter applied to the world. It relieved me to see the big digital billboard of the Akwesasne Casino. Its parking lot could hold five hundred cars. It was about half full.

Across the street, the Howlin' Wolf's parking lot held about fifty. There were only three cars.

I pulled in to add to that number. Parked out front. Ran in and bought a black coffee to go. The wide-faced, Native waitress took my order and delivered it with no pleasantries. Not even a smile. I tipped her a buck on the dollar-fifty coffee. Still no thank you.

I walked my coffee to the back of the building and up the

stairs to Jo Jo's office. The smell of bacon grease hung in the air. Even stronger than in the restaurant. I took deep breaths to savor it, between sips of my bitter coffee. Then I held my breath as I finished my trek to the office door. My way of battling high cholesterol.

Jo Jo wasn't in the office.

The lights were on. The place was empty, tempting me to inspect Jo Jo's digs. I often felt the same enticement when I found myself alone at Veronica's house. Sometimes, I rationalized my impulse by noting it was a common practice in my work. But snooping around Jo Jo's office wasn't part of this job. So, I fought the urge, just as I did at Veronica's home. I wouldn't want either of them digging around at my place. Though, the way Veronica cleaned my place it was impossible she hadn't seen everything.

I walked to the back wall and looked at his baseball picture. Jo Jo gripped the bat like he was trying to splinter it in his fists. Sinew corded his tanned forearms. The muscles in his jawline were bunched like bubble gum. I liked to think he was staring down a fastball, and that he was about to deposit it over the left field wall. I wasn't the one delivering the pitch. I knew this because in the fuzzy black and white background, standing at the top of the dugout steps, white hair peering out below the ball cap, was a young phenom. A local boy. Drafted out of high school in the 4th round by the Cincinnati Reds. Rather than taking the big-league money, he had decided to play for the Manatees. That young phenom threw the pill ten miles per hour faster than I did now. But I knew more about pitching now. I could give that kid a run for the money.

Closing of the office door interrupted my self-reflection. Jo Jo's face reminded me of how Audrey LaPage had stared at me.

"Fuzzy," he said. "What's up?"

I felt guilty of snooping. To hide the fact, I pointed to the photo on the wall. "Not much, Jo Jo. I was just thinking about what you were about to do to that fastball."

He held a clear plastic bag in his hand stuffed with a submarine sandwich wrapped in white butcher paper. He stepped forward. "Or what the curveball was about to do to me, eh?"

I had never heard Jo Jo use the 'eh' colloquialism. Because of this, it sounded foreign coming from his mouth. "You get anywhere today?" I asked.

He tossed the sandwich on the desk and walked over beside me. He put his arm around my shoulder and turned me to face the picture on the wall. "The days were few, my friend, but they were some of the best of my life."

It seemed an odd display of nostalgia from him, but how could I say? I didn't really know Jo Jo. "Mine, too."

He patted me on the shoulder, like I was an obedient dog.

I didn't care for the gesture. So, I sidestepped out of the reach of his arm.

He took on a look of contemplation. His watery, dark eyes stared at the picture, but he looked inward. "I do not feel like I learned anything new today. And we may have lost Gary."

"How so?"

"He is not speaking. I went by the Correctional Center this afternoon for my daily trip to see Gary. I like to let him know that I am still there for him. For someone like him..." He awaited my acknowledgement.

"I get it," I said.

He continued, "Jail has to be even more frightening. He often can go silent on my visits. I have learned to expect that, but today? He did not say a word. From the moment I arrived to the time I left. Through all the small talk. Through any of my question. Nothing. Not even a nod of the head or gesture. It was as if I was not there."

"I don't think he did it, Jo Jo."

He went to the desk and had a seat and dug into the bag. "You questioned his innocence? What changed your mind? If I may ask."

"I'm actually here to go through that box." I tapped my index finger on the cardboard banker's box that sat on the end of Jo Jo's desk, pushed up against the wall. "Things keep coming up that should have been identified as evidence. I don't think the prosecution is taking their duties seriously."

"And that hunch has convinced you of Gary's innocence?"

"Not my feelings about the prosecution, no. Just another piece of evidence. It was either missed or ignored."

Jo Jo peeled back the greasy paper from his sandwich, greeting me with the smell of oil, vinegar, and onions pouring out of the roll filled with Italian cold cuts. My stomach churned, reminding me I hadn't eaten anything since the cold eggs with Sonny LaPage. Jo Jo bent forward, but looked up before biting into his meal. "And?" he said.

"Katie Couture taught RCIA classes every week at the Church. Gary Pressley was one of her students. On the night before they found her body, Katie Couture did not show for obvious reasons. Gary Pressley did."

Jo Jo took a bite of his sub. He chewed on it and what I had just shared. When he had swallowed his bite, he shook his head. "Damn, I should have got myself something to drink." He set the sandwich down and wiped his hands on the thighs of his jeans. "Gary does not have the smarts to show up at class, when he knows Katie will not show."

"Nope."

"This seems like a question the police should ask, as part of their investigation."

"Yep."

"And that hunch has convinced you of Gary's innocence?"

"Yep."

He leaned into the sandwich again and ate it half down in

the time it would take me to have one nibble and a sip of drink.

I placed my coffee cup beside his elbow.

He glanced up from his meal. His lips glistened with oil and vinegar. A solitary shred of lettuce hung from his chin. He looked like a predatory bird disrupted while feasting on its kill. "I am glad you finally came around," he said. He took the coffee cup in his massive hand. "This from downstairs?"

"Yep."

"Lord help me," he said, and took a sip. His opinion of the coffee couldn't be determined by any facial reaction.

"Any idea what has caused Gary to clam up?"

He had filled his mouth with another half of sub. He held up a finger.

I waited for him to finish and tried not to think about my watering mouth.

He stopped and wiped his slick fingers with some paper napkins he pulled out of the plastic bag. "I asked to see the visitor log. Someone named Abraham Undie visited him today."

"Who's that?" I said.

He finished wiping his fingers, balled up the napkin, and tossed it with a flourish over my shoulder. It sank into the trash can beside the front door.

Two points.

"Beats me," he said. "We have no Undies on the rez, and we have none I know of in the Fort. I did a quick web search for Abraham Undie, and the closet listing I found was in Montreal."

I felt my throat parch. Father Cooper, Canada.

"They showed me a video of the visit. This Undie is black, which is notable. I am not sure if you have noticed, but we have no African-Americans walking around here."

I hadn't noticed it until he mentioned it. "Ok, so he's a brother, what of it?"

"Nothing, just an identifying feature. This Undie did most of the talking. Gary spoke a little, when he first arrived, but it was not long after that Gary went speechless. He was visibly disturbed. When I saw him two hours later, he wore the same look on his face."

"Did it seem like they knew each other?" I asked.

Jo Jo's eyes rolled up and to the right, as if ceiling held the answer. I thought it over for a few seconds. "I don't think so. Now that you mention it, Gary seemed confused when he walked into the visitation room, and saw Undie standing there. I don't think he had ever seen him before."

"Did Gary look threatened? Or did it appear that Undie was threatening him?"

"I don't know. Undie didn't appear to be especially threatening. But, like I said, you could tell it bothered Gary. And there was something else..."

"What's that?"

"It's hard to explain," he said. "Especially because we are talking about Gary Pressley, but it was almost as if Gary took on the mannerisms of a young boy while Undie was with him."

"I got some of that from him when I talked to him," I explained.

"I know, but he typically slips in and out of that mode, right?"

I thought it over for a second. "Yeah, I guess so."

Jo Jo leaned back in his roller chair. It croaked under his considerable weight. "With this Undie, Gary settled into the little kid mode. He wasn't like that when I saw him, but he was still messed up."

I wasn't sure what to make of Gary's silent treatment. It

could mean something. Maybe this Undie held the answer to what happened to Katie. Maybe he was behind her killing. Maybe Gary had succumbed to the stress of life in prison. But threads were breaking loose of the tightly knit ball that the prosecution had put together. Now we needed to pull on them until we found the one that tore the thing apart.

"Did you hear anything they discussed?" I said.

Jo Jo shook his head, clapped his knees with both hands, and hauled himself up out of his chair. "No volume on the video."

I expected as much. "Do you think they'd let me watch the video?"

Jo Jo fished around in his pockets. "I can arrange it." When he came up empty in his pockets, he searched his desk. Underneath the remains of his dinner, he found his keys.

"In a hurry to leave me, Jo Jo?"

I caught a peek of his brilliant white teeth.

"A lady friend awaits," he said. "Don't forget to lock up."

I felt his departure and descent down the outside stairs in the rumble of the floorboards.

The evidence box was crammed with manila folders stuffed with paper. Because of what I knew of all the oversights, it still seemed light for Katie's case.

Over the next hour, I removed each folder and fanned through the contents and made notes of those folders I wanted to return to for closer inspection. Ignorant of the County's file identification system, I included each of the unique numbers labeled on the folder tabs to my notes to locate the folder for my return visit.

After that initial scan, my growling stomach coaxed me to head down to the Howlin' Wolf for dinner. The same lovely waitress who served me coffee earlier, greeted me with all the charm of a sloth. To be fair, she was an efficient server, and I finished my dinner of microwaved Salisbury steak and mashed potatoes and carrots, and returned to my work upstairs in less than thirty minutes. I tipped her even better than before and received the same response.

I checked the time often as I dug into the evidence, standing and walking to the door to peek out at the weather occasionally. If the weather held off, I'd still make the hockey game.

Around 6:30, right before I called it a night, I opened the folder with scans from Katie's day planner. Evidently, Katie, like Veronica, was one of the few human beings who still relied on a written journal, rather than a digital calendar, to schedule her days. I saw nothing of significance in my original scan of the pages, but set it aside for a deep dive because I knew the patterns of one's days said something of the person. When you understood the pattern, the deviations of the pattern stood out. Deviations often meant clues.

In Katie's case, I never reviewed the file close enough to understand the rhythm of her life's days or weeks, because a name stood out of the page each Monday going back a year.

Undie.

MOST CLERGY TOOK Monday as their day off. If the Undie in her journal was the same one that visited Pressley, Katie Couture took that opportunity to travel up to Montreal.

Katie kept an appointment with him every Monday. Until the Monday before her death when she crossed out her appointment with him.

I was wrong when I said I hadn't recognized a pattern. Or deviations. Undie was a pattern. The cancelation was a deviation.

And his visit to Gary Pressley made him our best suspect.

I hoped FedEx delivered overnight to Fort Covington, New York.

I left the pile of paper on Jo Jo's desk, circling a few of the Undie appointments. If he was entertaining a lady friend, he probably wouldn't see it until the morning. I called it a night and went to watch the hockey game.

22

———

The ice arena at Salmon River Central School reminded me of the roller-skating palaces I attended in my youth before I realized there were better places to meet girls. It was a pre-engineered metal building with a light steel structure that would collapse like tinker toys in the face of anything approaching the hurricane-force winds we saw in the Strand. All the steel shined with glossy white paint, including the bottom of the roof deck. When combined with the ice of the rink, the effect was blinding and headache inducing. The green box bleachers, five deep on one side of the rink, provided a dash of color. The town citizens packed, like the poor souls in a DMV waiting room, provided the rest. They chattered like girls in the high school cafeteria.

I took the only seat I could find at the end of the top row beside two teen-aged lovers. Acne covered the boy's face. His dirty blond hair was unwashed and combed back in a duck's ass. The girl's auburn hair style came from somewhere it would take a tank of gas to reach. Her face unblemished. Make-up expertly applied with a light touch.

He knew he had out-kicked his coverage, but he stole kisses and let his nervous hands roam.

"Not here," she whispered repeatedly.

I considered handing over the key to my room at the Traveler's Rest to spare me seeing them in the reproductive process they learned about in Sex Ed.

I turned away from them and waited on hockey players to arrive on the ice.

A voice on the public announcement system informed us that the fireworks display would begin at 9 p.m. tomorrow night at the St. Lawrence Centre.

Little annoyed me more than giving out candy on October 30th; or lighting fireworks on the 3rd of July; or celebrating a New Year three hours before midnight.

Before I built up the gumption to share my opinion with the announcer's booth, the crowd roared as if the main act had arrived on stage at a rock concert. Nope, the Shamrocks squad clad in white jerseys and clover green trouser swept onto the rink.

"Ladies and Gentlemen, welcome your State Champion, Salmon River Shamrocks!" came over the house speakers, the voice like the guy hocking used cars on the local television stations. He was too late though. The place was already as loud as it would get. Even my lovebirds had quit necking long enough to stand and applaud the Shamrocks' arrival.

Korsakov's *Flight of the Bumblebee* replaced the announcer's voice. It was a perfect match as the Shamrocks weaved in and out in a complex choreography. The image of bees fit. Even the crowd quieted to a pleasant buzz.

The Governeur team's arrival broke the spell. A cacophony of boos and other more colorful chants greeted them. Where the Shamrocks glided like a team of figure skaters, the Wildcats lumbered like football players on skates. They were a much more physically imposing squad than

Salmon River's. I thought of Sugar Ray versus Hagler. A fight before my time, but that I had heard enough of from my father to know it fit. Boxer vs. Puncher. Salmon had to give up twenty pounds on average to the Governeur squad, and only one of their players had a build that would fit in on the Wildcats. Still my money was on the reigning champs.

As the teams scurried off the ice, and into their benches, two middle-aged gentlemen emerged and shuffled on street shoes to center ice. One wore a blue blazer with gold buttons and khakis and ox-blood loafers. He had gray hair glued to his scalp like a plastic shell. A stern Hagleresque look on his face. The other wore a green polo and stiff blue jeans like they had just come off the rack. His clothes fit snug on his fit physique. His skin unnaturally tanned for the dead of winter. He scooted on black and green running shoes. His straight blond mop of hair bouncing with each step. He approached Hagler smiling like a stumping politician. I'd seen the face before. Sugar Ray was Dave Hetfield.

Boos filled the room, again, as the referees skated out to center ice to deliver their instructions to the two coaches. A sarcastic smirk creeped onto Hetfield's face and remained there throughout the referee's briefing.

I didn't like the guy, and I needed to guard against that when I interviewed him tomorrow.

When the referee completed his diatribe, the two coaches shook hands and headed toward their respective benches. Hetfield smiled and waved to the crowd. Occasionally, he pointed someone out in the crowd, cranked the smile up an extra watt, and nodded his head like they had just shared a secret joke. It was a fake, political act.

After the coaches made it to their benches, Father Cooper struggled with his lame leg out onto the ice to lead the congregation in a moment of silence and prayer for Katie Couture and the entire community suffering the great loss of their dead Sister. Aimee Hetfield, a pretty, if slightly big-boned, Senior, sang an out-of-key rendition of the National Anthem. More ear-splitting cheers followed, cueing the Shamrocks to take the ice.

From the drop of the puck, it was clear Governeur had the two top skaters. Big, strong, fast boys, who hogged the puck, streaking the length of the ice and slapping wild shots, that the goalie seldom flinched at. In contrast, the smaller Salmon squad played boring, conservative hockey, passing the puck back and forth slowly advancing it until all of their skaters were set-up on the Governeur side of the ice and they fed shots to the Wildcats' goalie until one would rebound to a Shamrock camped out in front of the goal. Then, he would flip a wrist shot past the punch-drunk goalkeeper.

Hetfield positioned his most skilled players on defense, which frustrated the hell out of Governeur's two phenoms. Both would end up with full rides at hockey powerhouse universities. But tonight, they found themselves down 3-0 after one period.

At the break, I caught Hetfield walking off the ice with Salmon's largest player, whose blond hair matched his own. The student was a little on the soft-side, but when he burned off some baby fat, he would share Hetfield's build. The coach had a tight grip on the kid's arm. Red-faced, he shouted at the boy so violently that from the stands I saw the spittle flying from Hetfield's mouth.

The kid was Hetfield's son. Even the coach of a state championship team could not abuse a student in public. Unless the kid was his own.

I had wanted a vision of Hetfield, the man, through his interaction with his players. How he treated his own kid was more telling.

During the first intermission, the two lovers departed leaving me a little extra room to enjoy the game. It ended up a rout. Salmon tacked on two more score early in the second period before sitting their first line for the rest of the game and coasting to a 6-1 lead.

They impressed me with their disciplined approach to the game. Their tactics lacked excitement for a casual fan like me, but it worked. I had to give Hetfield that.

I filed out with the rest of the crowd in a single-file line out into a light falling snow.

Sonny LaPage saw me in the parking lot and waved me over to introduce me to his grandson Dylan. His pale face shone in the moonlight, and tiny snow crystals flecked his shiny black hair like dandruff. He wore baggy gray sweat pants tucked into brown leather work boots, and a red and black flannel coat with a white faux-fur collar. He was about grandpa's height, which meant I was more than a head taller. LaPage explained that he was a sophomore and on the Junior Varsity squad.

I asked, "What do you think of Coach Hetfield?"

The boy shifted his eyes from me to his shoes and shrugged his shoulders.

It meant nothing other than he was uncomfortable talking to an adult stranger.

LaPage patted him on the shoulder. "Answer the man." He frowned and explained, "He can be a little shy with new people."

Dylan stuffed his hands in his coat pockets and shuffled his feet.

Grandpa had now embarrassed him.

"No worries," I said, and took my leave.

As I walked to my car, I heard Sonny mumble to the kid, "You need to work on your confidence, Dylie. Coach looks for confident players."

I crawled into the Nova, turned the ignition, and coaxed

the heater into action. I rubbed my hands in front of the blower, trying to bring feeling back to my fingertips.

When most of the cars had left the arena, I still sat there watching the snow.

Besides me, only an over-sized, white SUV with gold spoked wheels and a bright yellow Toyota Tacoma truck with tires as tall as me, remained and sat side-by-side.

I had not seen Hetfield leave. My suspicions regarding his son were confirmed when Hetfield emerged from the arena's side doors. The boy he spat all over, the anthem singing girl, and a blonde trophy wife with manufactured boobs were in tow.

They huddled up between the two vehicles for a brief discussion. The chat ended with Hetfield tousling the boy's hair and faking a punch to the chin. The smile never left Hetfield's face. One never showed on the kid's face.

Mom gave the kid a peck on the cheek, then the boy climbed up into the truck and the rest of them got into the SUV.

They pulled out onto the Bombay-Fort Covington Road headed west towards Highway 37.

I wasn't sure what compelled me to wait around to see Hetfield leave. Nothing happened that meant anything, but I was glad I saw the whole family huddled around dad. I liked him even less. Mom was a fake. All I knew of Amy was she couldn't sing. And the boy hated his life. But was that really all that rare?

I headed to the Traveler's Rest. It was only 10 o'clock, but the American Legion would have to survive without me tonight.

23

Twenty minutes later, I was in bed reading a dog-eared Loren Estleman paperback by the dim light of a shadeless lamp which sat on the nightstand. In it, Estleman's detective followed behind his prey sloshing through snow-filled Detroit sidewalks, like the ones I had maneuvered for several days in the Fort. A long-legged spider pacing the ceiling made it difficult to focus on reading. I put the book aside and shut the light off.

Someone tapped on my door. I figured it for Stefanie Charles. I stayed in the safe darkness of my bed.

"Fuzzy, I know you are there," she whispered.

I turned my back to the window and door and played sleep.

More tapping.

She called my name one more time, tried the knob, and knocked louder.

Then silence for a few moments. Followed by the light smack on the door, and the sound of her receding footsteps.

I fell asleep and dreamed of a monkey in a cage wearing bright red lipstick. Dave Hetfield brandished a circus ringmaster's whip and snapped it at the bars of the cage. The monkey smiled dumbly back at him.

I AWOKE CHEWING on something that felt like a rubber inner tube patch. I realized it the flap of skin from my tongue, which had broken loose in the night. I ran to the sink and spat it out and dry heaved until my throat was raw.

My tongue felt funny without the baffle of flesh I had gotten used to.

The face looking back at me in the mirror was pallid and unshaven. I felt hungover, despite having come home early without a trip to the Legion. The old bear needed hibernation. Restless sleep, late drinking nights, and a beating will do that to you.

I remembered Stefanie Charles's visit in the night, and I went to the window, and peeked out the blinds at the office. No sight of her little red compact car.

I exhaled a breath I didn't realize I had held.

It was 8 o'clock. I had an appointment to meet Dave Hetfield at the school at ten. The drive to Malone was thirty minutes. If I skipped a shower, I could make it there, view the video of Undie's visit, maybe talk to Gary for a minute, and return to the Fort in time to meet Coach. Or, I could just hang around until ten, meet Hetfield, and then have the rest of the day to visit the prison. Except, I hoped my passport would arrive today. In which case, I planned to hunt down Abraham Undie in Montreal this afternoon.

I slid into the same jeans I had worn the day before, put on a bright yellow T-shirt advertising Kilgore Trout's Record Store, shrugged on my jacket, grabbed my keys, finger brushed my hair, and hit the door. My insides shouted for me to feed them. I ignored the pleas.

As I backed out the Nova, I saw a hot-pink post-it note stuck to the face of my room's door.

Stefanie Charles had slapped it on my door last night.

I threw the car into park, got out, and retrieved the note.

It read:

"We need to talk. A little birdie told me something about the good Sis'. — S."

Probably not worth the paper she wrote it on. I crumbled the slip and stuffed it into my front pocket.

24

I kept the needle pinned at seventy on the drive to Malone, fifteen miles-per-hour over the legal limit. A call to Jo Jo confirmed that he had arranged my viewing of the video. He told me good catch on Katie's journal entries. I asked again how nobody else caught this shit. He didn't know and didn't seem to care.

I remembered his demeanor at Garrow's office. Something about Jo Jo was like a wedge of apple skin burrowed between the teeth and into the gum line. No matter how much I worked at it with my tongue, I could not work it free. I knew if I remained persistent, I would succeed. The corresponding relief would be worth the effort.

I signed off with Jo Jo as I pulled into the drop-off circle at the Franklin Correctional Facility. I drove in front of the entrance to the left side of the circle and parked it with my tires brushing the curb.

A ticket would await me when I returned, but I was managing my time down to the minutes. Risk/Reward.

I hurried through the automatic sliding glass doors and to a heavy-set woman with hair teased to the moon and make-up the envy of circus clowns the world over. She oversaw a half-circle reception desk. A black plastic nameplate dubbed her Betsy Cochin. When she smiled, cracks formed in her lip gloss. "Welcome to Franklin Correctional. How may I help you?"

"I need to see Officer Whitaker," I said.

"May I tell him—"

I cut her off, "Fuzzy Koella, he is expecting me."

She rolled her eyes.

I jammed my hands into my coat pockets to keep them from wrapping around the sweaty folds in her neck.

She jammed a black plastic phone to her ear. "Hey, Steve. We have a Frizzy Koella here to see you." She looked to me. A frown splayed hairline fractures throughout her lips worse than the smile had.

I kept that observation to myself. Didn't correct my name, either.

She listened, nodded, listened more, nodded more. "All right, I'll tell him."

She dropped the phone in its cradle and directed her attention to a putty-colored computer monitor manufactured last century. She spoke to the screen. "He's in the middle of something, right now. Have a seat, and he will be with you in a moment."

I tried on my Southern charm, "Ma'am, I'm in a time crunch, any chance you can inform Mr. Whitaker?"

She tapped away at her keyboard. "Have a seat. He will be with you momentarily."

Momentarily, equaled five minutes and thirty-two seconds. I knew because that was how closely I watched the time crawl by on my phone.

I approved of the Franklin County definition of 'momentarily'. In Horry County, it was sometime that day.

Whitaker was a short, lean, poster-child for the Aryan

nation, without all the supremacy bullshit. Short cropped, blond hair. Blue sapphires, with whites so healthy it was almost as if some of the light blue from his irises had bled to the rest of his eyeballs. Chiseled jaw-line, and a brilliant smile to match his eye-whites. His beige uniform shirt snugly encased his canon-ball biceps and tapered to his narrow waist. His brown trousers seemed in danger of splitting at the seams from the pressure exerted by his powerful thighs with each step. He smiled a lot, and when I shook his hand, I didn't need to wipe mine clean on my jeans.

"Jo Jo says you want a look at that video?"

He was about shoulder height on me, but I still had the impression we spoke eye to eye. "That's right, and if time permits, maybe a short visit with Gary."

"Well come on," he said. "I set us up in a visitation room, so you can take a look-see, and then I can bring Gary in." He turned and strode off the way he had entered.

I walked twice my normal gait to keep up with him.

Over his shoulder, he said, "The kid still ain't talkin'. So, unless you're prepared for a long one-sided conversation, you will probably have no issue making your other engagement."

There was a pleasant cadence to the clap of his boot heels on the polished vinyl floor. It almost made me forget the struggle of keeping up with him.

When my breath became audible, he stopped before a gray steel door at the end of a corridor, pushed it open, and stood aside to allow me to pass.

The room was like the last interrogation room I had met Gary in, except it had no floor drain needing its trap primed. The place didn't smell like shit. It also had an old tube television on a metal cart. The cart held a DVD player the size of a small suitcase beneath the TV.

Whitaker must have caught me inspecting his gear,

because he beamed and said, "Only the top of the line technology here at Franklin County Correctional."

"Hey, I have an old stereo equipment fetish. No judgement here."

He pulled a chair back from the table. "Good, have a seat."

I did as commanded. He rolled the TV closer to the table, pressed play, and slid another chair over to my side of the table. Then, he remained standing with his hands on the seat back.

The picture was black and white and snowy. Gary sat slouched in a room just like the one we were in now. He had an unlit cigarette in his hand and he tapped the mouth end on the table.

"Gary smokes?"

"No idea," Whitaker said. "It's currency in here, but some come in non-smokers and leave three-pack-a-day guys."

"I wouldn't advertise that; some wise guy will get the idea to sue y'all."

He laughed a little too much. "You're probably right."

On the set, the door swung open and Whitaker entered with a black man dressed in traditional African garb. His sokoto was loose-fitting. The buba, similarly baggy, was untucked and hung over the waistline. He wore no headgear, and the tight springs of his coiled hair were cropped tight to his skull. His skin was as dark as the smoke from an oil fire.

"You met Undie?"

Whitaker dipped his chin. "He was quite a character. Not that I really spoke much too him, but you stroll into Malone, New York dressed like that, and you get a lot of folks talking. I think he did it for the attention. I mean I don't think he shows up at the office dressed like that."

Gary sat up in his seat on the video. He dropped the

cigarette and pushed himself back from the table with both hands on its edge.

"Did you get the impression Gary knew Undie? He looks a little scared."

He kept his eyes on the screen. "I think it's the first time Gary Pressley had seen a black man outside of television."

"C'mon? You have no brothers in here?"

"I don't know. We don't get many. I seldom note skin color. You'd think I would have, given how rare African-Americans are up here, but I don't. I noticed this dude, though, coming in here dressed like he stepped off the stage of some International Folk Festival."

"I guess it could disturb a guy like Gary," I said.

Undie leaned forward, hands flat on the table, speaking to Gary. Gary's eyes shifted often with whatever Undie said. He shook his head through a lot.

Undie paced back and forth like a politician working the stage, turning ninety degrees and speaking directly to Gary at specific points. Gary put both hands to the side of his head, like he was warding a headache.

Undie continued his delivery.

Gary dropped his arms to the tabletop, crossed them, and buried his head there.

Undie transformed. Gone was the fiery pastor from the pulpit act. He sat down across from Gary, patted him on the shoulder, and leaned in to whisper something to the sobbing kid.

I had forgotten Whitaker. In the picture, there beside the door he stood like a soldier at attention.

"What was Undie saying to him?"

"Weird shit. Psychic Reader Hotline stuff. Like that Ms. Cleo. You remember her?"

"I remember the commercials," I said. "But I don't get it, he came in here to give Gary a psychic reading?"

Whitaker stood and stepped over to the set and paused the playback.

No remote? They were old school.

"It wasn't reading shit. He kept saying some word repeatedly, and he was talking about Gary and Katie's son. Maybe reincarnation or something. What was that word?" He tilted his head back, searching the ceiling for an answer.

I tried it out, too, but I only noted the globe mounted light fixture and the massacres of insects revealed behind the burning glass. Did they feel pain, or was the death immediate?

Zap. Another one bit the dust.

Whitaker snapped his fingers and wagged his index finger at me. "*Ti bon ange,* he kept saying this. Then he'd call Gary, Beau. It freaked me out. I can only imagine what it did to the kid. Didn't Katie have a son named Beau, who died?"

Ti bon ange. What the hell was that? What language was it? French?

Whitaker waved his hand in front of my face. "Yoohoo, are you in there?"

I snapped out of it. "Yes, Katie had a son named Beau. *Ti bon ange*? Undie is from Montreal. Is that French?"

Whitaker nodded, "I took it in high school, it means 'good little angel'. To be honest, that creeps me out even more."

Goose pimples formed on my arms. I remembered Veronica's comment about woo-woo shit. I didn't believe in any of that stuff. I struggled with simple stuff like the New Testament. But the people who believed in that stuff? Those were the ones who spooked me.

Whitaker made an act of checking his wristwatch. It was one of those sportsmen's watches with GPS and miles per hour pace and more buttons than the latest video game consoles. "Hey, should I bring Gary in?"

"Yeah, probably a good idea."

I stopped Whitaker before the door shut about him. "Did Gary say anything, while all of this was going on?"

His lips turned down. The frown looked foreign on his good-natured face. "As soon as Undie spoke, Gary clammed up and hasn't spoken since. It was like he had cast a spell on him."

Great.

TI BON ANGE.

Good Little Angel.

Was Sister Katie Couture the good little angel? Or Gary Pressley? And why travel down from Montreal just to deliver that message?

Before I had my answer, Whitaker returned with a head-hung Gary with handcuffed wrists. What I could see of his face had taken on a sickly pallor, matching the forest green inmate's suit he wore. When the door closed behind them, Whitaker undid the bracelets.

I stood and extended my hand.

Gary ignored my hand and took a seat across from me.

Whitaker held his palms out at his side and shrugged his shoulders. He took a position beside the door, like he had in the video.

I sat down. "Gary, do you remember me?"

He rocked back and forth from the waist up.

I wasn't sure if that was a yes or a no. "Right," I said. "Well, I work for Jo Jo Bigtree, your attorney. I have a few more questions for you. Remember, Jo Jo and I are trying to get you out of here. So, anything you can give us to help us along those lines would be great."

I paused for a response from Gary.

He continued to rock with the cadence of a pendulum on

a grandfather clock. He glued his eyes to mine, and parted his lips like a stiff, horizontal coin slot.

"Gary," I waved my hand in front of his face.

Same dead, rocking stare.

"What can you tell me about the high truck?"

Nothing.

"Jo Jo said you mentioned a high truck. That it arrived when you found Katie's body."

Nothing. It was as if he wore headphones and rocked back and forth to the music, and could not hear me.

"*Ti bon ange*," I said. "You remember the black man that came to see you yesterday? *Ti bon ange*? He said this to you. What does that mean to you?"

Nothing. Same flat stare.

Whitaker smiled at me. Shook his head. Mouthed, "I told you so."

"Beau," I said.

There was a hitch in his rocking motion. He blinked, and his right eye twitched. His back-and-forth motion picked up speed.

"Did you know Katie's Beau, Gary?"

Picking up more speed. His hands cupped his ears.

"Gary, I'm trying to help." I leaned forward and took his wrists in my hands and lowered his hands.

When they reached the table, he yanked them from my grasp and settled them in his lap. Still, he rocked.

"Do you miss Katie?"

Nothing.

"How about Beau?"

He turned his head and squinted. The name was like a tuning fork. Still he said nothing.

I continued on for about five minutes. Every time I returned to the name Beau, he grimaced. I stopped short of the time frame I had given myself for the visit because I was getting nowhere. The name, Beau, bothered him, but Gary said nothing. Not one word. But it hurt him. The name Beau tortured him. I could take it no longer than Gary could.

I smacked both hands on the table and stood, "Ok Gary, I guess that will do it for now. If you want to talk about any of the questions I've asked, call Jo Jo, and we'll come right over. We'll probably stop by just about every day to visit, anyway."

He halted rocking and turned to Whitaker and held out his wrists.

Whitaker stepped forward, removing the cuffs from his belt. "If you'll wait here, Koella, I'll have another officer in here to escort you out."

"Any chance I can wait on you to return?"

That got a sideways glance from him as he tightened the cuffs onto Gary's wrists. "I thought you were in a hurry."

"This didn't take as long as I'd thought, and I have something I need to talk to you about."

"It has to be me?"

I shrugged. "I know you."

He put his hand on Gary's shoulder and directed him to the door. "Whatever you say," he said.

I spent the time working out a strategy to beat the Cracker Barrel peg game, but it was hard to do without the game or a pen and paper.

I counted three zaps from the light fixture during my wait. It unnerved me that I hadn't realized there were three insects flying around the room until they flew through the small gap between the lens of the fixture and the ceiling and met their demise at the hands of the scorching sixty-watt light bulb. I was working out my feelings about the slain insects, and had only determined that I was okay if they were spiders and not flying insects, when Whitaker returned.

The guy smiled too much.

"What's up," he said.

"Has a psychiatrist been to see Gary?"

He shoved his hands into his trouser pockets and rocked back on his boot heels.

If he started the rocking Gary routine, I'd need the psychiatrist.

"Well, has he seen one," I repeated.

"I'm sure the prosecution has had one or two in to see him, but you should talk to them about that. I'm just a lowly corrections officer."

"Believe it or not, I'm not asking about any doctors that y'all or Jo Jo would use for the case. I'm concerned about the kid."

The corner of his lips jacked up another quarter of an inch. "Right," he said. "I like you, Fuzzy, but I know how this works. I have one boss, and it ain't Fuzzy Koella. Find someone else to help you with your case."

I squeezed one hand with the other and popped each knuckle starting with the pinky.

"What, now you wanna throw down?"

I stopped and hid my hands behind my back. "Sorry, no, it's just a nervous habit. I'm not sure what to do here. Whatever you may think, I'm worried about Gary. And I don't think he needs the help that will come from lawyer appointed physicians."

I think he was coming around to my way of thinking. At least, that's what I took from the smile disappearing from his face.

"I don't know what I can do, unless he gets sick or acts like he might hurt himself," he said.

"Ok," I said. "But can you keep a close eye on him to see if he does any of those things?"

He opened the door. "Already doing that," he said, the smile returning. "I like Gary. He doesn't belong in here."

"Good."

25

Whitaker walked me back to the lobby, asking me about the weather in South Carolina, and why in the hell I had agreed to come up to New York this time of year. I asked him why he continued to live up there if it was so bad. He didn't have an answer for that. He patted me on the shoulder while he shook my hand and we said our goodbyes.

I strode half the Whitaker-pace through the lobby, passing Ms. Piggy's desk. I cocked my finger pistol, took aim, and shot her between the eyes. I gave the tip of my index finger a blow to clear the imaginary smoke and winked at her.

Piggy's nostrils flared and her throat contracted. She looked like she had just swallowed Kermit.

I continued out the doors.

Into more fucking snow.

The skies looked like the scene in one of those souvenir shop globes after being shaken by an over eager kid. The snow never seemed to fall to the ground. It fluttered around, defying the laws of gravity. But more filled the sky by the second, and by the time I reached the car I wasn't sure I'd be able to see past the hood on the trip back to Fort Covington.

A half-inch of it blanketed the windshield. I dug it out with clawed fingers. Surprisingly, I found no ticket underneath the stuff. Big fan of the Franklin County Sheriff's office. The frostbite settling into my fingertips and knuckles? Not so much.

I got in the car and called Dave Hetfield and told him I'd be a little late due to the weather. He asked if we wanted to make it another day. I told him no.

Something about Hetfield had my Spidey-sense tingling, and I didn't want to put him off any longer.

We agreed on ten-fifteen, and I began the treacherous trek back to the Fort.

Trying to make all the pieces work in Gary Pressley and Katie Couture's case was more difficult than that Cracker Barrel game.

I had hoped that my passport would come today. So, maybe, I could head up to Montreal in the afternoon. Now, I had no desire to chance icy roads in a foreign country. Undie was looking good for one of those question marks Jo Jo and I were seeking. I had to remind myself. We didn't need to find a killer. We needed to find a reasonable doubt.

An image of Katie struggling against her bindings in that sweltering basement came to life in my mind.

Nope, I needed to find a killer.

After a couple days of talking to people that seemed to have little bearing on the case, and save Garrow, weren't suspects, I felt excitement at the thought of talking to Hetfield and Undie.

They seemed like jumping pegs in the Cracker Barrel game.

I HAD SLOWED to twenty-five miles per hour and had passed two snow plows pulled off the side of the road, by the time the cream-colored stucco and brown bricks of the Salmon River Central School came into sight.

His titanic, white SUV idled in a drop-off circle before an aluminum awning that sagged under the weight of piled snow. The vehicle poured plumes of smoke out of its dual tailpipes.

I pulled in behind him and looked at my phone. A couple of missed calls from Hetfield. It was 10:25.

He'd probably burned through three gallons of gas, sitting there waiting on me.

I didn't look forward to stepping out into the cold, so I waited on him.

The phone rang.

It was him. The son of a bitch didn't even realize I was behind him.

"Fuzzy, where are you?"

"Look in the mirror," I said.

He cut the line.

He swung the door open and hopped down. He wore duck boots, and heavy blue ski pants and a matching jacket. A bright, orange toque covered his head, and a matching scarf wrapped around his mouth and lower face, leaving an inch-and-half strip of exposed flesh around his eyes.

He was certainly better at this winter stuff than I was.

He headed towards me in a Frankenstein walk. He was so wrapped up in winter clothes it limited movement of his joints.

I cranked down the window, something I had not done in a decade.

Dave Hetfield tugged the scarf loose from his mouth and leaned down to my window.

"Where do you want to do this?" I asked.

"Right to the point, eh?" He smiled and held out a gloved hand. "Dave Hetfield."

I shook his pillowed hand and gave it back to him.

"Fuzzy Koella. To the point out of necessity, Mr. Hetfield. I want to get somewhere that I can thaw out my toes. The heat in this bucket doesn't reach the floorboards."

He chuckled. "All right then. Come on, we'll find a classroom where we can chat."

I got out of the car, and he chuckled again.

"Damn, son. Someone needs to buy you some winter clothes and some boots. Or else, you're gonna die from exposure."

He stood there with his dumb smile searching for some reaction.

I waited on him to lead the way.

"Well, all right," he said, turned on his heels and walked off under the awning to a glass entryway covered with snow and ice.

At least I could walk without looking like someone had jammed a hockey stick up my ass.

When he reached the front doors, he fished out a ring of keys the envy of any school janitor, found the right one, and unlocked the door.

"What do you do at the school besides coach the hockey team, Mr. Hetfield?"

He pushed open the door and let me pass. "Oh nothing. I'm on the school board." He shook the keys at me. "Membership has its privileges."

I'm not sure I understood what the privilege was, but I flashed a smile no less fake than his.

Inside the two-story lobby, there were glass trophy cases filled with silver cups, trophies topped with the bronze figures of hockey skaters, and stained wood plaques with gold-etched placards.

Hetfield must have recognized my admiration. "Did you play?"

I shook my head. "Baseball. I've never ice skated in my life. Not really anyone down there to teach the game."

"Down there?"

"Ah, sorry, I'm up from South Carolina," I said.

"And Jo Jo flew you all the way up here to enjoy our weather, eh?"

I rubbed my hands on the front of my jeans to keep from balling them up into fists.

"Yes," he said.

I wasn't sure what he was answering 'yes' to.

He continued, "Well, we have quite the hockey tradition here at Salmon."

He held up both hands. Each ring finger had gold championship rings with marble-sized emeralds. He wasn't wearing a wedding band. "The trophies that came with these rings are somewhere in those cases."

I had two championship rings myself. One for state as a member of the Myrtle Beach High Seahawks. One for a conference championship with the Carolina Atlantic University Manatees. I gave up wearing them five years ago when I realized that a grown man flaunting his adolescent accomplishments looked like a douche-bag to other adults.

"I was at the game last night," I said.

He raised his pale white eyebrows, "Really? And what did you think?"

"Impressive," I said.

He pulled the toque off and shook his head like a dog coming in from the rain. His mop of blond hair fell into place. Perfect. He looked like a surfer misplaced on the Canadian border.

When he finished flouncing, I continued, "You're getting the most out of your talent, which even I know is limited."

"They become better players because of our puck move-ment strategy. Their eyes get better, and by the time they are Seniors no opportunity escapes them."

"Makes sense," I said. "Like I said, it's impressive."

"Have you ever seen that movie Jurassic Park?"

He realized there were more than one, right?

"Of course," I said.

"We attack like the raptors in the movie. We methodically set up the prey from all corners. It survives for a short time, but it is so frustrating that eventually it leaves its guard down. And there we are with the kill."

His face flushed with the excitement of talking about his strategy.

"Your guys don't have raptor speed, though."

He delivered his message with karate chop hand gestures. "Here's the thing. We've got a young team. We graduated five Seniors from last year's championship squad. We're left with two Seniors, but most of our talent are Juniors and Sopho-mores, getting their first real taste of playing time. They're getting to be better skaters. Talent isn't what you're born with, it's what you've worked for. Many of these kids will have scholarship offers by the time they have skated their last game for the Shamrocks."

The guy was good. I felt like I was in a locker room again, and ready to lace up my skates.

"I need to talk about Katie Couture," I said.

That killed the energy in his gesturing hands. He slid them into his pants pockets. "Right."

The other wall of the lobby was concrete block painted to match the exterior stucco and had a sliding receptionist's window with a small banker's counter. Taped in the window was a letter-sized sheet of white paper. Printed on it was "Office". Punch windows looked down on the lobby from the second story. Forest green metal doors were on either side of the office window.

Hetfield led us through the door on the left.

Through that door was a hallway that could have existed one thousand miles south and twenty-five years in the past. It was comforting to know not much had changed in the American high school. The walls were striped with the green school colors. The floor tiles were green and white checkered. The forgotten ceiling tiles were plain white and stained and were only about eight feet above the floor. Many of the class room doors were decorated — Mrs. Metcalf's class, Ms. Sheehan's English, Mrs. Sawyer's room. Mr. Thomas', Mr. Selmon's, and Coach Dudley's doors were not decorated.

Hetfield chattered on about the Shamrock's record over the years. "Fourteen state championships. This last one was the first in ten years."

He walked us deep into the guts of the school.

Why couldn't we use any of these classrooms? Surely Mrs. Sawyer didn't care if we squatted in her abandoned room on New Year's Eve.

"Forty-two all-state players…"

This guy loved his Shamrocks. Maybe, Katie Couture was a closet Massena fan?

He stopped at a scarred, primer coated door that couldn't have seen a kid pass through it since the Shamrock's prior championship.

Hetfield grinned, as he hunted for the key. "We haven't had a kid make it all the way to the NHL yet, but it's only a matter of time."

I finished it for him, "With you as their coach, I'm sure it will happen."

He found the key and let us in.

The room seemed dark even after he turned the lights on.

Two-foot-high awning windows lined the opposite wall where it met the ceiling. If the skies weren't so overcast, the windows would allow natural light to enter, but we were stuck with the faint light coming from fluorescent troffers. White throw sheets covered all the room's furniture. The pieces were huddled in a chaotic array in the center of the room.

An old blackboard hung from the wall to our left. A faint smell of chalk dust lingered in the air. Or maybe it was just dust.

Hetfield slid the sheets off two pieces of furniture with a flourish and smiled like a game show hostess showing me my prize.

The furniture looked like a bastard hybrid of an easel and a bench lacquered with a dark mahogany stain.

"I don't know whether to sit on it or take a picture to send to the Smithsonian," I said.

"They're artists' benches," he patted the bench portion. "The artist straddles the bench here." He pointed to a vertical plywood element attached to one end of the contraption. "Then they put their drawing pad or canvas on this easel. Or," he took the bench in his hand, rotated it ninety degrees, and stood it up on one end. "If they want to work standing up, they do like this here, eh?"

"Any reason you brought me to the art room?"

He waved his arm over the room's contents. "This is all abandoned due to tax cuts to the arts programs," he said. "No teacher can complain about us using their room."

"That's a shame," I said.

"You haven't heard them complain."

"I was talking about the cuts, not the teachers."

He returned the bench to the seated position and dropped down on it.

I took the other one facing him.

I went with the curve ball. "Do you own any traditional Mohawk war clubs?"

His chest expanded and contracted with silent laughter. "What the hell does that have to do with Katie Couture?" His head tilted and craned forward as he studied my face. "Say, what happened to your face, Fuzzy?"

Before I had registered for my private investigator's license and after a drunk driver had killed my fiancé, I had toiled as a campus cop at my alma mater (or whatever they call the university that you attended but never received a degree). I hadn't been subjected to the low-lives of society that my Uncle Rod dealt with daily, but I had come into contact with my share of sociopaths. They were frat boys, jocks, or social outcasts brought in for questioning for sexual assault on campus. None of them did it, of course. They said this convincingly, but the nasty feeling you got crawling down the skin over your spine told you there was some truth in the accusations brought against them.

It was slithering down my back now. I touched the scabs on my face left there from the crushed stone parking lot at the Legion. A bitter taste settled on the open wound on my tongue. I bore my eyes deep into his gaze. "I cut myself shaving."

He didn't flinch. "You ought to be careful. Did you shave after a night of drinking?"

The serpent's tongue was flicking on the nape of my neck. I stood and rolled my shoulders. "You never answered my question about the war club?"

He stood, too. He was a few inches shorter than me and he didn't garner the respect of a Steve Whitaker, so I still felt like I was looking down on him.

"I have to assume that if you ask that question you already know the answer. Now perhaps you can answer my question about what a Mohawk club has to do with Katie Couture."

"How well did you know Ms. Couture?"

He shook his head. "You're a piece of work." He picked away at a splinter in the easel of his bench. "I knew her as well as anyone else in the Fort I suppose. But how does that help you? Hasn't everyone pretty much answered the same?"

"What did you think of her?"

"She was actually kind of hot, if you could get around the stupid Holly Hobbie clothes she took to wearing."

The blood was drumming in the veins of my temple. Pounding away, making it difficult to think of anything other than my fist connecting with Dave Hetfield's chiseled jawline. But the other thing I learned from those miscreants in the police station at Carolina Atlantic University was that there was nothing more a sociopath wanted than to bring you into their fold. They would happily sacrifice a beating at your hands if it meant that you had stooped to their level. Once you are down there with them, it was a long, steep climb in the blazing heat of hell to get back to just being a human being.

"There's new evidence in the case of Katie Couture. A war club found at the scene. Someone told me only you or Garrow would have such a thing."

His Adam's apple bobbed two times, and his lips pursed as if he were holding down bile that had traveled up his esophagus.

His knees had buckled, and my curve ball dropped right over the middle.

Strike One.

"Do you go to Church, Mr. Hetfield?"

He held his chin up. His blond mop fell back from his forehead. His hairline was receding. "Never believed in it," he said.

"God or going to Church?"

"Neither," he said. "Jesus, it's hot in here." He unzipped

his coat, shrugged it from his shoulders, and hung it over his easel. "I'm my own God, Mr. Koella. All this luck and superstition stuff?" He waved his arm over the room again.

There wasn't one religious item in the room.

"I make my own luck. Everything I've earned in life has been through my own doing."

"Outside the school board, what do you do?"

"I invest," he said. "You oughta try it. It might get you out of that heap you're driving around."

I sat down and gripped my knees with my hands. Took a deep breath.

"What's the matter, Mr. Koella, did that sting?"

I pictured Gary Pressley rocking back and forth. A coping mechanism. I resisted the urge to do the same. "What year is your son?"

"Excuse me?" He said.

"That was your son you humiliated at the game last night, wasn't it?"

He took a seat in front of me. "Look here, you bastard, you keep my son out of this."

Did it sting? I wanted to ask him to turn the knife deep to the hilt. Instead I went with, "What year?"

"Junior," he said. "Watch it, Koella. I said leave my son out of this."

"And you think he'll come around and get a scholarship?"

Cartilage bunched in the back of his jaw, and his face flushed with hypertension.

I'd delivered my inside fastball. Time to try another pitch. "Did you and Katie Couture ever have a relationship beyond just knowing her as well as the rest of town?"

"Fuck you, Koella. I'm married."

"I notice you don't wear a ring. Well you do, but they have nothing to do with your wedding vows."

That hung in the air. He clenched and released fists in his lap. He probably hated me as much as I hated him.

Good.

"I meant before you were married," I said.

He scoffed. "I don't think it was a relationship," he said. "Half of town balled that whore."

"So, you did? Interesting. Did you father any of her kids?"

His eyes squinted and slid from me and scanned the wall to his right. There was nothing on the wall but the door exiting the room.

"No worries. We can let the DNA sort that out if it comes to it."

He snorted and shook his head and kept his eyes on that door.

"How many of those war clubs do you own, Hetfield?"

He didn't answer.

"What interest do you have in them? I don't see the slightest trace of Indian descent in you."

He mumbled something.

I leaned forward and turned an ear toward him. "What's that, Mr. Hetfield?"

"History," he said.

"You are interested in Native American history?" I smirked to let him know, I was calling bullshit.

"The town's history, Koella. You may not get that. Coming from the city."

This guy had obviously never been to Myrtle Beach. The city?

"But we have a proud heritage here. I honor that by collecting artifacts of that heritage."

"Is that why you still wear rings from state championships from twenty-five years ago? To honor the history of the town? Its heritage?"

He faced me again. He jacked his smile up to eighty watts. "I wear those because I earned them. Something you could never understand."

"Matteo Garrow may be a better person to honor the heritage of the Mohawks. Don't you think?"

"Mr. Garrow doesn't have a monopoly on honor, Mr. Koella." He scoffed. "Don't be so impressed by the authenticity of his Native blood. It does not buy him honor."

Hetfield stood, lightly slapped the thighs of his ski pants, and grabbed his jacket. "Now then, Mr. Koella. If you have no further questions, I need to get back to the family. It is after all New Year's Eve, and there are plans to be made."

As we headed down the hallways, I said, "Speaking of family. I'll need to speak with your wife and kids. Could you arrange that for me?"

I got to give the guy credit. I had dealt the punch out pitch, and he kept his head high as he walked to the dugout. The smile remained on his face. "I told you to keep my son out of this. That goes for Dawn and Amy, too."

Of course, this only meant that I would definitely speak with them.

26

I had to goose the Nova into action. And once started, its tires weren't up to the challenge of the worsening road conditions. The ass end fish-tailed and almost deposited me in the roadside ditch as I pulled out onto Ft. Covington-Bombay Road. The skies were electric with dancing snow and the slush piled on the roads hid a thin layer of ice. I steadied the needle at twenty miles per hour, and I still slid the car halfway past the stop at Route 37. Fortunately, everyone else in town was smart enough to not chance the roads, and I survived that sitting duck ordeal.

I turned left on the highway and the tires slid close to another ditch.

A mile later I was at the entrance to the Traveler's Rest. It took three attempts to climb the icy incline of the driveway leading up to the motor court, but I was triumphant and with great relief deposited my car in the spot before Unit 3.

The flip sign in the window of the office read, "Open."

I remembered the crumbled note from Stefanie Charles in my pocket. She needed to speak.

Why the hell not?

I jammed by hands in my pockets, and shuffled to the office on the slick pavement, my shoulders pinched high against my neck to ward off the cold.

I tapped on the door.

"Come in," she croaked.

I opened the door and released a cloud of smoke.

The monkey face looked out at me from above the pile of magazines sitting on the counter. A thin, feminine cigarette hung from her lower lip, glued there by her lipstick. Another butt rested in a tin ashtray on top of the magazines, its filtered end stained coral pink. The same shade lipstick as Stefanie wore.

This lady was a poster child for the American Lung Association.

Deep smile lines formed from her nose to her jawline on either side of her mouth. "Lookie, here." The cigarette see-sawed on her lower lip. "It's Mr. Private Eye." She frowned, the monkey lines etching deeper into her face. "Or do they call you private dick?"

I detected a faint slur. She hung on to the end of the sentence a fraction of a second longer than she should. Maybe, it was just the trying to speak around the cancer stick hanging from her lip. I remained one step inside the door. "Good afternoon, Stefanie. You left a note on my door last night?"

She peeled the cigarette from her lip and rested it in the ashtray beside the other one she had burning. "You were home, too. I know you were." She said it like wur-uh.

It wasn't the cigarette. She was hung over. Good thing I didn't answer the door last night.

"I must have been asleep."

She lifted a white coffee mug to her mouth. It had a black and white cow painted on its side. Above the cow read, "Hayberg's Dairy Farm." Above the advertisement, upside-down, pink half-arched stains lined the edge of the mug like bunting.

Maybe it wasn't a hangover. Maybe it was whiskey spiked coffee.

"Sleeping beauty, couldn't be bothered last night or this morning, but now he comes sniffing' around my door, eh?"

I reached for the door lever behind me.

"No, No, No, Dick. You're gonna like this." She put the coffee down and snatched a cigarette between two fingers. A column of ash dropped onto her as she jammed the cigarette home in her mouth. She jumped to her feet and swiped the ashes off the shelf formed by her silicone reinforced globes. She wore a low-cut, tight-fitting Shamrock-green shirt.

This girl was proud of her plastic surgeon's work. I wondered if she used the same doctor as Dawn Hetfield. My hand settled on the door lever, but I left it there, and waited for her to continue.

"The birdies are talking," she said. "And they do like tweeting away up here. They start them young, and by the time they are in high school, there isn't one of them can keep from chirping." She removed the cigarette and blew a plume of smoke out the side of her mouth. Crossed an arm under her bust, rested the other elbow on her hand, and held the cigarette pointing to the ceiling like they teach young cadets to hold their drawn weapon at the Academy.

I stepped away from the door.

She smiled like a chimp at feeding time. One of her front teeth was stained like her mug. "Lookie here, Dickie's interested in what the birdies had to say."

"I'm interested if it helps Gary Pressley," I said.

She shrugged, "Probably just the small-town gossip. You wouldn't be interested."

I walked up to the counter, leaned an elbow there, and said, "Why don't you let me be the judge of that?"

"Ooh, Dickie's all smooth-operator."

Through the heavy tobacco odor, I smelled the shot of whiskey buried in her coffee. "What have you got for me, Stef?"

She leaned back and picked imaginary pieces of lint from her shirt, drawing attention to her boobs. Wrinkles webbed the orange-tan flesh of her cleavage. "Tara Latulieppe's daughter heard from a friend who heard from Amy Hetfield that her brother caught something off of the good Sister."

Shit.

It must have shown on my face, because Stefanie took a drag on her stogie, blew a smoke ring, and stabbed the center of it with the end of her cigarette.

It had the same effect as the gunfighter blowing off the end of his pistol after he'd outdrawn his opponent.

"You're sure you heard right?"

"Sweetie, it's made it from the high school cafeteria to the door of the Traveler's Rest office. If the good Lord himself had it scrawled on stone slabs, it wouldn't hold any more weight than the gossip of the folks in Fort Covington."

I tried to work that out in my head.

"It's true, honey."

"I just got done speaking with Dave Hetfield. Do you think he knows?"

"He knows," she said. "Amy overheard it from Hetfield, while he was beating the shit out of Parker."

That fit. If Hetfield found out his boy had contracted chlamydia from Katie, he would beat on him. Would he also turn his anger on Katie?

He could.

"What is this Amy like? Is she like most teen-aged girls? Does she exaggerate things for effect?"

"Honey, what is there to exaggerate? He either got the clap, or he did not get the clap."

I rubbed the stubble on the end of my chin. "The clap? Parker Hetfield caught gonorrhea?"

"Look at him, with the chin rubbing. Like he's Sherlock Holmes, and he's caught the scent." She paused to admire her joke. "I don't know what Parker caught. I assumed it was the clap because that shit spreads like wildfire around here. I think Dr. Sheffield makes enough to tide him over for the whole year when the carnies come into town for the Franklin County Fair. That's summer-time, but it's like his Black Friday."

I caught myself before I shared that Katie Couture had chlamydia when she died. Like Stefanie said, the birdies couldn't keep shit to themselves. And Stefanie was definitely a bird. "I need to talk to the Hetfield kids."

"They won't talk to you unless Daddy says it's ok."

I hadn't realized I had spoken out loud.

Stefanie corrected herself, "Parker won't talk to you. But you're good looking enough, and young enough that you could get Amy Hetfield to talk."

"I'm 31, Stefanie. I have a limit to how low I'll stoop."

"It isn't nothing for a guy your age to get with a girl like Amy. If she thinks you're interested, she'll talk."

Stefanie Charles had become a better partner than the person who hired me. "You think this weather will stop at all today?"

"Nope." She checked to be sure she was displaying the right amount of breast flesh and leaned forward, "What are your plans tonight for New Year's?"

"What's that?" I said, clearing my mind with a shake of the head. "Oh nothing, I was just thinking I needed to get over to the office and look over some evidence."

"You have an office, honey?"

"Jo Jo's," I said. "With this weather though, I guess I'll just have to wait until tomorrow."

She got up and flipped the sign in the window. "I can take you, but it might mean you watch the fireworks with me tonight." She winked at me. The slur had slipped away from her voice.

For a second, I saw her in her twenties in her tight jeans and a tight shirt and tight body. Before the slipper factory had shut down and before the persistence of time had taken its toll and before she fought its attrition by scraping together what little she had and handing it over to a smiling doctor with a knife, Stefanie Charles probably had been something to see. As it is, I was learning she was more than I had given her credit for.

She looked over her shoulder. Her simian face came into view and brought me out of my revelry. "I almost forgot," she said. "Reach over the counter. There's a FedEx envelope there for you that came this morning."

My passport.

––––––

KEEPING the focus on what I had learned proved difficult on the way to Jo Jo's. Stefanie spent the drive tossing flirtatious pickup lines over the bow at me. Each delivery, she looked my way and winked or grinned or played with her hair or all of that, and slipped over one of the lines framing our lane. Oncoming traffic on one side, the maw of the storm ditch on the other. The quips she cast my way depressed me.

"You have nice shoulders," she said, as she squeezed one. "I bet you give good hugs."

Or.

"I've got something you can investigate, Dickie."

You get the picture. I understood the trials of an attractive young woman at a singles' bar. Or the shit Veronica put up with every night on the job.

She slid to a stop at the light before Jo Jo's place. The car's rear end slid forward, and we were perpendicular to the direction we should be while we waited on the light.

I gripped the plastic door handle with such force I could feel my fingers leaving impressions in it.

"You never opened your package, honey?"

I steadied my hammering heart by concentrating on slow intakes and releases of breath.

She tapped on the envelope in my lap. "And who is this Veronica Townsend?"

"Light," I said.

And she pulled forward, and around the deserted restaurant to the back, where Jo Jo's truck grazed like a mammoth, white elephant. The snow cloaking the parking lot, and the diesel fuel pumps and the barren trees beyond the property looked like the ashen remains of a desolate, post-apocalyptic wasteland.

I kept that observation to myself.

When I opened the door, Stefanie Charles shut off the car and got out, too.

She must have seen disappointment in my reaction, because an "oh" escaped her, and she reached back for the handle.

Recognizing how much she'd done for our case, I recovered quickly, "Come on up, Stef. There may be stuff we cannot discuss openly with you, but you've been a lot of help so far."

She patted at her black hair like she had to work it back into shape. "Really?" She said. "I'd be glad to help."

She realized what kind of help I was looking for, right?

I ignored her question regarding Veronica. There was an acidic taste rising from my stomach. But I clamped the diaphragm down on it. I had to play the game. Fireworks were a small price to pay. Keeping her out of my bed after the display would take some nifty maneuvering of the pegs on that triangular wooden board.

As we climbed the sagging stairs, I lightly put my hand on Stefanie's elbow.

"Aren't you sweet," I said.

"If keeping you from falling through the hole at the top of these stairs makes me sweet, so be it."

When I guided her around the hole, her shoulders shivered. "Oh, my."

I used my key to unlock the door, and found Jo Jo leaned back in his seat, his head tilted back over the seat back, facing the ceiling. His mouth was wide open. He wheezed, followed by a gargling sound, which almost sounded like he would choke himself on his own drool. The cartoons with the exaggerated snoring character with the Z's escaping the mouth were not far removed from Jo Jo's current state.

I tossed the keys on the desk.

His swivel chair groaned when he sat up, shaking the sleep from his head. He wiped the crust from his eyes with the heels of his hands.

"Hey Jo Jo!" Stefanie said a couple octaves too high for Jo Jo's current state.

But I saw a slight uptick in the corner of his mouth when he saw her standing there. "Ms. Charles," he said. "What brings you here?"

She hitchhiked a thumb my way. "This one."

"I see you're hard at work," I said.

"Yeah." He still dug away at the corner of one eye with his middle finger.

Was it a coincidence it looked like he was flipping me off?

"What have you been doing, Cochise?"

"Went to Malone. Spoke with Whitaker. Spoke with Gary. Back to the Fort, met with Hetfield. He's a work of art."

Jo Jo nodded his agreement.

"Then I stopped to see this one," I returned the favor of the thumb jab in her direction. "And she came up money."

Jo Jo stopped digging in his eye and wiped the finger on the front of his jeans. He looked to Stefanie, "If I got you, what am I paying him for?"

I pulled out the chair for her. She removed her coat, handed it to me, checked her cleavage, patted her hair, and sat down.

I stood holding her coat because I didn't know what to do with it.

"He's the brains of the operation," she said. "I'm just the ears."

I explained to Jo Jo the gossip about Parker Hetfield and Katie Couture. I studied his face for any reaction. What I found, seemed unimpressed.

Stephanie must have seen it, too, because she followed up my explanation with, "It's true, Jo Jo. I know it sounds like petty gossip, but there's no way Amy would let that out and risk her daddy's wrath unless it was true."

And with that I began to have my doubts. I didn't know Amy Hetfield, but I knew teenage girls, and they weren't above twisting the truth as punishment when their fathers disappointed them.

"How can I talk to Amy Sheffield without her dad knowing?"

They both looked at me like I had asked about getting time alone with the Pope.

"What?" I said. "She's seventeen or eighteen? Not twelve, this can't be that difficult."

"Just be careful, Fuzzy. If it gets back to Het you're harassing his family, I may not work in this town again."

There's the Jo Jo that met Matteo Garrow with me.

"School would be the easiest place to track her down, but

that shit would get back to him before you pull out of the parking lot," Stefanie said.

"What about work? Does she have an after-school job?"

Jo Jo shook his head, but Stefanie snapped her fingers and wagged her pointer at me. "Dr. Sheffield's office. I hear she's working the front desk, answering the phones, and sitting there looking pretty." She fidgeted with her shirt, and adjusted her silicone. "Though I don't think she's all that pretty."

"Any idea what days she works?"

"Not tomorrow," she said. "He won't be open on New Year's. Other than that? No clue."

I turned my attention to Jo Jo. "Did you talk to Whitaker about anything overheard from Undie when he visited Gary?"

His eyes dilated.

It was like he was working for the prosecution. I shook my head. "I take it that's a no? Okay, so Undie repeated the term *Ti Bon Ange* several times, and also used the name of Beau, Katie's deceased son. I talked to Gary, and he's still silent, but when I used the term, Beau, he became visibly upset."

Jo Jo stood and paced the short width of his office. "And this *Ti Bon Ange*? How did he react to it?"

"He didn't," I said.

"*Ti Bon Ange*," he said, scratching his forehead. "What does it mean? I wonder."

"Little Good Angel," Stefanie said.

Jo Jo looked at her. He shared my surprise.

She shrugged, "I took two years of French. They required it to get into college."

She was full of surprises. "Where did you go?"

She swiveled her head to look up at me. Giggled. "Clarkson. For three weeks."

"I will need to talk to this Undie," Jo Jo said.

"I'm already on it," I said. "My girlfriend sent my passport. It arrived today."

Stefanie scowled at the mention of a girlfriend.

Jo Jo tilted his head. Thought lines appeared on his forehead. "If you just talked to Gary today, how did you know to have a passport sent up?"

Jo Jo asked better questions of me than he did of any of our suspects. I kept Father Cooper's advice to myself. "A hunch," I said. "We found an Undie in Montreal yesterday."

He searched my face for a moment. Then went back to pacing. "Okay, day after tomorrow, you and I pay Mr. Undie a visit."

"It's off the Rez, Jo Jo. I get to talk this time."

He chuckled. "I seem to remember you could not keep quiet last time."

I let that pass. "There's someone else we need to talk to."

"Who? The boy?" Jo Jo said.

"Parker? Yes, we'll have to talk to him, too."

Jo Jo grimaced.

I ignored it, and continued, "But that isn't who I was suggesting. Frankly, we have a lot of oversights on evidence here. Who's leading this investigation?"

Jo Jo frowned, looked down to Stefanie, and answered, "Cliffie."

There was a brief moment of silence shared between them. Then Stefanie looked up over her shoulder to me. Her mouth was open.

"Cliffie?" I said. "Just Cliffie, the guy doesn't have a last name?"

Stefanie closed her eyes.

"Detective Cliff Hetfield," Jo Jo said.

"Are you fucking kidding me?" I said. "Jo Jo, you are just now telling me this? What is he, Dave Hetfield's brother?"

"No, it is nothing like that," he said. "They are cousins."

It was now my turn to pace. I made two passes, and turned, my fists grinding into my hips. "It is exactly like that, Jo Jo!"

His jaw unhinged.

Before he could respond, Stefanie added, "He's right, Jo Jo," she looked to both of us in turn. "In the North Country family is family. Cousins are like brothers. Hell, half the Fort is a Couture, LaPage, Latulieppe, or a Hetfield."

I stopped behind her and rested a hand on her shoulder. "What about Charles?"

She looked up at me with a toothy, monkey grin. "Honey, I'm an original."

No argument here.

"Okay," I said. "Now I know what we're up against." I bore my eyes deep into Jo Jo's all the way back to the optic nerve. "We need to talk to this Cliffie, and we aren't until after the holiday."

"Whatever we say to him will go straight to Dave," Jo Jo said.

I dropped both fists on his desk blotter and leaned into him. "Help me understand why that matters, Jo Jo."

He looked away. "I have to live here, Fuzzy. Work here."

I looked to Stefanie Charles, who sat listening. Her arms hugged her chest and her legs crossed. She looked like she was waiting on a drink. "Give us a minute, Stef."

My knuckles showed in relief on the desk calendar when I pushed myself back from his desk. I walked around the desk and headed to the rear of the office and stopped when I got to the two back rooms.

Jo Jo remained standing behind his desk, looking at me.

I pointed to the ground at my feet. "Jo Jo."

He hurried over.

I led him into the room with the filing cabinets and computer. Shut the door behind us.

"What the fuck is going on, Jo Jo? You either try to help Gary Pressley or you protect your job. One or the other. You can't have both."

He studied the tops of his boots.

"What is it Jo Jo?"

"I uncovered something I should not have."

"Good," I said. "Will it help Gary?"

"I do not think so, but it could very much hurt me."

"Ok, Jo Jo. I live one thousand miles away. I could give two shits about this place. You can tell me."

He lifted his chin. His black eyes were glassy. "Garrow and Hetfield make on like they hate each other. Hetfield flaunts how he has this collection of Mohawk artifacts as impressive or more than Garrow keeps for the Pow-wows. Garrow talks Hetfield down like he should not have this stuff. Like he does not respect the heritage. It is all bullshit. Neither of them respects the heritage."

I waited on him to continue. When he didn't, "Help me connect the dots, Jo Jo."

"Matteo is selling the shit to Hetfield, or he is giving it to him. They may be partners. And Hetfield is feeding it to some online auction house."

"Dave Hetfield is selling ancient Mohawk weapons on eBay?"

He sighed. "It is not eBay. You know how every occasionally you will hear about someone selling a souvenir ball worth ten grand on some auction house? A number five hundred or something?"

"Sure," I said.

"It is like one of those sports memorabilia auctions sites, but more for..." He searched for the right word. "Museum pieces."

"So, it's just like those sports memorabilia auction sites?" I smiled.

"I guess so, but they do not deal in sports."

"Okay," I said. "So, what?"

"Garrow wants to maintain that appearance of a rivalry between him and Hetfield. If the tribe found out he was buddy-buddy with Hetfield, he would lose face. If they found out he was feeding Hetfield their heritage, they would run him off the reservation. When I stumbled on to this… arrangement, Garrow warned me off."

"In what way?"

He swiped a finger on one eye. "He has something on me, that could end me."

"End you? That's a little too doomsday for me, Jo Jo. Very little in this world could end you."

His chest expanded. He sighed. "When I came back up here after CAU did not work out, there was an incident. I made a horrible mistake."

He stopped there. I waited. "Again Jo Jo, I don't give a shit about the Fort. Don't give a shit about the Rez."

"I had an accident after a night of drinking. A girl was in the passenger seat with me. She was still in high school, and drinking in the bars with a face ID. I knew she was underage, but, hell, so was I. Twenty years old, but I should not have been in the bars. I knew I should not be with a seventeen-year-old girl, but when did that ever stop us when we were twenty?"

It didn't.

"Garrow kept the drinking under wraps. And the identification of the mysterious driver. He sold the story that when he arrived on the scene, the driver had disappeared leaving poor Robin Cree behind. Dead."

I felt a vise tighten on either side of my head. "Jesus, Jo Jo."

"I know," he said. "Not a day goes by I do not think about what I did, and about the life I stole from her. Matteo said at the time he was doing it to save me from a life ruined due to one mistake. I set about changing my life the next day. It is part of why I felt so connected to Sister and it is why I am helping Gary. I am not trying to save him from his mistake. I am trying to save him from others' mistakes."

For days, I had fought the temptation of punching someone, something. The urge came so quickly this time I could not push it back down. I swung and landed my blow in the wall. The jolt of pain ran all the way up my arm through the shoulder and hit home in the base of my neck. Given how little thought I had given my target, I was fortunate. The wall was gypsum board, and I had landed my punch on a space of board between the stud bracing. The broken board exposed insulation blankets, electrical wiring, and wall studs spaced too far apart.

I bent at the waist holding my busted hand between my legs.

Jo Jo rested his hand on my back. "Next time hit me, my friend. I am sorry to have brought you into this. I never expected that this case would expose old and current wounds. Matteo Garrow has held the events of that night over my head for many years, but I did not realize that this case would lead me to his door. I was dumb."

I stood up on wobbly legs. The pain throbbing in my arm disoriented me. "You said Matteo Garrow could end you, Jo Jo. It seems you have just as much leverage on him with the knowledge of his partnership with Hetfield. Don't lose sight of that."

"I will not," he said. "I will do my job. Thanks to you and Ms. Charles I am more convinced we are doing the right thing with Gary."

"Good," I said. "We will need to talk to Cliff Hetfield tomorrow."

"He has a hunting camp in the woods north of Malone. They won't be hunting, but they will be drinking beer and watching bowl games."

"They?"

"A bunch of single guys," he said. "I get invited by him every year. I have only gone once. I am not much for drinking to inebriation these days, and I have never come under the spell of college football. He did not invite me this year, but that probably has more to do with my work to free Gary Pressley. He is still single. I am sure he will be there."

I repeated, "Good."

Jo Jo squeezed my aching shoulder. It sent a fresh jolt of electric pain down my arm into my busted fingers.

I fought back a groan, grinding my teeth together. My raw tongue pasted to the top of my mouth.

"There is one more thing, my friend." His stern face showed no emotion. "A month back I was treated for chlamydia."

The world tilted on its axis. Fresh pain in my hand bent me over again. I lost my footing, then my consciousness.

27

———

I awoke in my room at the Traveler's Rest with my head in the lap of Stefanie Charles. Or at least I assumed it was the underside of her breasts that shielded the dim light from the lamp on the nightstand. Her jeans smelled of tobacco smoke.

"Where's Jo Jo?"

"Probably back at home, honey. He helped me get you into the car and then followed me here, so he could help me get you into bed. I'm a little too petite to carry a giant like you around."

Her monkey face peered down at me over her twin peaks.

I patted myself down. Fortunately, both of us were still fully clothed.

"I think you got a concussion with that beating you took the other night, honey. Your mind is all scrambled." She frowned. "And you're too stubborn to go to the hospital to get checked out."

I lifted my head out of her lap and propped myself up on my two elbows at my sides. "I've spent enough time in hospitals."

She laid her hands on either side of my head and massaged my temples with icy fingers.

"What about the fireworks?" I asked.

"Listen, sweetie."

Pop. Pop. I recalled the dream. Bombs. I had thought it was my subconscious warning me of the minefield I was walking through in Jo Jo's case. It was no warning. Just fireworks announcing a New Year three hours too early.

"Veronica has called a couple of times."

I sat straight up, and scanned the room for my phone.

"Don't worry, honey. I didn't answer. But return her call. She's phoned twice with no answer. She's probably worried about you." There was something warm in her grin, like a Momma Chimp's. "It's what us girls do. Worry about our men."

She pointed to my phone sitting on the nightstand and stood. "You seem to be okay. I'll leave you be. I entered my number in your phone. Call me if you need anything."

She strode across the room with her chin held high. When she opened the door to leave she turned and said, "Jo Jo said he'd be by to pick you up at ten, he wants to catch Cliffie before there's too much of a crowd, and before he starts drinking."

STEFANIE CHARLES WAS CORRECT. Veronica was worried. When she got over her initial worry, she tried sexy talk. I told her I was tired. And she worried again.

"What's wrong, Fuzzy? Is everything okay up there?"

I lied, "It's fine, V. This place is just fucking boring and cold. I think all the snow and lack of sunlight is tiring me out."

"Ok, old bear. How much longer do you think you'll be?"

"I don't know. I think we're close, but it depends on how the pieces come together."

"Do you want to talk about it?"

"I want to talk about you," I said. "But I'm too tired."

Silence.

"Ok, old bear. Call me tomorrow?"

"Absolutely," I said. "And V, Happy New Year's."

Her giggle sounded like home. Like waves splashing on the beach at sunrise. "You still have two hours, old bear."

"Your old bear won't make it the two hours."

We exchanged *good nights* and *love yous*. I felt good for about thirty seconds, and then I remembered Jo Jo Bigtree, Dave Hetfield, and Matteo Garrow.

I fell asleep with bombs going off in my head.

The fireworks had ended sometime during my call with Veronica.

28

The next morning, Jo Jo's knock came while I was bent over the vanity, scraping heavy stubble away from my scabbed face. When I didn't answer the door, he came through.

He wore a red, snap-button, corduroy shirt, and blue jeans stretched over his powerful thighs. "Happy New Year, my friend."

I tapped the shavings loose of my razor, wiped my face clean with a stained hand towel, and put on an American Aquarium T-shirt. "What's the weather like?" I said.

He held his arms out at his side. "A new day. It is warm." He pointed at me. "What is that? American Aquarium?"

"A band," I said. "A good one." But he'd never seek them out. So, the less said the better. "You say it's warm?"

"It is above freezing and the snow is melting."

That's rich. Above freezing. I grabbed my coat. "All right, let's go."

It was a high blue sky. The kind that wreaked havoc on middle-infielders fielding pop flies. Empty of clouds. The sun like a punched hole in a baby blue blanket. It was far from warm. My breath still flickered before me in steamy wisps, but Jo Jo was correct. It was a new day. Like nothing I had seen from Upstate New York to date.

We spent most of the silence.

What do you say to an old friend after he has confessed to vehicular manslaughter and sleeping with a nun?

He gazed out the windshield, making all the turns as if he were on autopilot.

I watched the melting snow break free of its great sheets and drift like tiny icebergs on the rivulets running down the edge of the street.

Two deer buried their noses in the snow seeking a meal. They were both spike horns, not much more than fawns, but bigger than any deer we'd see in the Carolinas. Beautiful animals. Veronica would love to see them, and then she would bitch about hunters.

"What is it, my friend?" He turned onto a dirt road. Pebbles clanged off the underside of his truck like birdshot. The fence-lined campus of Franklin County Correctional was in the distance, off set against a craggy tree-rimmed horizon. Jo Jo had taken a route that didn't run us through the town of Franklin. "You laughed about something."

"I thought about my girl, is all." I pointed at the prison. "Cliffie's camp is out there by the jail?"

Jo Jo waved his hand across the tree-line in the distance. "We still have a couple of miles north to go." He faintly smiled. "But yes, both jails and hunting camps like to set-up shop a little out in the boonies."

Silence returned for those remaining two miles.

When the tree-line came into closer view, and it became dotted with cabins leaking faint smoke from stove-pipe chimneys, Jo Jo pulled into the weeds alongside the dirt road. "We should probably discuss how we want to play this."

He had a point. I had spent the entire ride focused on

ignoring the uneasiness between us and admiring the view of the countryside. I had given no thought to our meeting with Cliffie Hetfield. I continued to give no thought, when I said, "Fuck it, Jo Jo. Let's show our hand, and see how he reacts."

His lower lip hung open, protruded, giving him the look of a Neanderthal. It was a look I had never noticed in Jo Jo. Even as a young man, when he was tossing frat boys over his back, I had seen nothing but intelligence in his dark, Native eyes. That I was seeing something less than intellect in him now saddened me.

"We know he's overlooked or suppressed the war club evidence at the crime scene. There's the canceled appointment with Undie the week of Katie's death. And there's the autopsy findings of Katie's disease," I said. "There may be more, but I think we'll have just as much luck hitting him over the head, as pussy-footing around. Plus, we get the added benefit of seeing how he'll react. We show our hand. He shows his."

Jo Jo released his grip on the wheel and dropped his hands to his lap.

"What?" I said.

"I had something to do with suppressing the news about her disease."

"Jo Jo…"

"I was not protecting myself, honest. I simply suggested to Cliffie that Katie was a good person, and I did not want her name soiled by all the speculation that would follow."

"Does Cliffie know about you and Katie?"

His chin dropped to his chest. "He does not."

"How do you want to play this now?" I said.

I could almost hear the hinges creak as he lifted his head upright. His enormous chest inflated, much to the chagrin of the struggling snap buttons on his shirt. "Katie would not want to see Gary rotting away in a cell. She would care nothing of her name if it meant Gary's suffering. We will do what needs to be done to free Gary with no thought of myself or Katie's reputation."

I had missed something when Jo Jo kicked the wind out of me last night with the news of Hetfield's brother working the case and of his relationship with Katie. Jo Jo had been as close to Katie as anyone I'd questioned. But I hadn't questioned him, yet.

It would have to wait until after we spoke with Cliff Hetfield.

We looked at each other and nodded.

Jo Jo wheeled us back out onto the street, and less than a minute later pulled up beside a forest green Chevy Silverado. There was a luster to the paint that showed through the snow and the salt. The chrome wheels caught the sunlight and flashed stars of piercing light.

"Nice truck," I said.

Jo Jo climbed out of the cab. "His pride and joy. With this break in the weather, he will probably be out here washing and waxing it sometime today."

I hopped down and landed in a slurry of melted snow. The cold water seeped through the cloth of my tennis shoes, freezing my already numb toes. I walked up beside Jo Jo.

"Who washes a car in the dead of winter?" He said.

I draped an arm over Jo Jo and patted him on the shoulder. This case would get very difficult for him. He was a man of great pride, and I could only imagine the beating it would take. "We can ask him that, but first let's talk to him about the case."

The cabin was sheathed in mismatched planks of cementitious board of various shades of gray. Two rows of concrete blocks served as steps leading up to a battleship gray door. There were two windows on either side of the door. They were framed by fake, white, vinyl shutters hung askew. The pleasant smell of a wood stove reminded me of the campfires of my youth. As we got closer, the thump of a bass drum and the growl of an electric guitar rattled through the windows. Warren Zevon's "Play It All Night Long". Cliff Hetfield had taken Zevon's advice. He had turned his speakers up full blast.

Jo Jo shook his head. "What the hell is that shit?"

I stepped up the concrete blocks and looked down on him. "That, my friend, is a dead man's song."

He didn't get the reference.

I knocked on the door.

Nothing.

I pounded on the door with the side of my fist like a hammer.

Warren died all over again.

The door cracked open, and a creased face, spotted with bronze stubble, appeared in the doorway. The Hetfield mop was disheveled atop his head. "Who are you?"

The smell of sour mash whiskey emanated from a mouth filled with rotted teeth like jagged pebbles pressed into swollen pink bubble gum. His inflamed eyes slid from me down to Jo Jo, who had not made his way up the steps.

"Jo Jo? You here for the ballgames?" He looked up at me. His eyes were the same shade of blue as his brother's, but the whites were road-mapped with blood red veins. "Who's your friend?"

"This is not a social call, Cliff. We are here to discuss the Couture case," Jo Jo said.

His face pinched. "In that case, this can wait until tomorrow. I am on holiday."

His head vanished behind the door, and he tried to swing the door shut.

I slid my wet shoe between it and the jamb. Then, I shoved the door open with my forearm.

I stepped into a living room like something from my college days.

Crushed beer cans littered soiled carpet, a table made from an old cable spool, and a vinyl couch held together with duct tape. A pile of six pizza boxes, all from different pizzerias, were against the wall opposite us. A wooden salad bowl sat atop the stack, filled to the brim with cigarette butts and ashes. An old, tube TV encased in molded black plastic displayed a smiling game show hostess in a sparkling gown with a neckline that plunged halfway to her navel. A couple of dead soldiers stood on top of the TV trying to get a peek down her neckline. Between them lay a pack of Marlboro Reds and a matching plastic lighter. On the ground at my feet, a dozen plastic CD cases were strewn about, including Zevon's *Bad Luck Streak at Dancing School* with its fuzzy ballerinas encircling Warren on the cover. The stereo was one of those cheap shelf unit jobs popular in big box discount stores in the 90s. It sat on a red plastic milk crate pushed against the wall under a shadeless window. The speakers were on the floor on either side of the crate.

"I like what you've done with the place," I said.

Cliff Hetfield jabbed a thumb in my direction. "Get a load of Phil Donahue here. Will you, Jo Jo?" He stood with hands on waist, smiling, and shaking his head. "What's up with the hair dude?"

I'd heard the Donahue crack before. It went with the territory when you're prematurely gray, trending towards white, in your early 30s. I waited on him to quit admiring his own joke. Jo Jo was a tougher audience than me, and after a few awkward seconds of silence, Cliffie clapped his hands, "Well, we've already established this is a holiday." He made to walk past me to the door.

I laid my hand on his soiled white T-shirt. "Not before we

have a few words on the investigation or I should say the lack of investigation into the Katie Couture murder."

He looked at my hand on his chest. The muscles in his jawline flexed. He swayed back and telescoped a roundhouse right.

I snatched his punch out of the air, twisted his arm back and up behind his back, and cop-walked him across the room. I tossed him onto the vinyl couch. He landed with a metallic crunch a top the pile of Budweiser cans.

His eyes widened as did his mouth. His head shivered like a boxer trying to steady himself before trying to climb up from the canvas. Spittle helicoptered in my direction when he said, "Do you realize what you just did to an officer of the law?"

I stepped aside to let his saliva drop amongst the aluminum cans and cigarette ashes. "Self-defense, Cliffie," I said. "You swung first."

His face flushed. He sat up, "That may not be how they hear it down at County."

Jo Jo stepped between us to mediate. "Easy fellows, we're here to talk. Not to play out the Hetfields vs. the Koellas."

"Koellas?"

I extended my hand to him, "Fuzzy Koella. I am helping Jo Jo out with the Pressley case."

He ignored my hand. "So, you're trying to free a murderer, too?"

I let my hand drop to my side. "We only free Gary, if we can show reasonable doubt. In that regard, Cliffie, we're here to help you. Because if this case went to trial, today, Gary would go free. There is enough oversight on the evidence that reasonable doubt would free the kid."

He looked at Jo Jo. "What is he talking about, Jo Jo?"

Jo Jo looked to me.

I had wanted to deliver the news to Cliffie, because I wanted it to come like an anvil over the head, but the way things were shaking, Jo Jo was the man. I nodded.

"Cliff, an ancient Mohawk war club is leaning against the wall behind Katie in one of the crime scene photos. The log of evidence does not mention this artifact."

Cliffie's mouth hung open, saliva stringing between his open lips.

"A few nights ago, someone beat me with one of those clubs down in the Fort." I circled my palm in front of my face. "We've established that only two individuals in the area would possess such a weapon. Matteo Garrow or…." I gave it a second.

He closed his mouth. His Adam's apple bobbed.

I continued, "Your brother, Dave Hetfield."

Jo Jo looked at me from the corner of his eye, "We have established nothing, Fuzzy." He turned his attention back to Cliffie, "We simply would like an explanation, Cliffie. Was this an oversight, suppression, what?" He paused.

Cliffie's dumb look did not change.

"Where's that club now, Cliff?" Jo Jo asked.

Cliffie planted a palm on his forehead, and dragged it down over his eyes, past his mouth to his chin, where he let it hang. "How the hell should I know?" His eyes jumped from Jo Jo to me, and back to Jo Jo. "You say there's a picture with a club, but I haven't seen no picture, and I haven't seen no club."

"You don't recall seeing it at the crime scene?" I said.

"Clean the wax out of your ears, eh? Didn't I just say I haven't seen no club?" He paused. "And I would be very careful about slinging accusations my brother's way, eh? You aren't from around here. So, you probably don't know no better, but that kind of shit doesn't fly around here, eh, Jo Jo?"

Jo Jo didn't respond to Cliffie's request for affirmation.

I let the threat pass.

The rest of the conversation went much the same way. Jo Jo went through the list of oversights.

Cliffie played dumb and acknowledged no wrong doing.

I added splashes of color along the way.

Cliffie flung idle threats.

Jo Jo did a good job. He even ticked off one I had forgotten. "Cliffie, did you know Katie taught RCIA classes at St. Mary's?"

"What the fu-," he caught himself. "What are RCIA classes?"

"Adult religion classes," I added.

Cliffie adjusted himself on the couch, "I did not know she taught classes." He reached behind his back and produced a crushed Miller Lite can and tossed it to the floor with several of its brethren. "But, she was a nun, I guess it doesn't surprise me she would teach classes at the church."

Jo Jo said, "She'd been teaching them for years, and never missed a class."

Cliffie cut in, "Let me guess, she missed a class right before her body was found." His torso jiggled with silent laughter. "Yes, we knew that. It's kind of hard to make class, when you're tied up in some basement and being tortured by some retarded kid."

Jo Jo's fists clenched at his sides.

I'd been fighting off the temptation to pummel someone for days, and could relate. Cliff had within the span of two sentences claimed to not know Katie was a teacher, but proudly state they knew she missed class. Sometimes you had to choose the right time to let a chronic liar die on his sword. I stepped in to let Jo Jo cool down. "Gary was in class that night."

Cliff's head tilted, and he closed his eyes. When he opened them again he said, "The kid was taking religion? So, what?"

"Yes, he was," I said. I stepped forward, and crouched before the couch, so I was eye level with Cliff Hetfield. "Does Gary Pressley strike you as a person who would think to attend a class he knew would not be taught? Do you think he would think to create an alibi?"

He didn't answer right away. He opened his mouth to speak, but he bit it back. His eyes slid from me to the television where some sweet voice hocked No More Tears baby shampoo. "I would have no way of knowing if Gary would think to do that or not. I'm not a shrink."

I clenched a beer can in my hand, stood up, and tossed it onto Cliff Hetfield's chest, "You are a detective, though, eh?"

God help me. I was talking like them.

Jo Jo never added the chlamydia piece to his list of oversights. I let him have that, after all, the birdies liked to chirp. It would no doubt get to Cliff Hetfield. If it hadn't already.

We left Cliffie lying there on his ratty couch, without saying goodbye.

In the yard, Jo Jo said, "I'm not sure we accomplished anything."

"We rattled the branches on the tree," I said. "Now we just wait for the vipers to drop and slither our way."

And how they did.

29

I spent the afternoon and most of the evening at the American Legion. There were no vacant seats at the bar. So, I sat at a table a comfortable distance between a group of six senior citizens playing penny ante poker and two young lovers playing tongue hockey between swigs from a shared bottle of Labatt's.

They weren't making much progress on the beer, but my tongue ached from watching them.

None of the regular crowd was there, except Jeanie behind the bar. A peroxide blonde with a mismatching torso and lower body joined her behind the stick. She was as thin as Jeanie from the waist up, but had elephantine legs and ankles.

It seemed like the rest of Fort Covington, having the day off and wanting to continue their New Year's celebration, had headed to the Legion. And that chased away the regulars, which left me isolated by my lonesome. It amused me. I had only been coming to the Legion for less than a week, and I already thought of myself as a regular.

Jeanie slinked into a chair opposite me. Her eyeshadow was green today.

Perhaps her resolution was to try different colors and not be so rigid about the blue?

She smiled.

I smiled.

"Look at you over here all by yourself like a sad hound dog." She propped an elbow on the table and leaned a cheek against her palm.

If she wasn't made up like a circus clown, it would pass as a pose for the cover of one of those glamor magazines. "I wouldn't say sad," I said. "I'd say contemplative."

"Oh," she said. "Deep thinker. Are we, eh?"

I considered continuing work, but pushed that thought away. I hadn't asked Jeanie her thoughts on Katie Couture, but I needed a break from all that. "None of my friends are here today."

She winked. "I'm here."

That tied my tongue.

A look of horror must have passed my face, because she reached across the table and patted my forearm, "But you're right, holidays bring in the tool bags and scare away the Regular Joes."

I noticed that the boy half of the young lovers now cupped his girl's breast. She wore three or four layers of clothing. So, I wasn't sure what either of them were getting out of his groping. Tool bags, indeed.

"What can I get you?" Jeanie said.

Sonny and Audrey LaPage sat at the bar, and I felt guilty by association from Jeanie's tool bag comment. "I'll have a Labatt's," I said. "And Jeanie, get Sonny and Audrey whatever it is they're drinking on me."

She rolled her eyes, "They may have reached their limit. Sonny's been nursing the same PBR for over an hour, and

Audrey's switched over from some Seagram's fruity drink in a bottle to Diet Coke."

"Whatever," I said. "Buy 'em a drink for me."

She stood up, patted her hips. "You got it," she said. "And don't be a stranger sitting over here all by yourself."

Sonny saluted me with a fresh can of PBR when Jeanie delivered it. Audrey whispered something in his ear. They never came over to visit.

The rest of the day and the night was a blur. I drank beer. Played billiards. Drank more beer. Played darts.

By around ten o'clock, I had no business tossing sharp, pointy objects. I inquired at the bar about getting a cab.

Jeanie had clocked out sometime in the night, leaving me with her colleague. Acnes scars dotted her face, which she did not touch up with make-up. Fresh black heads peppered her bulbous nose. I longed for Jeanie's Kabuki-like face paint.

"A cab? In Fort Covington?" She laughed. "Honey, this isn't the city."

A familiar voice from my side said, "Mr. Koella, I will be happy to see you home."

Derry Trong had snuck in sometime in the night. His eyes were clear. His face friendly.

"Mr. Trong, how kind of you."

DERRY TRONG DROVE A RUSTY, old Pontiac Grand Prix that smelled of air freshener. Probably to cover up whatever Patty Pill-popper and he smoked for pleasure. In the night sky, starlight had replaced the sparkle of snowflakes in the beams of headlights. The beautiful day had extended into night. Even with a head that felt stuffed full of cotton candy, I could appreciate it. Halfway to the Traveler's Rest, Mr. Trong broke the silence, "Mr. Koella, could I provide you with some advice?"

"I don't know, Mr. Trong. You are already providing me a drive home. Now you wish to provide me with advice? That may be a step too far," I slurred.

His face remained a stony profile as he watched the road. "Choose your words wisely, and who you speak them to."

"Whoa, Mr. Trong, are you threatening me?"

Cords of muscle formed on his forearms. "I am not threatening you at all, Mr. Koella. Quite the opposite. I am trying to steer you clear of trouble."

I studied his face. It was like trying to read Jo Jo's.

Somewhere deep in the caverns of my drunken mind, Mr. Private Eye whispered sweet nothings. Something I had forgotten from my visit with Dave Hetfield. "Mr. Trong, are your friends with Dave Hetfield?"

His face remained blank. His voice monotonous. "I'm not sure I would describe my relationship with Mr. Hetfield in such a way."

Thank you. That's very helpful. "Mr. Hetfield's on the school board, isn't he?"

Trong took his eyes off the road and turned to me. "Yes."

I pointed out the windshield.

He obliged by turning his attention back to the road.

"Ok, don't drive us off the road or anything. But do you know what Mr. Hetfield's opinion was of Katie running for a seat on the board?"

He slowed and pulled us to the right as we approached the entrance to the Traveler's Rest. "Mr. Hetfield's opinion aligned with my own."

There's a surprise. "Is there something else you want to tell me, Mr. Trong?"

He pressed the accelerator to the floor as the tires sprayed loose pebble against the undercarriage. When the tires caught, the Pontiac shook its ass and darted up the hill. "What room?"

I pointed to my unit off to the right. "Number three."

He brought us to rest in front of my place, and turned to face me like he had when driving. "I only wished to share with you the advice about giving mind to who you spoke to, and what you shared. This is a small town. Word gets around." He tilted his head in my direction. "As you have already learned on at least one occasion."

Without thought, my hand went to my face, and my middle finger scratched at one of the scaly souvenirs from my first night in town. "So, speaking with Cliff Hetfield? This was an example of the wrong person to speak to?"

He adjusted himself in his seat. His eyes locked on mine. "That would be an example."

"Did Dave put you up to this little warning?"

His mouth formed an Oh. His eyes rapidly blinked. "I hope you will not share our discussion with Mr. Hetfield."

"Okay, not a problem, Mr. Trong. But in case you are bullshitting me. I have a message for you to take back to your almost friend. You tell him I will speak to anyone. Anyone! That can help me prove Gary Pressley's innocence. And next time he wants to scare me off, he had better bring something better than an old wooden club." Or an old Asian dude, I added silently.

Trong turned, so he faced the wheel again. "We aren't such close friends, Mr. Koella, but I see you have decided to ignore my advice." He pressed the button to unlock the passenger door. "I'm afraid your message will never reach Mr. Hetfield. I try to avoid contact with him for my own reasons of self-preservation."

I opened the door, but remained in my seat. Cold crisp air poured inside the car. "Would you mind explaining that to me? Self-preservation? What does Hetfield have on you?"

He stared at the door of my unit. No reaction. We could have been discussing how many weeks were left of winter. "I do not," he said. Something like a frown. Then he said, "Wish to explain anything about my relationship with Dave Hetfield."

30

J o Jo picked me up after sunrise the next morning. Lavender and pale orange clouds were stacked atop the silhouetted trees on the horizon. Despite all the melted snow from the day before, the stuff still blanketed the world, and the sky's colors splashed highlights across its pale shroud.

I clicked off a couple photos on my phone with hands shaky from last night's drinks.

"What are you taking pictures of, my friend?"

I slid my phone into my coat pocket.

A tight-lipped grin formed on Jo Jo's profile. I wasn't sure I had ever seen his teeth.

"Did you see a deer?" He added.

"No. I'm finally noticing the beauty of this place," I said. "Most of my picture taking is for work. But I wanted to share this with Veronica," I tapped the window with a knuckle. "She would appreciate it. Hell, she'll probably plan our next vacation up here, when she sees this." I knocked on the window again.

We drove past the Legion on our left. The Nova sat like a

scorned child alone in the parking lot. Jo Jo watched it as we drove by, but said nothing.

"Veronica?" He said. "I bet she is something to see. You always had an eye for the ladies, my friend."

We were getting close to a topic I had no interest in discussing. "You'll have to come down and visit us sometime," I said to change the focus from the past to the future. Digging through my past was like reaching into a box of spiders. I hated spiders.

We approached a glass box the size of an outhouse. The arm of a security gate spanned our lane. A red stop sign beside it. Jo Jo slowed to a stop beside the outhouse and dropped his window.

A smiling woman with Asian eyes, dressed like a school crossing guard, leaned through the window of the booth. In a sexy French accent, she said, "To where are you going today?"

"Montreal," Jo Jo said.

She spoke through her smile, "And what is the purpose of your visit to Montreal?"

Jo Jo handed her his driver's license and a card for his business and reached to me with his other hand. "Work," he said. "I need to speak to someone in Montreal regarding a case I am working."

I slid my passport out of my coat pocket and handed it to Jo Jo, and bent down so the border agent could see my smiling face. "We're going to a see a voodoo doctor," I said.

She kept the smile plastered on her face and looked at Jo Jo. "A voodoo doctor, eh?"

"I understand that the gentleman we will meet practices Vodun, yes," Jo Jo said.

She didn't seem to register his answer. Instead, she leaned in for a closer look at me, holding up my passport for comparison. "What brings you up to Canada from South Carolina, Mr. Koella?"

I thumbed Jo Jo's shoulder. "This one," I said. "I'm working for him."

Her eyes shifted back to Jo Jo. "Is this your vehicle, Mr. Bigtree?"

"It is."

"And are you bringing anything of value into Canada?"

He shook his head, "No."

"Do you plan to bring anything back?"

"No."

She handed our paperwork back to Jo Jo. The gate-arm rose. "Enjoy your visit," she said.

Before she disappeared behind the sliding window of her booth, I called across the cab, "Excuse me, ma'am."

Jo Jo mouthed something but I could not read his lips.

The window halted halfway on its track. "Yes, sir?"

"I wonder," I said. "Did you know Miss Katie Couture?"

Her hand tightened on the edge of the window. "The young lady who was killed?"

"Yes," I said.

"Did you know her?" I repeated.

The agent frowned and shut her eyes for a moment. As she nodded, she said, "I did not know Sister. But she regularly came through here. I knew nothing of her, other than she was always such a pleasant person." She stopped to inhale deeply and closed her eyes again. "Then I saw her face in the papers, such a sad situation." She opened her eyes and directed them towards Jo Jo, "Is this the case you are working? Is this why you go to Montreal?"

Jo Jo's puffy face tightened over his cheek and jaw bones. "It is the case," he said.

"May I see your papers again?"

Jo Jo shook his head as I handed him my passport. He mouthed, "What the fuck?"

This time I read his lips.

"And may I see your vehicle registration?"

Jo Jo reached across to the glove, jabbing me in the side with his elbow in the process, and gathered his papers.

She took my passport, his license and registration, and tapped the pile on her window sill. "Okay, if you will park over there in the lot to your right. I will be with you shortly."

Jo Jo parked the truck in a cracked pavement lot. Snow filled the cracks like white veins. He slid his window back up against the cold and turned his attention to me, "Fuzzy, are you drunk?"

Valid question. I was hungover, at least. "What? She's seen Katie come through here often. How much you want to bet it was once a week on Mondays?"

"We already know that." He smacked the steering wheel with the heel of his hand. "And why the hell did you tell her we are going to see a voodoo doctor? What good could possibly come of that?"

She's cute and has a sexy accent, I thought. What more reason do I need? Plus, I had a swollen head from the night before. "Okay, that was of questionable benefit," I said. "But did you see her smile?"

"We may not make it over the border now. I hope the flirting was worth it."

It was a nice reversal of roles that Jo Jo now questioned my motives. However, before I could point this out, the agent appeared at his window.

Jo Jo's look dropped the temperature in the cab ten degrees. "You better hope she does not send us back home, my friend." He slid the window down.

The agent smiled through the window. She had donned a shiny black officer's cap, completing the school patrol look. With a smile like hers, I wasn't sure what Jo Jo worried about. "Gentlemen, Miss Couture came through here every Monday for what seemed like over a year. As I said before she was always pleasant, but she was also contemplative. Like something bothered her. The last few weeks on her return she was visibly upset, crying."

I backhanded Jo Jo on his shoulder, and leaned across the seat to get a closer look at the guard's name badge, Elise Aillet. Good luck getting me to pronounce that last name. "Miss — Elise. Were you concerned for Katie's well-being at that time?"

Her chin dimpled as she frowned. "No," she said. "I am ashamed to admit I thought her tears were the result of an affair coming to an end."

I remembered Stefanie Charles's suggestion that Katie had taken to her old ways across the border. Jo Jo's confession. The sexually transmitted disease. How much did this town really know about Katie's return to promiscuity? "Were you aware of Sister's religious position?"

"I did not know anything of her, other than she was the Monday morning woman, until I saw her face in the paper." An incisor appeared in the corner of her mouth, and dug into her lip.

I gave her something else to chew on, "When she showed up in the papers, did you contact anyone with the law to report how upset Katie seemed lately on the return from her Monday trips?"

Her eyes dilated and three fingers capped with bright red polish went to her dimpled chin. "I did not even think to do so."

I had forgotten Jo Jo in my discussion with Elise Aillet, but I felt his eyes poking at me. I didn't share his concern that Ms. Aillet may block our border passage, but I realized that things could go south quickly. A border guard needed nothing more than their own intuition to bar entry.

Her hand rested on the truck's door clutching our papers.

I wagged a finger at them, "So, are we free to go? Or are we being held for further questioning?"

"No, Mr. Koella," she looked at Jo Jo. "Mr. Bigtree. No further questions. Please enjoy your time in Canada." She handed Jo Jo the papers, turned on her heels like a cadet, and marched back to her station.

Jo Jo backed out and pulled to the gate arm. He kept his eyes on the road ahead. I watched Elise Aillet from behind as she disappeared into her booth.

Jo Jo pulled under the lifting gate arm. He said nothing to me on the hour and a half drive through the Canadian countryside.

MONTREAL STOOD like Metropolis before us. Its gleaming crystalline skyscrapers jutted out of the snow-covered farmland. We crawled up a steep bridge crossing the St. Lawrence River. The cars all looked like props from the Jetsons. The muscles in Jo Jo's forearms stiffened as he swung us up to the peak of the curving raised highway. He took his foot off the accelerator as we crested the peak and began our descent. The truck still reached speeds that would be the envy of the Swamp Fox, our wooden roller coaster back home. Highway 20 leveled out at a height that still put us higher than many of the buildings on the outskirts of downtown Montreal and some five stories above the St. Lawrence, which now flowed on our right, all black water and whitecaps and barges floating like shoe boxes on its choppy surface.

I looked at the speedometer, and it read seventy-five miles per hour. Jo Jo had us half a car length off the bumper of a rusty Volkswagen Jetta of indiscernible color. Over my shoulder I saw a semi following at the same distance. I couldn't recall the last breath I'd taken.

Jo Jo followed our leader onto 720, which led into the heart of downtown Montreal. The semi remained on our tail.

"I hate driving in the city," Jo Jo said with all the emotion of a mortician. "I have come away with fender benders my last two trips here."

I gripped the door handle and almost did the sign of the cross until I pictured Katie Couture's dead eyes.

We dipped below the city's surface into a tunnel. It swallowed the city sounds, leaving us with only the sound of our tires clipping the expansion joints in the concrete road. The fake light was blinding in contrast to the overcast skies of the real world. Jo Jo slowed a few meters behind the Jetta, and the semi followed suit. A bleat of a car horn penetrated the relative silence as we vomited out of the tunnel.

Jo Jo slipped from between our escorts onto an exit ramp for the Bell Centre, "Home of the Montreal Canadiens. Hockey's Greatest Tradition."

"You know your way around the city well?"

"No," Jo Jo said. "I know the way to the hockey arena, that is all."

"Is there a game tonight?" I asked.

"It does not matter. We will be home by early afternoon."

Where's the fun in that?

The exit ramp dropped us onto a pedestrian level road that was lined with… pedestrians. Before I could take in the sights, Jo Jo made an abrupt right into the mouth of a parking garage.

An attendant with a fluorescent yellow vest pulled over a lumberjack flannel shirt stood from a chair beside a glass and aluminum booth. Jo Jo dropped the window, *"Parle vous, Anglais?"*

Jo Jo needed to get with Elise Aillet and work on his French accent.

"It is ten U.S. for the entire day," the attendant said in perfect English.

Jo Jo paid him and parked us on the ground level where two sedans sat amongst many empty spaces. Jo Jo pointed to the concrete structure above, "We are beneath the ice."

"No kidding?" I said. "Undie works at the hockey arena?"

He opened the door, "If Google was correct, he is within walking distance."

Jo Jo led us out of the garage and into the view of a McDonald's restaurant that must have been five stories tall. Jo Jo shrugged, "The Canadians like their fast food, too. I guess."

The sidewalks were teaming with pedestrians. I noticed the women were thin, and stylish. Most of them smoked. All of them were attractive.

Jo Jo chuckled. He punched an address into his phone, and we followed a GPS app around the glass and brick marquee of the Bell Centre onto the Avenues des Canadiens de Montreal. The next home game was a week away.

With any luck I'd be in the friendly confines of Veronica's arms by then.

Jo Jo led us across the street behind two chatting blondes, who both wore matching red scarves and skin-tight jeans. Jo Jo tugged me out of my hypnotism when the women headed to a Starbucks, and I made to follow them. "Come on, Lover boy." He pointed to the street sign, "Rue Stanley, Undie is in this direction, I believe."

I took one last look at the girls of the red scarves and their swaying denim clad hips and followed Jo Jo down the tavern lined Rue Stanley. As we got more than a block off the Avenue, the bars got seedier. Less glass storefronts. More hand-painted signs. More door men.

The street remained clean of litter.

One bar stood out. Its marquee hung over the sidewalk and was back lit and lined with glowing light bulbs even in the morning. The marquee read, "Live Nude Girls - 24 hours a day."

Jo Jo stopped under its canopy. Studied his phone. Looked at me, "It is pointing us here."

"Undie works at a strip club?" I said.

Jo Jo's thumb slid up and down across the screen of his phone. "It cannot be."

"Why?" I said. "Is it against his religion?"

He looked up from his phone. His face a mask, save for the way his lower lip hinged open and jutted out. I did not like the Neanderthal look on Jo Jo, but I kept that observation to myself. I stepped past him to the club's black doors. I grabbed a brass handle and looked over my shoulder, "You coming?"

I swung the door open and stepped over the threshold. The door shut behind me, then re-opened when Jo Jo made his decision. We stood in a vacant foyer. A metal detector stood before another set of doors. A waist-high glass display case to the right served its purpose of showing merchandise for Le Lune Bleue and acted as the clerk's counter. The room was finished in burgundy and gold. Which I felt was a miss, given the club's name. Then again, I wasn't paid to criticize interior design decisions.

"I thought it was 24-7?" Jo Jo said, as he scanned the vacant lobby. His eyes fell on a framed glass display hanging on the left wall. Inside a poster for Le Lune Bleue announced the appearance of one, Trixie LaRue, for a one-night engagement. On the same night as the next Canadien's home game. Shrewd scheduling by the club. If the poster was truth in advertising, Trixie was making the most of her looks and age before it would all go downhill when gravity would take over and she would be left with lower back issues in her middle-age years. She was blonde, well-endowed, and tiny-waisted.

Jo Jo's tongue moistened his lower lip.

As we stood there admiring Trixie, a stereotypical stripper door man entered from the doors behind the metal detector.

"Gentlemen, are you looking for some morning excitement?"

He had a dirty blond mullet pulled back tight to the skull in a pony tail. The rusty stubble on his face was on the verge of crossing over to a beard. Though, it would never quite get there, because he would keep it clipped just so. They all did. He stood a few inches short of me. Say, six-two. His belly lapped over the belt of his blue jeans and tested the limit of his tight black T-shirt. Over the shirt he wore an unbuttoned, matching blazer.

I decided against asking him how tall he was in metric. Jo Jo still looked dumbfounded as if he'd never been inside a club. When it was clear he would not answer, I said, "We are looking for Abraham Undie."

The bouncer grinned, showing off a black gap where one incisor belonged. He shook his head. "You would be in the wrong place, friends. That crazy bastard rents a tiny office off the courtyard around back."

Jo Jo's front teeth were biting his lip now. Not sure if he was holding his tongue, or was still thinking about Trixie LaRue's upcoming show.

"Thank you," I said. "And how do we get to this courtyard?"

The pink end of the bouncer's tongue appeared in the gap where his tooth belonged. When he was done playing with the recess in his gum, he said, "There's a narrow alley beside us. You passed it on the way here if you came up from the Avenue. It'll take you there. When it empties you into the courtyard, look to the right and you'll see Undie's place. But look closely or you'll miss it." His eyes shifted to Jo Jo. "And fellas, when you are done speaking with Mr. Undie, come back and see us. You'll probably need it."

I clapped Jo Jo on the back. "Let's go."

He nodded and followed me to the door.

Before we got there, a thought occurred to me. "Did you bring any photos of Katie?"

"Yes," Jo Jo said. "On my phone. Why?"

He found a good representation of Katie in life, between pictures of the crime scene.

I took the phone from him and approached the bouncer. "Has this woman ever danced here?"

"Fuzzy—" Jo Jo called from behind.

The bouncer chuckled, "Boy, would we like that. She's a looker, if you can get past her outfits."

"So, you've seen her before?"

"All the time. She comes to see the same guy you're going to see. It's a shame. A girl that looks like that filling her head with that voodoo mumbo jumbo."

He had something against Undie, but I didn't inquire further on it. I had better things to do than talk religion with a strip club bouncer. Jo Jo and I took leave of him, as a bespectacled man with a hairline that had receded half way back his head entered. He avoided eye contact and walked directly to the bouncer.

"Mr. Wilcott, good to see you again," the bouncer said.

We left Mr. Wilcott to his fun.

The alley was where the bouncer said it would be. It was barely as wide as a common doorway, and the concrete pavement was cracked, but clear of litter. Similarly, the wall of the buildings, the club on our right and an Irish pub called the Harp and Thistle on the left, were losing their paint and chinked in spots, but free of graffiti.

Halfway down the alley, Jo Jo grasped my bicep. "Fuzzy,

why did you ask about Katie dancing here?" He pointed a thumb at the club's wall. "Surely, you do not think she would stoop so low."

"Jo Jo, I am through tiptoeing around Katie's image. Three days ago, I would have never suspected her of spreading chlamydia around the north country."

He said nothing, but I could see the hurt in his eyes. He started us back down the alley at a brisker pace.

When we made it to the courtyard, it was a disappointment. A concrete yard closed in on all sides. Air conditioning units sat beside garbage cans, which ironically arose from junk each tenant had set out to die. Old business signs. Rusty shopping carts. Tables missing legs. Bar stools with gouged vinyl seat covers. It was like we entered the alley in Canada and exited it in the streets of New Orleans the morning of Ash Wednesday.

To our immediate right, two doors. A garbage pail rested beside the door to the left. Posters from a previous performance at Le Lune Bleue were littered at its feet.

A wooden sign the size of a desk placard identified the other door as belonging to "Dr. Abraham Undie."

No M.D. Undie was one of those doctors, who had lived most of his adult life at some college with his nose in books.

Below the sign was a door bell, below that on the ground was a used condom. Jo Jo and I tiptoed around the spent casing. Jo Jo rang the bell.

No answer.

I tried my luck.

Again silence.

"Maybe we should have called for an appointment?" I said.

"Under what guise? That we wanted to discuss his relationship with the deceased? He never would accept that appointment."

I studied his face, there wasn't a trace of humor. "We could lie," I said, retrieving my phone from my coat pocket. "Hell, we still can. Maybe we can set something up with him, today."

Jo Jo pointed to the door. "He is not there, my friend. Who do you think will answer the phone?"

He was right, but I continued to search for a number. Maybe he had call forwarding. I caught sight of the condom as I had that thought.

"Besides, what reason would you give for an appointment?" Jo Jo said.

"I don't know, Jo Jo,' I said. "A palm reading? Jesus, I'm a private investigator, I've lied to get my way past a door before."

Miracle of miracles, the door to Undie's place opened halfway, and a beautiful, slim redhead dressed in a pinstriped jumpsuit back stepped out of the door. A pair of black hands clasped one of hers. She leaned in and pecked a face behind the door. "Thank you so much, Undie."

Jo Jo and I shared a look. I'm not sure what was on his mind, but I contemplated getting into the voodoo game. First Katie, and now this knockout?

She gasped when she turned and saw us standing there. Her eyes were the color of sea water and stood out against her face's porcelain skin. Her hand went to her heart.

"Ma'am, we did not mean to startle you," I said.

She lowered her head and squeezed between Jo Jo and I and hurried to the alley. The condom clung to one of her four-inch heels like a dryer sheet.

We turned back to Undie's door, and he stood there. Tall, lean, black as midnight, and dressed in colorful, green African garb. His smile seemed authentic, and his eyes were bright and intelligent. He wore no hat, and his little black springs of hair were speckled with gray like metal shavings.

"Gentlemen, how may I help you?" His accent sounded like it came from a Caribbean island. He looked to a gold watch on his wrist. "I do not believe I have an appointment at this hour."

Jo Jo said, "No, Mr. Undie, we do not have an appointment. We have driven up from New York in hopes of speaking with you about Katie Couture."

His smile disappeared, and left a flat slit in its place. "I see." He stood aside from the doorway. "Well, I guess I knew it would come to this. Come along."

As we approached him, Undie studied his watch again, "I do have a hard stop at noon. My next appointment is at 12:30," his other hand went to his flat abdomen. "And I will need to get something to eat prior to then."

We slid past him. He was only a couple of inches shorter than Jo Jo and I, but he had a much leaner frame than even I. So, he was a good hundred pounds lighter than Jo Jo. "Thank you for taking the time with us, Mr. Undie," I said.

"Please," he said. "No mister, just Undie."

We entered into a hallway with dark wood paneling all the way to a cracked plaster ceiling. Dim wall sconces casted faint yellow light over the path.

"Please continue back to my consultation room," he held his arm out beside us. "Go. Go."

Jo Jo shrugged.

I couldn't seem to get my feet to work.

Undie stepped past us, "Come. I assure you there is nothing to fear."

He walked off down the hall, and we followed.

Over his shoulder he said, "You are police officers investigating Katie's sad misfortune?"

Jo Jo looked to me, and said nothing.

He probably wanted me to be the liar. I threw him a curveball, "Actually, Jo Jo is Gary Pressley's attorney. We know you visited Mr. Pressley a few days ago. He hasn't spoken since. We'd like to talk to you about that."

Jo Jo backhanded me across the shoulder, and narrowed his eyes.

Undie chuckled. He had reached the entrance into his voodoo chamber, and stood aside so we could enter. "Do you think I cast a spell over him?"

The consultation room was more of the same. Dark wood paneling. No windows. Yellow light thrown from wall sconces, and a globe ceiling fixture mounted above a mahogany table. All the walls were lined with bookcases stuffed with leather bound books with gold lettering on their spines. The space had the dusty odor of a used book store.

The table was circled with simple wooden chairs. There was a yellow legal pad on its surface, and a black fountain pen on top of it.

No crystal ball. No deck of tarot cards.

It looked like a spartan lawyer's office. Not a voodoo doctor's place of business. But then, outside of a trip to a voodoo shop on Bourbon Street when I was in college, what did I know about voodoo?

Jo Jo and I stood there taking in the place, and Undie arrived at my side. "Well, did you?"

"What's that?" I said.

"Spell? Did you think I worked some black magic on the boy?"

I noticed plaque and bits of food lodged in the crevices between his teeth. "You tell me, Undie." I waved my hand at the books lining the room. "I know nothing of your religion."

He pulled two chairs back from the table. "Here," he said. "Have a seat. We will talk."

There were four chairs set up around the round table. I took the seat to the left adjacent to the yellow pad. The writing on the pad was clean penmanship, almost beautiful cursive script. A skill lost in today's world of word processors, text messaging, and tweets.

Undie eased into the seat in front of the pad. Smiled at me and flipped it over. "Sorry, while I am not under the confidentiality obligations of a traditional doctor or a Catholic priest, I do take my clients' privacy seriously."

I locked onto his brilliant eyes. "My apologies," I said. "I did not read anything. I just admired the penmanship."

Undie splayed his hands on the table before him. "Ah yes, well this is something I also take pride in." He looked up to Jo Jo, who still hadn't taken a seat, and drummed his fingertips on the table. His fingernails glistened with clear nail polish. "I am at a disadvantage in that you know who I am, but I do not know who you are."

Jo Jo produced a business card from his wallet.

I slid my license card across the table to him.

He left the cards on the table but lined them up corner to corner.

I scanned the room and noticed the tidiness of it. Fairly spartan, but all the books were neatly lined. Each shelf filled, save for one case at the other end of the room, where one shelf had space for half a dozen more tomes. This kind of neatness, and the manicured fingernails disturbed me.

"To answer the question, Mr. Koella. The one you did not ask." He smiled. "I did not subject Mr. Pressley to any magic." He looked around the room. "And I do not have any dolls laying around that I would use as a pin cushion."

"I—"

He held his hand up. "I know you did not ask these questions. They are common misconceptions about Vodun, however. So, I suspect that even if you would never vocalize these thoughts, they were your thoughts nonetheless."

I'm not sure if he was right or not. I certainly felt uncomfortable in Undie's presence, and I felt the same way when I watched him grill Gary. "Why did you visit Gary Pressley, Undie?"

"I wanted to know if he was the young man that caused Katie so much grief." He clasped his hands together, and rested them on the backside of the pad. "Will you not have a seat, Mr. Bigtree?"

"Excuse me, Doctor, but I have sat behind the wheel for a couple of hours on our trip, and I prefer to stand."

Undie frowned and turned to me. "Gary did not kill Katie."

Jo Jo said, "We agree, doctor. However, we need something to establish reasonable doubt."

We had established plenty of reasonable doubt. What we needed was overwhelming doubt to rise above the small-town corruption that had put a scared kid behind bars. I returned to something Undie just shared, "You said a young man was causing Katie grief. In what way was this young man doing this? Was Katie seeing her deceased son in this young man?"

He started to say something, took a deep breath, and continued. "You have quite the intuition, Mr. Koella. I am sure you are a fine investigator." He broke eye contact with me. "The answers to your questions are," he held up one finger. "Katie had long repressed urges. Ones we all have, but some of us are better at repressing. She was struggling with this urge with this boy."

Parker Hetfield.

Undie held up a second finger. "Yes, she had visions of Beau. But as I am convinced Gary is not the boy she was fornicating with—," he inhaled deeply, and audibly released it. "She did not see Beau in this boy. She saw her son in Gary."

I looked to Jo Jo. His face remained flat. I put both palms to my face, and tried to rub my confusion away. *"Ti bon ange,"* I said. "You said this repeatedly to Gary."

The smile returned to his face, and he nodded.

"What does it mean?"

"Little good angel," he said, crossing his arms across his chest.

"I realize that," I said. "But what does it mean?"

"Are you a Christian, Mr. Koella?"

The edge of the wooden seat dug into the back of my thighs. I shifted to another position, but still found no comfort. "I don't know," I confessed.

"Ah, so you are agnostic?" he said. "Your discomfort in the current surroundings is understandable."

Somehow, I figured my uneasiness would be greater if I were a devout Catholic. "I don't know if I am agnostic either," I said.

"Very well," Undie said, as he tilted his head, his eyes probing. "But is it safe to say you most understand the Christian faith?"

I nodded.

"Very well. Then you have heard the terms the 'flesh' and the 'spirit'?"

"Undie, can we quit Sunday school lessons, and just answer the question?" I said.

He continued undeterred, "We have a similar dichotomy in the Vodun faith, as it applies to the individual's soul. They are the *gros bon ange*, or big good angel, and —," he held out his left palm like a magician revealing the coin he had disappeared up his sleeve. "*Ti bon ange*," he said. "The *gros bon ange* is what a Christian would call the 'flesh'. It is the biological function that keeps us," he made a quotation marks gesture with his hands, "Alive."

"And *ti bon ange* is the soul?"

Undie's head danced on his shoulders. "Not exactly. In Vodun, we think of the 'flesh' and the 'spirit', the *ti bon ange*, as two aspects of the soul. But to connect it to your religion, yes.

The *ti bon ange* is that aspect of the soul which continues on into the afterlife."

"Are you saying that Katie believed that Gary Pressley was her son Beau reincarnated?" I said. "How is that possible? Gary was born several years before Beau."

"Reincarnation is not really what we talk about when we talk about the afterlife and the *ti bon ange*." Undie looked to Jo Jo. "Mr. Bigtree, am I correct in thinking you are of the Akwesasne tribe?"

Jo Jo slid both hands in the front pockets of his jeans and rocked back on his heels. He held his chin high, and said, "I am."

"And you understand the primordial philosophy of your people's traditional religion?"

"I am not much for religion, I am afraid."

"Okay," Undie said. "I am sure some of this will ring true to you nonetheless." He returned his gaze to me. "In Vodun, we believe that the *ti bon ange* lies in rest for a year and a day after the *gros bon ange's* passing. We believe that the *ti bon ange* lies in wait in a nearby body of water." Undie held a palm out to Jo Jo. "Much like the Mohawks, we believe all elements are imbued with a soul, a spirit."

"And after a year and one day?" I asked.

"A ceremony is performed," Undie said. "It would almost appear like a second funeral to those of another faith. The *ti bon ange* is called from the recesses of waters into a *govi*." Undie pointed to two clay jars set atop one of his bookcases. "Those are the *govis* of my parents. I keep them here in my consultation quarters so their wisdom will guide me in helping others."

"So, you trap souls in a clay urn?"

"Trap is not the word I would use," Undie said. "I would say we welcome the *ti bon ange* to return to their loved ones, so they are not corrupted by the less loving elements of the world."

I gave Undie the roll-on gesture. "Okay, what does this have to do with Katie Couture. She didn't participate in these rituals, did she?"

Undie frowned, "I'm afraid that Katie did participate in the initial funeral ritual for Beau."

I looked to Jo Jo. "She had a voodoo funeral, Jo Jo?"

"Please don't misunderstand me, Mr. Koella. Katie participated in the standard, and very valid, funeral rites of the Catholic Church. Yet, within that first week after Beau's death she was tormented spiritually. She felt herself slipping to long subdued urges. I do not know what exactly led her to my door, but we did execute the first funeral rites of the Vodun faith. These lead the *ti bon ange* to its resting place in the waters."

I felt the effect of the previous night's drinking, and I had a difficult time processing all of this. I pinched the bridge of my nose to ward off a headache that I did not feel, but was confident was in my future.

Undie continued, "The issue is that Katie never returned for the *govi* ritual."

Jo Jo asked, "And why is that an issue?"

Undie's chest inflated and receded. He leaned forward, and slapped the tabletop. "Because, the *ti bon ange* expelled from the waters after a year and a day did not have the safe quarters of its loved one to return to. When this happens, the *ti bon ange* will often find another element to inhabit. One perhaps with a weak current *ti bon ange*. Often times this is in a safe host such as a stone or possibly a tree. It appears that in Beau's case, we have a rare case of a *ti bon ange* inhabiting another human being, Gary Pressley."

A smile crept onto Undie's face again. He seemed to enjoy giving us this lesson in his faith.

I thought about the *govis* sitting here in Undie's chambers, and how they brought him comfort. How he felt they brought wisdom to his practice. "I don't understand, Undie. The little good angel tormented Katie? What is good and angelic about that?"

"It is not the *ti bon ange's* fault, Mr. Koella. It is Beau in his purest sense. It is his truest nature. There is nothing good or bad about that. However, Katie like most addicts when presented with something uncomfortable such as the return of her lost son's soul, returned to her base nature."

I remembered Derry Trong's lecture at the Legion on addiction, and his assertion that Katie had always been in danger of returning to her old ways. His campaign against Katie's school council run was not looking so petty, now. "Undie, how long had Katie been coming to see you?"

"Shortly after she became convinced that Beau had returned." One of his clear coated nails traced circles on the back of his legal pad. He shrugged. "I don't know. Two years, maybe?"

"You say a young man was causing her grief? When did that start happening?"

Jo Jo sat in his chair.

Undie said, "About a month ago, she came to me upset. More upset than usual. Without her saying anything, I knew she had succumbed to her compulsions. I pressed her on it, and she admitted that she had slipped."

Jo Jo's chair screeched on the hardwood floor. When I looked to him, he dropped his eyes to his hands on the table-top. His fingertips pressed together forming a steeple.

Was Jo Jo Katie's initial slip up? I kept my eyes on Jo Jo, "Did she share who she slept with or anything about him?"

"Not on this first traumatic visit," he said. "But Katie continued to slip. Each time she came she was more upset.

And she confessed things, that are almost unthinkable of someone like her with her ties to the Church."

"Do we really need to drag her name through the mud?" Jo Jo said. "Can we not cast enough doubt on Gary's guilt without digging into Katie's past?"

I've been on the receiving end of a fair share of the dagger eyes. Veronica was masterful with them. I'm not sure I quite reached that level of mastery, but Jo Jo stopped his line of questioning right away.

"What did she confess, Undie?" I said.

He stopped tracing circles on the pad, and looked to the ceiling. "God, help me," he muttered. He closed his eyes and spoke to the ceiling. "There was more than just one time," he said.

"I gathered as much," I said.

Tears leaked from the corner of his shut eyes. "She was such a sweet soul. I hated that her past tormented her. I hated that something as sweet as the opportunity to see her son's *ti bon ange* caused her to suffer."

Jo Jo's elbows were on the table now. His hands on either side of his head rubbed his temples.

"What was it, Undie?"

"She had an affair with a school-aged boy," he said.

I let my jaw hinge open in pretend shock. He hadn't told me anything I didn't know, but he didn't need to know that. "A kid? My God, I guess that would tear her up," I said. "Not to mention the kid."

Undie's close-lipped frown seemed sincere. He nodded his agreement. Jo Jo slouched back in his chair.

I continued, "Why do you think she chose to sleep with a minor?"

Undie squinted. Pain on his face. "In anyone else, I would suggest that she found easy prey. With Katie it goes deeper than that. Whether she knew it or not, I think there were some deep-seated psychological reasons for not only choosing a child, but the one she chose."

"Wait a minute," I said. "You told us that you went to see Gary to determine if he was the boy causing her grief. Which by the way is a poor choice of words given the circumstances. Are you saying you know who the boy is?"

Undie gave me an easy-does-it gesture, "I do not know the boy's identity." He went back to counting out his explanation on fingers. One finger, "I think Katie sought out a teen-aged boy or young man, because her first encounter did not satisfy the appetite of her awakening addiction."

Jo Jo tugged at his collar. His chair squeaked again under his shifting, mammoth weight.

Two fingers, "Sex with teen-aged boys and college-aged kids is what she left behind. Never mind that when she was doing it she was of an appropriate age. There is a certain logic to her returning to that age group. Not a logic that you or I would acknowledge, but to the addict?" His watery eyes searched me. Two fingers remained up. "But it was more than just an age group, I got the impression there was a reason behind her specific choice."

My stomach turned. I was going on an empty stomach, after a night of drinking, but none of that had my insides doing somersaults like the story of Katie Couture's fall from grace. With Jo Jo's shame. Undie's sorrow. My disgust. The room was reaching critical mass when it came to angst. "What was the reason, Undie?" I said. "And why did you initially assume Gary?"

Undie dropped his hand, lowering the rabbit ears. "I do not know the reason. She mentioned 'bookends' and something 'poetic' about it. I do not know what could be considered poetic about her actions. There surely could not be any beauty in it. But the 'book ends' comment led me to Gary. Erroneously, of course. But my thought was she gave birth to

Beau, perhaps in her sick mind she felt sleeping with Gary would close the book on Beau's *ti bon ange*. I see now that it was quite a reach on my part. After visiting Gary, I am convinced that the *ti bon ange* is there. But I know Katie did not sleep with him."

I wasn't sure how he could say with any certainty, but I was reaching my daily quota of voodoo talk. I asked Jo Jo, "Do they do blood tests on inmates when they book them?"

"Yes," Jo Jo said. "I don't recall seeing anything on Gary, but I also don't remember looking at the test report."

Fair enough. Except once he became aware of Katie's disease, why didn't he think to check on Gary's blood work. Hell, if Gary came back positive, he could drop the *pro bono* work. But Jo Jo, no matter what he claimed, had his image at the front of his head. Digging into Katie's STD not only dragged her name through the mud, but could drag his name down into the ditch with her.

Parker Hetfield. How did he form a bookend?

"Do we know if Katie had any other kids out of wedlock besides the three?" I asked.

Thought lines formed on Jo Jo's forehead. "It is not possible. The Fort is a small town, everybody knows your business. Katie never left the Fort for any length of time. She could not hide a pregnancy."

Leonard Cohen crooned *Everybody Knows* in the back of my mind.

Undie wagged a finger to draw my attention. "If I may," he said. Tears trailed down both cheeks, and his voice was thick with saliva. "Despite my initial query of Gary, I am of a mind that Katie would not seek out one of her own children. I would perhaps look to the parents."

No problem. I was happy to keep Dave Hetfield number one on my list.

"Does anyone know who Beau's father was?" I said.

"No," Jo Jo said. "Father's name was blank on the birth certificate."

"What about the girls?"

He shook his head. "Same thing."

"Do we even know if they were all by the same dad?" I said.

Undie's chin had fallen to his chest, and he swiped tears from his cheek with the back of his middle finger. "Undie, did she ever talk of her kids' father?"

He muttered to the tabletop, "She—"

I leaned in to hear.

"—I never pushed her, and she never shared a name." His hands dropped to the table. When he lifted his head, his eyes bulged to the size of ping-pong balls sliced in half. "Beau's father is still in that town. She used to say, 'At least with the girls, I don't have the constant reminder.' I'm not sure why I did not think of this until now."

Jo Jo shrugged. "None of the kids really resemble each other. Beau was blond haired, blue-eyed like his momma. Maddie and Lilly are both brunette, but the similarities end there."

"Jo Jo!" I smacked the table. "You said everyone knows your business in the Fort. Yet, somehow, nobody knows the dirt on Katie's babies' daddies?"

He slid back in his chair. The sound of it gouging the floorboards brought goose-flesh to my forearms. He stared at a book case. "Do not raise your voice to me, Fuzzy."

Whatever. "Surely, there are rumors?"

"He is somebody big in the community," Undie said. "Katie thought he was behind the vile postings on the newspaper."

Derry Trong?

Jo Jo remained silent, but he shook his head.

"It could not be Trong," I said. "That ship has sailed."

"Katie said this person got others to do his dirty work," Undie said.

I stood, and paced from Undie to Jo Jo. I leaned into Jo Jo's ear, and whispered, "I will talk to Amy Hetfield today."

<hr>

When we took our leave of him, Undie clasped each of our hands, almost as if we were in group prayer. He asked us to work our hardest to free Gary, and to find justice for Katie. We had eaten up all of Undie's free time, and his client (another attractive woman in her late twenties to early thirties) approached from the alley when we left him.

Her heels were clean of used condoms.

31

Undie had given us a lot to digest. So, we spent half of the trip home in silence. If investigating Katie's murder concerned us beyond just providing reasonable doubt of Gary's guilt, then what we learned from Undie would be more valuable. However, I'm not even sure we needed to make the trip. We already had enough reasonable doubt to free Gary without going to trial. It felt like we were spinning our wheels, and I believed it had to do with Jo Jo's sensitivity to his own revelations. As we pulled through Cazaville, a town with a Main Street like Bedford Falls, snow fell like the dandruff of the gods. It put a damper on my already grumpy mood, and I'd had enough of the silence.

"Jo Jo, did you sleep with Katie before or after Parker Hetfield?"

His hands tightened on the wheel. "What does that matter, my friend?"

"Humor me, Jo Jo," I said. "What does any of this matter? We've had enough to cast reasonable doubt on Gary Pressley's conviction for days. I cannot believe we are just now having this conversation."

"I am not so sure we have enough to secure Gary's release," he said. The one traffic light in Cazaville turned yellow, but Jo Jo continued at the same speed. "You do not understand the reach of some people in a small town."

Unbelievable. A kid is rotting away in a cell. Tormented by a voodoo priest with accusations he is the spirit of a dead kid. And we're concerned about the 'reach' of some people in town. Jo Jo didn't need a private eye for his job. He needed someone from outside the influence of the small-town politics, and he needed someone he could trust to keep his skeletons neatly tucked away. "You're a coward, Jo Jo. What was all of that about doing the right thing by Gary and Katie regardless of your past?"

He sped through the light as it turned red. Someone laid on the horn to my right.

Great, get me killed in the process.

"This has nothing to do with that, Fuzzy." A slight grin crawled onto his face. "Guys like Hetfield and Garrow are so deep into the local politics and law. Their grip is strong. We almost need to prove Gary's innocence to free him. It sucks, but that is the way it is."

"You realize that in all likelihood it was Parker Hetfield that killed Katie, right?"

He shrugged, "I do not know that."

"Jo Jo! I know you are not that ignorant. She passed an STD onto him. Not to mention the abuse she visited on him with the affair to begin with. His dad is one of two people that owned a club like the one found at the scene."

We were outside town now, driving through a post-apocalyptic countryside of dead, leafless trees, and snow falling like ash drifting down from blighted skies.

"The club was not used in the execution of the crime," Jo Jo said without a trace of humor.

"You're kidding me right now?"

He glanced at me. "There was no evidence of blunt force trauma."

I put my fingers to my scabby face. "What about this, Jo Jo? Any evidence of blunt force trauma, here?" I opened my mouth and wagged my tongue, and spoke like a dental patient, "Wuhabow dis?"

His face pinched. "Jesus, Fuzzy, that will get infected."

I snapped my mouth shut. "We need not protect Katie's good name any longer, Jo Jo. She was a shit. She was the whore that Wrath of Trong said she was."

"Do not say that."

"She has no good name to protect, Jo Jo. We have to find someone besides Cliffie Hetfield to listen. If we don't do that now, we are letting your pride impede saving a scared, mentally disabled kid."

He opened his mouth, then clamped it shut again.

He didn't open it up again until we pulled up behind a bright yellow Toyota with tires jacked to the moon.

32

______

I was busy trying to work out where I had seen the truck before while Jo Jo beat out the rhythm to some unheard song on the steering wheel. An image formed of the Hetfield family emerging from the high school hockey arena. Hetfield's white teeth as bright as the snow, his arm slung around the waist of his trophy wife. Cute Amy Hetfield, the star of the pre-game activities, walked beside them trying her best not to acknowledge their existence. And then, there was the boy. Parker Hetfield. The rest of the family crawled into Dave Hetfield's environmental nightmare. Parker continued past me to a tall bright yellow Toyota truck.

Jo Jo abruptly halted the drumming. He faced me.

"Parker Hetfield," I said.

At the same time, he stated, "High truck."

Elise Aillet smiled at the driver of the truck. I may be mistaken, but it looked like her cheeks blushed. This kid's good, I thought. First a nun, now the hot border agent. She handed papers back to a beefy arm that reached from the tinted window.

The truck's license plate read PRKHET.

I guess that left no mystery.

"Pull him over, Jo Jo."

"What?" he said. "How do you expect me to do that? I am not a police officer."

"Just do it."

The Toyota coughed blue exhaust as it pulled away.

"Follow him, Jo Jo!"

"I cannot. We have to stop for the agent."

"Go now, before the gate drops!"

And to my surprise, Jo Jo floored it. It threw me back in my seat and my tender head smacked the headrest. Pain like ice on an exposed tooth root shot from the back of my skull down into my neck. My eyes went blurry. The gate arm came into view, but somehow, we slid underneath it. There was a clunk and metallic scrape when it came down on the truck's bed.

I caught Elise Aillet's blurry face hanging out the booth window. Her mouth formed in an *Oh*.

Jo Jo continued forward, and pulled within inches of the Toyota's back bumper, which loomed eye-height before us. Jo Jo flashed the high beams off and on.

I wasn't sure it would work. The high beams basically flashed the Toyota's undercarriage.

"Stay with him," I said. "He has to stop somewhere."

"Yes," he said. "Probably the Hetfield residence. Then we will have the pleasure of explaining ourselves to Dave Hetfield."

"Fuck Hetfield. Stay with him."

And Jo Jo did. Parker passed the Legion with my car still in the lot (now with a handful of company), and drove alongside the Little Salmon River until he reached Highway 37. He rolled through the stop sign and turned right in the direction of Massena. The Library, where Katie Couture was killed, watched us from the left like an accusatory librarian.

I was just about to concede that Jo Jo was right when our luck changed and Parker caught red at Fort Covington's lone traffic light.

Parker Hetfield, despite being a murderer, was a law-abiding citizen when it came to following the traffic laws of the land. Jo Jo and Parker's vehicles were the only ones in sight. Yet the kid sat at the light knowing we were following him.

I swung my door open and stepped out onto the street. My foot slipped, and the meniscus in my knee popped like a champagne bottle. I held onto the car door and got my feet under me.

"Fuzzy, what the—"

I slammed the door shut on him, cutting off the obscenity.

The squeals and chatter of little kids came from the ice rink at Rainbow Park off to the left. I did my best skating up to Parker Hetfield's passenger door. I'm not sure what was going through the kid's mind. He obviously watched from his rear-view mirror, but he neither pulled through the light nor locked his doors, as I scooted up to him.

I reached up and opened the door and climbed up. The cab smelled of marijuana and fast food. Greasy food wrappers littered the floor board. Some hip-hop music blared from the stereo, rattling the windows.

I hopped onto the bench seat.

His eyes looked as if they would leap from their sockets, and his lips trembled as if he were about to cry.

I held out my hand to him. "Fuzzy Koella."

He gave me his dead fish. "Um, Parker."

In my peripheral vision, I saw the light turn green. "Hetfield, right?"

He slid his clammy hand from me. "Um, what do you want?" he said. "I don't have much money on me." He reached for his hip pocket.

"Start with turning that shit down." I smiled and pointed to the light. "It's green, Parker."

He scanned my torso. "Um, where are we going?"

"I don't know. Where were you headed?"

"Um, home. I guess."

"Okay," I said, pointing to the light again. "I don't want to go there. And with the cannabis I smell in here, I don't think you want to head right home."

Parker rolled slowly through the light. I faced the kid and saw Jo Jo following in the corner of my eye. I reached over and turned the stereo off. "I'm staying at the Traveler's Rest," I said. "Maybe you can drop me off there?"

"Um, Mister. I don't know what you are doing, but my dad—"

I held up my hand. "Your dad would love to catch a whiff of this reefer," I said. "Look, kid, just give me a ride to my place. All right?"

"That's all?" he said.

"That's all," I said. "When we get there, we can talk about that shit you caught off Katie Couture."

His shoulders dropped, and his face flushed. The lips stopped trembling, but only because the tightening of the cartilage in his jaw had his lips clamped shut.

The tires weren't up for the road conditions, and I held onto the handle above my window as we fishtailed down Route 37 at a speed of twenty-five miles per hour.

"Is it true about what they say about people who own these huge trucks?" He glanced at me sideways, but kept quiet.

"You know? That you're compensating for other areas which may be undersized."

His face looked sunburned.

"I guess Katie Couture will never weigh in on that," I said.

As we drove by the Willow Creek, Sonny LaPage was

in an animated conversation with Parker's father. Sonny waved his arms, and tilted his head back to look up at Hetfield. I couldn't tell if he was angry or just excited about something. Audrey stood behind them. Her hands jammed into her coat pockets and her shoulders hunched against the cold.

Hetfield looked over to the road just as we passed. His permanently fixed smile remained but his eyes widened.

I waved to him and returned the smile.

Dave Hetfield's mouth opened wide, as he shouted something unable to penetrate the glass of the shut window. He strode in our direction. Behind him Sonny LaPage's hands went to his hips, a toothless grin on his face. Audrey remained motionless, braced against the cold.

Parker either hadn't seen his father or pretended not to. He kept his foot on the pedal. Even at twenty-five, Dave Hetfield had no hope of walking up on us.

"Look, Mister —"

"Stop it with the Mister, shit, kid," I said. "Just get me to the Traveler's Rest, okay?"

He nodded and did what I had asked.

His monster truck wasn't up to the challenge of climbing the incline at the entry to the Traveler's Rest. Parker admirably tried three times with Jo Jo looking on from the shoulder before quitting and letting it roll back down right before Jo Jo. He took his hands off the wheel and looked to me. The tremble returned to his lips.

"Kid, don't cry on me, okay?" I said. "I'm a private investigator. And I'm trying to free Gary Pressley. You know him?"

His eyes searched me, again. And he fought a losing battle with his shivering lips.

"I'm not carrying, Parker. I will not shoot you. I will not rob you. And I will not take you into the law, yet. I need answers though."

He hung his head, shoulders slouched. "I know Gary," he said.

"Great," I said. "Now we're cooking. You and I both know Gary didn't kill Katie Couture, right?"

He slowly nodded his head, and his blond bangs dropped over his eyes. He looked ridiculous. Like a schnauzer, whose owner didn't keep up with the grooming.

"And how do we both know this?" I said, holding out both palms. "Because we know who did it—"

The kid finger-combed his hair back off his forehead. His eyes narrowed, and he tilted his head.

"You." Now his entire face shook. His mouth opened, but he was speechless.

The kid was the best actor the world has ever seen, or he really had nothing to do with Katie's death.

"Gary saw you pull up at the scene of the crime, and drive away when you knew something was wrong," I explained. "Look, nobody will think you purposefully killed Katie. They will understand you were trying to scare her. To punish her for what she had done to you."

The waterworks came, and they were a gusher. His eyes leaked. His nose blew snot bubbles.

Crying angered me. In its presence, it made me uncomfortable. I hated that feeling. I tightened the grip on my kneecaps.

"I loved Katie," he said. "I didn't kill her."

"Parker, then who did?" I said. "Who drove up to the crime scene in your car? Who knew what she had done to you? Who hated her enough to torture her for it?"

Parker Hetfield was a good kid caught in an impossible situation. The face convulsions stopped as he figured out what I implied. He bit off something he said.

I couldn't stand the thought of sitting there watching him cry. So, I opened my door.

It thumped as it slammed into the angry face of Dave Hetfield.

I couldn't have timed it any better had I known he had hurried up behind us.

Jo Jo shuffled up beside him. "Mr. Hetfield, Jesus. Are you okay?"

"Oh," I said. "Sorry, I didn't see you there, Mr. Hetfield." I winked at Jo Jo.

Hetfield looked up, his hand covered the lower half of his face. Blood seeped between his fingers. He removed his hand and sprayed blood across the virgin snow with a flip of his wrist. A fresh batch of the stuff pumped out of his nostrils. "I told you to steer clear of my family, Fuzz-ball."

"Parker here was just giving me a ride home," I said turning my attention to the kid, whose face had turned a whiter shade than the snow. "Isn't that right, Parker?"

Parker stared at me, searching my face for an answer to my question. His eyes slid from me to his father's bloody face. He frowned and nodded. "That's right," he said.

Hetfield's eyes narrowed, as he withdrew his cell phone out of the front pocket of his jeans. "Oh yeah? And why exactly is the fucking Indian following you if you needed a ride from Parker?" Blood coated his teeth, and he looked like a character from a Stephen King novel. "I'm calling the law, Fuzz-ball. You can think about harassing my family again while cooling it behind bars." He punched in numbers on his phone with his thumb.

I swatted the phone out of his hand. It missed the blanket of snow on the road shoulder and clattered on the pavement beneath Parker's truck.

Hetfield's nostrils flared and pulsed bloody bubbles like a rabid dog. I saw the punch coming, but the uncertainty of my footing on the slick ground slowed my reaction. He buried a short body blow six inches deep in my sore kidney. The punch unleashed a blast of air and saliva from my face that landed on the side of Hetfield's face.

I bent over at the waist and hugged my arms around my bruised abdomen.

Hetfield seized the opportunity with a rabbit punch to the back of my neck followed by a blow from his knee to the point of my chin that threw me back off my feet.

My teeth buried into my wounded tongue, and I felt sure I had bitten clean through. I landed on the seat of my pants, and skidded back ten feet on the slushy pavement. Warm blood filled my mouth. I spat a sticky clump of it in the snowy drainage ditch. Fortunately, I saw no fleshy bits.

Hetfield crab-walked towards me, his arm slung low between his legs like a linebacker waiting on the snap. His eyes like slits. A bloody grin on his face. I'm not sure I've ever looked into a psychopath's eyes, but I'd bet good money they would look something like what I saw in Dave Hetfield.

A giant sped past me, its features a blur. Shoulders down, it slammed into Hetfield's chest. He wrapped his arms around Hetfield's mid-section after the initial hit and took him down in a perfect form tackle. They both went down in a pile in the snowy ditch. The wrestling that followed was Greco-Roman style. Jo Jo had the upper hand, grinding Hetfield further into the mud and snow. Overpowering him with the hundred pounds of extra body mass he possessed. Hetfield wiggled and grunted trying to break free of the F.B.I.'s grasp.

Happy the big guy was on my side, I pushed myself up from the ground.

Jo Jo rose with Hetfield in a bear hug, lifting him clear off the ground. Hetfield's bloody face turned an unhealthy shade of blue, as Jo Jo tightened his clasp around his abdomen.

Hetfield's legs kicked at air like a kid in a tantrum.

"Easy, Dave. We cannot have a rumble in the streets.

Relax, and I will let you go and we can discuss this like adults."

Hetfield opened his mouth, but only produced a rasp. Jo Jo's clench on his insides was limiting his air supply. Hetfield landed a boot heel onto Jo Jo's shin.

Jo Jo grimaced, but kept his tight grip.

Hetfield's head lulled to one side.

"Jo Jo—" I called

The loud clap of a passing car backfiring cut me off.

Except there were no cars passing.

Parker Hetfield stood at the grill of his truck, the hood as tall as him, with a gleaming, nickel-plated, snub-nosed revolver held above his head. Black smoke curled from the tip of its barrel. His eyes looked no different than Hetfield's had as he approached me in his crab walk. There was murder in them.

And I questioned my inclination that Hetfield and not Parker had killed Katie Couture.

"Let him go," he said. "You fat skin. Or you will catch the next bullet."

The term "skin" was about as offensive a word, as you could use with a Native-American. Jo Jo gave his dad one swift squeeze at the skin comment, and there was a nauseating crunch of rib bone, before he dropped Hetfield like the sack of garbage he was.

Hetfield crawled under Parker's truck, and retrieved his cell phone, while Parker kept the pistol trained on Jo Jo.

I considered a running tackle of my own on Parker, but I realized my tennis shoes weren't up for that on the slick ground. I held my hands up in surrender. "Take it easy, Parker," I said. "We don't need to add murder in cold blood to the charges building against you."

The handgun wagged in Parker's hand.

The kid was nervous. I knew he didn't want to shoot, but I couldn't be sure he would not.

His father knelt beside the tire of his truck with his phone to his ear, "Cliffie, we have an attempted abduction here."

"Parker?" I called to him.

He found my eyes, and I held them there for a second.

"Yeah, it's that city boy Koella. Trying to run off with Parker."

I shook my head. Trying my best, "don't do this," look.

He lowered his gun, and with a flick of his wrist used it to fling Hetfield's phone from his ear. It landed at my feet.

"C'mon Dad," he said. "Let's get out of here."

The shattered phone trumpeted Cliff Hetfield's whiny voice. "Dave, are you there? What's going on?"

I reached down and cut the connection and tossed the phone to Parker Hetfield.

He caught it with one hand while the other grasped his father's coat collar and lifted him to his feet.

I walked over beside Jo Jo, and said, "Thanks, partner."

But he was in deep thought and didn't acknowledge my gratitude.

We stood side by side in the bloody snow, and watched Parker Hetfield help his dad into the cab of the Toyota, and drive off spraying slush and loose pebbles which felt like birdshot against my shins.

33

It felt good knowing Jo Jo had my back against Dave Hetfield. He took his leave of me shortly after Parker Hetfield had driven off. I had lied and told him I wanted to turn in for the day. As much as it would feel good to jump in my bed and sleep off my battle wounds and shame at getting beaten by Dave Hetfield, I still had a visit to make.

Instead of going to Unit 3, I went to see Stefanie Charles in the office. The one thing we had forgotten in all the activity with the Hetfields was to retrieve my car from the Legion parking lot.

I found Stefanie just inside the door wiping the venetian blinds clean with a wadded-up paper towel. Poised on one foot, and leaning over a waist high bookcase, my entry startled her and she pirouetted and fell back into my arms. In the movies, this is where I would have kissed her, and she would spend the rest of the film giving me the heavy eyes. Instead, I caught her under each armpit, got her back on her feet, and swatted her on the fanny. "Nice try, Charles."

She batted her eyes, "A girl's gotta try."

"If you give me a ride to my car, I'll only have eyes for you for the next fifteen minutes."

That got a monkey grin that would be the envy of Tarzan. "Where did you leave your car, love?"

I explained my long night at the Legion. She explained how she was sorry to have missed it. And during all that exposition, she closed down the office and got us into her little red car.

"You look like shit, Fuzzy."

"For all the talk of the small-town hospitality, I have received little of it," I said.

She tooled us through town like an Indy car driver, not once threatened by the slippery roads. She kept the innuendo up, and I swatted each away like pre-game batting practice.

When she dropped me off at the Legion, it was half-past three. She asked, "So where's my favorite dick off to now?"

"It's time I spoke to Amy Hetfield," I said.

She winked, "Don't knock her up."

* * *

DR. GARY SHEFFIELD'S office was a white clapboard job, with a full front gallery complete with a porch swing hanging by rusty chains from the rafters. I would have taken it for the house of one of the Fort's well-to-do families had I not seen the small black sign with the brass, calligraphic letters beside the green door. It announced the offices of Dr. Sheffield and gave the office hours as "M-F, 8-5."

It was a few minutes before four. I considered giving Father Cooper a visit to share some of my latest findings and watch the contortions of his face, but my better angel prevailed and I settled in the parking lot off the back of the house to figure out my game plan before Amy Hetfield emerged.

I ended up trying to recall the starting lineup of the 1998 Yankees. The team that won all those games.

I was working on the left-fielder when Amy Hetfield emerged and broke my concentration.

She wore skin tight yoga pants revealing muscular, if a little heavy, legs tucked into brown, calfskin boots with a faux-fur fringe. Her camel-hair coat matched the color of her boots. The red, white, and blue Buffalo Bills toque she wore did nothing to hide the unmistakably Hetfield blonde locks. Her skin was flushed pink with the cold, and her eyes were the color of a robin's egg. She walked across the lot with the confidence of someone who had walked across ice all of her life and scrolled through something on her phone.

I rolled down the window of the Nova. Tried on a flirtatious smile, "Hey, are you Amy Hetfield?"

She looked up from her phone, thought lines burrowing into her forehead. She considered me with the healthy skepticism any young girl should give a man of my age.

The #metoo movement had worked. My flirtatious smile had not.

"I saw you sing the Anthem the other night," I said. "It was beautiful."

She dropped her chin and pretended to look at her phone again. "Thanks," she mumbled, and continued on her way.

But I caught her peeking at me from the corner of her eye. Maybe, Stefanie Charles was right. These girls were so eager for some way out of town that they became an easy prey for an outsider like me or some carny. "Say, Amy. Maybe you can help me."

She stopped and turned and mocked impatience.

"Do you think the Doc may see me on such short notice?"

"We're closed, buddy. Call in the morning?"

"Will you be working?" I said.

She ground a fist into her hip.

I feared I had taken it too far.

She kept her head tilted forward, but she looked at me like a sad puppy. "Maybe," she said. She walked towards me. "What is it you need to see the doctor for? We're booked pretty heavy because of the holidays, eh?"

I opened my mouth and wagged my tongue at her.

"Oh, gross," she said.

I wanted to explain that I wasn't flirting or giving her the Gene Simmons treatment, but then I realized she had commented on the gash in my tongue. I hadn't inspected it yet, but I imagined it was disgusting. "So, you think it's worth seeing the doctor for?"

"Honey, I think you need to get to the hospital," she said. She came close for a better look.

I kept my tongue out like a thirsty dog.

She took my head in her hands and tilted it back and forth to get a closer look.

I resisted the temptation to moan in pain. It wasn't just my wounded tongue. My melon and neck had taken a beating, too. Why the hell was I letting this eighteen-year-old girl examine me like a nurse? It was probably the way her hair smelled like a candy cane. I don't even like candy canes, but I must like hair that smells like them.

"Maybe we can catch Doctor before he leaves, and I can get him to see you," she smiled and shook her head. "How on earth did you manage to do this to yourself? It looks like someone scooped out a chunk of your tongue and then cut a slash through it."

As much I would have loved to tell her that her father was responsible for both of those wounds, I kept it to myself. "I bit my tongue." I shrugged.

She play slapped my shoulder, "No kidding, silly." She stepped back from the car door. "Come on, Balboa. Let's see if the doctor is still in, eh?"

When I crawled out of the car, it felt like a fresh kick to the kidney.

I must have grimaced, because she said, "Oh God, does it hurt that bad?"

"Only when I breathe," I said and winked at her. "Don't worry. I'll survive, and when I do I owe you dinner and a movie."

She giggled, "I might take you up on that."

She escorted me to the front porch, her hand on my elbow. "You really liked my singing? I thought I was a little out of key."

I thought she was, too, but I didn't share that.

THE LOBBY of Sheffield's office looked like Miss Havisham had decorated it. The walls were papered white with some blue and gold paisley print, and were stained with nicotine from another era, when it was acceptable to smoke in the waiting room of a doctor's office. Is this the Great America we longed for?

Dusty, lacy curtains draped the windows, and the worn, cut-pile carpet was navy gone to black, and in need of replacing sometime last century.

"Not much like the offices in the city, eh?"

I marveled at all these small townees concluding that I was from the "city." I hadn't shared where I was from with Amy Hetfield. Hell, I hadn't even told her my name. Yet, she assumed I was a city boy. I fluttered my fingers at her. "Go find the doctor, please."

Her smile disappeared. "Right." And she disappeared through a door with a header that was eye height on me.

I sat down on a burgundy wing-back chair. Miss Havisham needed lessons in color theory. The chair sagged with my weight, but I stayed put and grabbed a copy of a National Geographic from 1985 off the nightstand. The cover displayed an Afghan woman with a scarf draped over head that would match the chair I sat in better than the carpet. The woman stared out at me with the most stunning green eyes I had ever seen.

I was thumbing through the magazine to find other photographs of the girl with the sea-green eyes, when Amy Hetfield peeked her head around the door and said, "You're in luck."

I followed her down a corridor with more of the same decor, except that the doctor had gone against Havisham's best advice and added black and white photos of old-time Yankees framed in bargain store plastic frames. It gave the place a facelift.

Amy deposited me in an observation room.

Immediately after we entered, Doctor Sheffield entered. He was an old walrus of a man with wireless spectacles and a Wilford Brimley mustache. He held a clipboard in his hand and studied it over the top edge of his glasses. "Well then, Mister--?"

"Koella," I said. "Francois, but you can call me Fuzzy."

Amy giggled. "Fuzzy? I love it!"

Sheff stared at her and frowned. "Mr. Koella, I don't normally take out-of-town patients. I don't normally see someone without an appointment. And I never see someone after hours." He took his eyes off Amy and looked at me. "But Miss Hetfield was persistent and persuasive."

She giggled again. "Sorry. But, Fuzzy?"

I turned the smile up a notch, and said with the affirmative nod of a cheerleader, "Fuzzy."

"I'm not gonna go through all the insurance stuff, but this will cost you fifty bucks assuming I don't have to do any stitches, and a hundred bucks if it does."

"Suits me fine, Doc," I said. "I have none anyway. Insurance, that is."

"All right," he said. "Let's have a look."

As I opened my mouth, Amy's cell phone went off with a ringtone of that song, "Happy" by Pharrell Williams. She stepped out of the room and closed the door behind her to take the call.

Doctor Sheffield grabbed a hold of my tongue with all the care of a dairy farmer squeezing an udder.

He pulled it left and right and grabbed it by its tip and tugged it straight out.

If he had wanted to know if it still held true on the other end, I could have shared that without all the pomp and circumstance.

He released it and it crawled back into place like a turtle retracting its head.

"You need to get to the hospital and get this stitched up," Sheffield said.

"Ain't happening, Doc," I said. "But I appreciate your accepting fifty bucks for advising me that."

"This is a nasty wound you have here, Mr. Koella. You really need the expertise and resources of the hospital."

I smiled at him. "Sorry, I've reached my quota of trips to the hospital over the last twelve months."

His eyes seemed to magnify on the other side of his spectacles. "Very well," he said. "I told you a hundred if I had to stitch. A hundred it is."

"Now we're talking."

Sheffield went about collecting instrument in a metal pan which looked like the pan my mother used to bake my birthday cake every year. It was a sad reminder. My birthday was a few months away, but once again mom wouldn't be baking a cake for me this year. Cabinet doors slammed as did drawers. The guy was as subtle as a shark in a pool of beef blood.

As I questioned my decision to let him stitch up my tongue, Amy returned with a frown on her face and her eyes watching some film playing in the recesses of her mind.

"Everything all right?" I asked.

She shook her head as if someone had thrown cold water in her face. "Huh? Yeah, everything is okay."

Sheffield pried open my mouth, yanked the tongue into view, and jabbed a needle into the center of my gash. It was no worse than the sting I felt in my toes every morning when I stepped outside in this god-forsaken place. He pressed the plunger home, and a blanket of numbness spread over my tongue and the roof of my mouth.

"Well, get over here, Amy," Sheffield croaked. "This was all your idea. The least you could do is help me out with the instruments."

She hadn't scrubbed her hands clean, but with Sheffield still gripping my tongue and brandishing a needle I was in no position to point that out.

Amy shuffled into position. Her eyes had gone back to that place deep in her thoughts, but she handed the good doctor a needle threaded with what looked like cat gut tennis racket string.

Amy must have caught fear in my eyes because she came back to earth. Smiled and laid her soft hand on the side of my head.

Sheffield went to work sewing me up.

Her robin's egg eyes had flecks of amber, as if the kid painting the Easter egg had flicked specks of paint on his masterpiece to add character.

Swallowed up in Amy Hetfield's eyes, I had forgotten about Sheffield working in my mouth until I heard the metal pan tossed on the counter, and Sheffield starting the sink to wash his hands.

It occurred to me he hadn't washed his hands before working on me either.

IN THE PARKING LOT, afterwards with Amy Hetfield hanging from my arm, she jammed a pink prescription slip into my hand. "Doctor says to get this filled as soon as you can or you will be a sad camper when the Novocain wears off."

Her smile was one of those frowning ones where the person can't help but smile despite something eating themselves up inside.

I unfolded the pink slip, on the prescription side there was the typical doctor chicken scratch. On the flip, a phone number in neat penmanship with two cute hearts doodled beside it.

"Why don't we do that movie tomorrow night?" I said. "You pick the flick and the restaurant."

She chewed away on the corner of her lip.

"Or not," I said. "What's wrong, Amy?"

She rested her head against my shoulder. "Oh nothing," she said. "Just, my dad called while you were in there to warn me that some tall man with gray hair named Koella may be by to see me, and that I should steer clear of him."

I stopped us in our tracks.

"He's probably right, you know?"

She patted me on my chest. "I know," she said. "But that's never stopped me before."

"So, dinner and a movie?" I said. "Tomorrow night?"

She rose up on tiptoes and planted one on my cheek. "You betcha. There's a new Nicholas Sparks movie, and The Hotel

Massena has a great bar and grill." She clapped her hands together. "And they even serve me."

I had forgotten that I hadn't even asked Amy my question. To do so now would throw cold water over her. Not to mention, I wasn't sure I even needed Amy's confirmation of Parker's infliction after the afternoon's proceedings.

Which begged the question why was I setting up a jail bait date with Amy Hetfield?

I pictured Dave Hetfield's bloody grin, as he approached me like a gorilla at feeding time. I had my answer.

34

———

I decided against stopping in to see Father Cooper, and drove back to my room as the sun dipped beneath the craggy, black silhouette of the horizon. The Office was closed and there was no sign of Stefanie Charles's car. I remember sliding the key into the door, and entering, and kicking my shoes off. I remember nothing else until my phone rang three hours later at nine.

It was Jo Jo.

"Fuzzy?" he said. "Did I wake you? You sound funny."

I tried to shake life into my face, and clear the cotton candy stuffed in my mind. "No, I'm good," I said. "What's up?"

There was a pause, and I could hear his breath wheeze. "Garrow wants to meet me," he said. "I am heading over to see him in a few minutes."

"Great," I said. "I can be ready in thirty seconds. Swing by and pick me up."

"That is not how it will work, my friend," he said. "He has asked to see me alone."

"Piss on what Matteo Garrow wants, I'm coming." I said.

"Sorry, Fuzzy," he said. "I need to have this conversation with him alone."

"Then, why in the hell did you call me?" I shouted.

"Take it easy, my friend. We are working this case together, and I am tired of keeping things from you. I thought you should know."

I could feel my cell phone flexing in my hand, under the pressure of my grip. "Know? Hell, I should be there, Jo Jo!"

"I have to do this on my own, my friend."

"Where are you meet—"

The line went dead.

I tossed my phone against the wall. A chunk of plaster broke free of the ceiling and landed in a powdery white pile on the floor.

I FIGURED I had a few options:

I could drive aimlessly about Franklin and St. Lawrence Counties searching for Matteo Garrow and Jo Jo.

I could go to the Legion and drink my disturbing thoughts into submission.

I could go back to sleep and try to make sense of everything tomorrow.

Looking back, I wish I had chosen one of the first two options. The first, I could have stumbled upon Jo Jo and Garrow in that barren corn field off a dirt road I didn't know existed. The second, I would have heard almost immediately from the drunks at the Legion when it came over the scanners.

Instead, I woke to knocking on my door, and the frantic voice of Stefanie Charles imploring me to, "Open up, Fuzzy. Oh God, open up."

I opened the door on what looked like dawn, but was

honestly difficult to tell in the land of overcast skies and electric snow. Stephanie stood shivering, knees locked together, arms folded tightly below her bust. Wet mascara smeared her cheeks, and fresh tears poured from her eyes.

I knew it without her saying a thing. I took her into my arms and buried her head into my chest.

"Oh God," she mumbled. "How the hell is this happening here?"

"It happens everywhere, honey," I said. "Where did they find him?"

"Way off a dirt road behind the school campus," she said.

I had to resist the tightening of my arms to keep from crushing Stefanie in my embrace. My teeth clamped so tight I could feel the give in them. There was a dull ache in my tongue from yesterday's operation, but filling that prescription would have to wait.

Garrow.

Hetfield.

A partnership made in hell.

"So, you had already heard?" Stefanie asked.

Her voice was like a whisper trying to wake you during an intense dream. Your dreaming mind senses that the voice is part of the dream and doesn't initially heed its call.

"Fuzzy?"

The voice heightens, crystallizes. The subconscious mind detects that there are two realities. The dream and the voice.

The voice wins.

"Huh?" I said. "Um, no I hadn't heard. I just guessed."

She wiggled out of my embrace. "How could you guess such a horrible thing?" she said. "And that look on your face — "

"What?"

"It scares me," she said, and she started back stepping from me.

I held my palms out in surrender. "Easy, Stefanie. I guessed because Jo Jo called last night to tell me of a secret meet. It seemed fishy. You show up like this at my door at the crack of dawn?" I gave it a chance to sink in. "I guessed."

"Secret meet?" she said. "Oh God, Fuzzy. Who was it with? We need to tell the police."

I had already told her too much. If I wanted Garrow and Hetfield, I couldn't give her any more. As soon as word got out I knew where Jo Jo headed on the night of his murder, the wheels would be put in motion. Leonard Cohen was right. The dice are loaded. "He didn't say," I lied.

She stepped towards me, again, and laid her cheek on my chest. She sobbed, "We should still go to the police."

I rest my chin on the top of her head. Her hair felt like strings of gooey plastic. "What police, Stefanie? The tribal police? Do you think they would even hear us?"

She blew snot on my white T-shirt. "I don't know, but we have to do something. Someone has to know who Jo Jo was going to see last night."

"Who? If he didn't tell me, who was he gonna tell?"

She shuddered against me like a shivering baby chick. "Why did this have to happen?"

It was a good question.

35

I sent Stefanie Charles on her way and suffered my way through the chain of events that led to Jo Jo's demise. Nothing from the Undie visit caused this. But before that there was our visit to Garrow, and my visit to Hetfield. Both seemed too benign to result in Jo Jo's slaying. Then there was our trip out to Cliffie Hetfield's hunting camp. That seemed to be a trigger. I made it all worse with my little trick with Parker Hetfield. Then I poured salt on the wounds when I double downed by asking out Amy Hetfield. It still seemed light for motivation to kill Jo Jo. Hetfield was no doubt ashamed of the rag doll treatment he got from Jo Jo, but I still couldn't see what he would see worth killing for. Surely, I was a bigger target for his hatred.

I recalled Jo Jo telling me about the wrongs of his past. The girl he accidentally killed in a drunk driving incident. Matteo Garrow's role in the coverup. But I also recalled Jo Jo's leverage on Garrow. How the Native police chief was in some sweetheart deal with his supposed enemy that involved feeding him with Native artifacts. I suspected some of that came up in last night's conversation.

I dressed in jeans, a turquoise t-shirt for Kilgore Trout's record shop, and the light windbreaker that served as my heavy winter coat. The sun had risen, and the world glistened with melting snow. The temperature probably was still subfreezing, but I felt warm. Either I was building up my tolerance to the place, or my anger was boiling my blood.

I took a ride to Jo Jo's place.

A BANKER'S box sat atop Jo Jo's desk. Scrawled on the side in black Sharpie marker was, "Couture Evidence." I sat on Jo Jo's side of the desk and squinted my eyes against a building urge to cry. They stung with salty tears, but I clenched them until the tears' need to flow subsided. When I opened them, they fell on Jo Jo's picture on the wall. The one with me in the background, and he about to deposit the ball over the left field wall.

The cops would get around to tossing Jo Jo's place soon. In fact, it surprised me that Garrow and his goons hadn't already been by. With that in mind, I went about digging through Jo Jo's filing cabinets.

They were about half full with manila folders tagged colorful translucent plastic tabs. Meeting minutes filled most. He had defended a lot of drunk drivers. I wondered if the irony was lost on him.

There were also several jet-black legal document-sized envelopes, which seemed to designate last will and testaments, death certificates, estate management, that sort of thing. The subject matter was too morbid given the circumstances for me to look any closer than to peek into two of the envelopes to confirm the pattern.

The short of it was that he did not seem to have any evidence against Garrow or Hetfield filed away in the cabinets. I sat down at his desk, and yanked drawers out only to find typical contents such as ballpoint pens, post-it notes, and rubber bands. No safe deposit keys. No incriminatory photographs. No personal photographs, for that matter. The realization that my friend had lived such a lonely existence saddened me.

I was about to give up and hurry back to the Traveler's Rest, when the doorknob wobbled and broke.

The door swung in and a lean man of about six feet dressed in the brown uniform of the tribal police stepped in. He had a cowboy hat in his hand, with a light pink feather tucked in its band. His hair was jet black and buzzed down to a high-and-tight flat-top. His brown face shone like a newly oiled saddle. His eyes were Mohawk dark. He had the broad nose. He fit the stereotype to a tee, except for the wide smile which spread across his face.

I reached for the handles on the evidence box.

"You must be Mr. Koella," he said, striding towards me with his hand held before him. "Tony American Horse."

I took his hand.

He had a firm, confident handshake to match the smile.

"Yes, I'm Koella," I said. "Do you make a habit of breaking the lock off a man's door?"

He continued to grin. It wasn't the fake politician's smile that Hetfield wore. It was the smile of the young man who had lost nothing he'd truly loved yet. And he was young. I'd card him before serving him. "I wanted to get here to take a look before the cavalry arrived," he said. His eyes fell on the evidence box, which I had now lifted off the desktop. "It appears you beat me to it."

I shrugged. "Jo Jo hired me to help him free Gary Pressley. In honor of him, I intend to continue that job."

American Horse dropped his hat on the desktop and hooked his thumbs in belt loops on either side of his pelvis. "Did you talk to Jo Jo last night?"

I shook my head. "You need a warrant to be here, Horse."

That brought a chuckle. "You know better than that, Koella. I'm not here to arrest anyone. Hell, the owner of this place, or I should say the renter, is dead. I am allowed to be here on grounds that this is a homicide investigation."

"Kid, you look like you just stepped off the stage at Salmon River with your diploma in your hand. What do you know about homicide?"

He took the seat opposite me. My seat. Leaned back, propped his feet up on the desktop, ankles crossed. He hooked his fingers behind his head as if he were about to begin an abdominal work-out. "I know this whole place is dirty."

I scanned the office. Spartan yes, but not dirty.

"Not the office. The Rez, the Fort. Hell, all of Franklin County."

"You do realize that your boss is caught under that wide net you're casting?"

He dropped his feet to the floor, and leaner forward, smile still wide, "Hell, he is like the Godfather."

I didn't know what to make of him, and I was still punch drunk from the news of Jo Jo's death. "How did you all know where to find Jo Jo?"

He looked over my shoulder to Jo Jo's photograph. He stood, and studied it. "I did not know Jo Jo played baseball. I would have taken him for a football player. Then again, we do not have a scholastic football program." He peeled his gaze away from the picture, and his eyes dropped to the box in my hands.

I set it down on the desktop, but I could not release my tight grip on handle holds on either side.

"Anonymous call," Horse said. "I was sitting in the dark at my desk alone. Meditating." His smile disappeared. "I took the call, radioed Matteo, and we met there right where the caller said Jo Jo would be found."

"Male or female caller?"

He scratched his clean-shaven skin.

It brought an itch to my day-old stubble.

"Are you going to help me?" he asked. "Because you are asking a lot of questions that do not have anything to do with freeing Gary Pressley."

I shook my head. "You're not that stupid, Horse. The two cases are obviously connected. Besides, Jo Jo was my friend and teammate." I hitchhiked my thumb over my shoulder at the photograph on the wall.

"Holy shit, is that you?" he said. His smile crept onto his face again. "You even had that gray hair back then."

The kid smiled too much for having just found a dead body. Plus, his hair was black and shined like a wet Labrador's hide. I envied him it. "So how was Jo Jo killed?"

"Shot," he said. "Probably a hunting rifle. Took it between the eyes, blew out the back half of his head." His shoulders shook and his lips pinched. He tried to cover it by inspecting a cuticle on his middle finger, digging at it with his thumbnail.

But I caught it, he was disturbed. And who wouldn't be? He was just a kid, doing a job he probably thought would be glamorous, and was probably one of the better jobs available to him, and then someone calls in a dead body. And shit ain't what it seemed just minutes before.

"Male caller," he said. "And before you ask, no. It was not the Chief."

"But you know he was behind it, right?"

He sat. "That's why I'm here. I need to toss this place. There has to be something here that can shed some light into why Jo Jo was out in that field."

I locked my eyes on his. "He was meeting Garrow," I said.

There was no twitch in his eyes or anywhere else on his face. The smile disappeared, again. Otherwise he took the news like I had just told him they had forgotten to deliver the paper.

I continued, "Jo Jo called me last night to tell me he was meeting Garrow."

Tony American Horse's eyes widened. He wagged his index finger at me. "Did he say where?" He paused, tilted his head. "Why was he going to meet him?"

Much as I'd like the help, I wasn't quite ready to air Jo Jo's dirty laundry. There was something about Horse's interest that seemed beyond straight police work.

He wanted Garrow out, because he figured it would open a path up the ladder to him.

As if he had read my mind, he stood and turned away and slid both hands in the back pockets of his brown trousers. Studying the ceiling, he said, "Look, I am ambitious. Sue me. But I did respect Mr. Bigtree, and I would like to bring some justice to the killer. Rather than just sweep the whole thing under the rug like I fear Matteo will do." He turned back to me. For effect, he kept the smile tucked away. "We can help each other."

The kid had watched one too many Bogey films, but I happened to like Humphrey Bogart. "You and I both know Garrow is behind Jo Jo's death."

He nodded. "We need evidence." His eyes settled on the box still in my hands.

"This is for the Couture case," I said, and a thought occurred to me. "Cliff Heffield is the primary detective on that case. It's dirty like everything else. Do you think you could connect me with his superior?"

His face went deadpan. Like Jo Jo's. Like Matteo

Garrow's. "I can try, but I am Native. They have the respect you give to the kid on school patrol to us."

I saw his point. "Nonetheless," I said. "Perhaps they will extend a little profession courtesy."

He shrugged, "As I said, I will try."

"Okay," I said. "What do you need from me?"

He winked, "Move your ass and let me toss the place."

I explained that I had just done the same and found nothing, but he wanted to convince himself. I left my cell number with him and left him behind in Jo Jo's office.

I HAD PICKED up another teammate in Tony American Horse. However, I wasn't sure how far I could trust him. He had political aspirations after all, and I trusted politicians like I trusted the basket that housed a cobra. I returned to the Traveler's Rest in hopes of visiting with my other teammate. The one I trusted.

But the Office was closed, and there was no sign of Stefanie Charles. So, I entered my unit and tossed the evidence box on the bed.

Vengeance was on my mind.

For the ass kicking Hetfield had given me. Probably twice.

For Jo Jo's murder.

But finishing what I had set out to do was also on my mind. Gary Pressley was still behind bars, and didn't belong there.

As the pulse pounded in my temples, and I set about grinding my teeth to chalk dust, I tried to remember that.

Where the kid once had the two of us working to release him, he was now stuck with only me.

The glasses sitting on the vanity were traced with the salty stains of effervescence, and one of them had the permanent pink imprint of some long-lost tenant's lip gloss. I chose that one, and filled my glass with cloudy water.

It tasted the way skunk spray smells.

I drank it down.

I remembered the box. For all the honorable qualities Tony American Horse credited him, Jo Jo had never seemed to pay much attention to the evidence file. I had pointed out all the inaccuracies and oversights, and Jo Jo swatted them away like a goalie defending against the power play. But the box had sat on top of his desk. He had left it there when he visited Matteo Garrow. Had he found something? Something, that when shared with Garrow, had led to his death?

I sat on the bed beside the evidence box, and tossed the cardboard lid aside. On top of all the folders neatly jammed into the box sat a black envelope, like the ones he used for the last will and testaments in his filing cabinet. A while label was fastened to it. Lettered on it in the fine penmanship of a draftsman was "Fuzzy."

I lifted it, and held by the edges between both hands. I was reluctant to open it. I feared there would be one of those, "If you are reading this I am gone" notes. My eyes squinted back tears, and in the darkness of my closed eyes, an image appeared. Jo Jo trotting around third in the full teal and gold uni of the Manatees. He grabs the offered hand of the third base coach, whose name I cannot recall, but he had Popeye forearms covered with coarse dark hair. Jo Jo released his hand and continued his slow stroll to homeplate where we awaited him. As he entered the batter's box, Action Jackson, our close, smacked Jo Jo's helmet. Jo Jo hopped into the air, and came down with both spikes on the plate. And we swarmed him.

It was all fantasy. Jo Jo had never played a game for the

Manatees. He had come home after his red-shirt season. A failure.

I tapped the corner of the envelope on my thigh.

Opened my eyes, and ran a fingernail under the glued flap of the envelope and tore it open.

To my relief, there was no note from Jo Jo.

There was a stack of glossy 3 x 5 photographs. Printouts from an auction site called, artifactsbay.com. The site's log looked suspiciously familiar to the world's most popular auction site. There was also an old 4" floppy disk, and a thumb-drive.

A floppy disk? Jo Jo had held onto to something, very long.

I swallowed a deep gulp of the dusty, Traveler's Rest air, and dug into the stack of pictures.

They looked like my handiwork. I wondered if Jo Jo had another PI on retainer or if my friend had a streak of peeper in him, as well. All the pictures had either Matteo Garrow or Dave Hetfield in them. Most of them had both of them in the composition. But I couldn't see the importance in that. Other than in most of the pictures, they did not look like the heated enemies they made out to be, they were just a couple of talking heads. The conversations took place in cornfields, the parking lots of deserted convenience stores, or expansive black top pavement with weeds penetrating cracks in the surface. But that described much of the landscape up here.

I was about to set the stack of glossies aside, when I flipped to a shot of Dave Hetfield standing and smiling beside his behemoth SUV, and Matteo Garrow approaching, back turned to the camera, long black hair trailing behind him in the breeze. He carried a blue plastic tote, the kind the college kids carry home their dormitory belongings in. The lid was off the tote, and it appeared to contain a pile of those souvenir mini-baseball bats.

I thumbed to the next shot. Matteo Garrow stood over the tote, at his feet, and had one of the bats in his hands held out to Smilin' Dave Hetfield. Except it wasn't a bat. My fingers went to a tender spot on the back of my head. It was pulpy flesh like that of a bruised banana. The back of my neck heated up, and my probing fingers became slick with sweat that beaded in my hair. I crumbled the picture in my hand. The one of him holding the weapon used to assault me.

Sometime the next year, I came back to my senses. I wasn't sure what I had other than the same leverage Jo Jo had over Garrow, without Jo Jo's personal baggage. The same leverage that had gotten his head blown away.

My fingers continued to prod at my wounded scalp, until I had worked the scab away and held a different kind of moisture in them.

I found my phone and called Franklin County Correctional, and asked to speak to Steve Whitaker.

He was prompt in coming to the phone, "Mr. Koella, what's up?"

I started with the formalities, "How's Gary?"

Silence on the line.

Oh shit. They didn't get to Gary, too. Did they?

"He's without an attorney, I hear," Whitaker said. The background noise of the bullpen got swallowed up, followed by the sound of a door latch. "Sorry to hear about your friend, Fuzzy."

I closed my eyes, and waited on the tear ducts to shut. "Thanks," I said, and moved along, "Listen, I need to get to someone above Cliff Hetfield. Gary's never going to get a fair shake with Cliffie running the show."

Whitaker huffed. "What do you think I am, Fuzzy?" He didn't wait for me to answer. "I'm just a lowly correctional office."

My grip tightened on the phone. "And I'm a low out-of-state private investigator. Who do you think has the better shot?"

There was a stretch of silence on his end, and I thought we had lost our connection, but there was a metallic scraping sound.

"C'mon, Whitaker. You must have some connection with the force."

"What makes you think getting to one of Cliffie's superiors will make any difference?"

Good question. "I don't know," I said. "Maybe there's a decent person that lives above the Mason-Dixon line." I regretted it, even before I had finished saying it.

"Ouch," he said. More silence followed.

"Look, I'm sorry—"

"Forget it," he said. "Give me a couple of hours, I'll call you back when I find someone."

"Thanks," I said.

"Don't thank me yet. And Fuzzy? Sorry again about Jo Jo. He was a good shit."

WHITAKER CUT THE CONNECTION, and I recalled my conduit to the Hetfields. I unfolded the pink slip, which sat on the night stand, to Amy Hetfield's phone number, and texted her. "What time do I pick you up tonight?"

The response was immediate. Good sign. "Fuzzy?"

"Yes, Fuzzy. How many guys you have taking you out to dinner and a movie, tonight?"

Moments passed. Not so good a sign. Did she really have a handful of boys or men courting her? And why should I care? She was probably having second thoughts due to something her father had said about me.

"Oh God, Fuzzy," showed up on the screen. "I would have called you if I had your number."

There was nothing in her response that should elicit any concern. She could just be having second thoughts about going out on a date with a man over ten years her senior. And she should have those doubts, but something curdling deep in my stomach told me that it wasn't as simple as Amy Hetfield showing some smarts. My hand tightened around the phone. I punched in, "Is there something wrong? Can't do tonight? Second thoughts?"

The screen remained blank. No sign she was typing a response.

I added one of those stupid frowning emoticons.

Now there was typing. A lot, too. I waited for what seemed like the writing of *Don Quixote.*

"You will not believe this. When I got home last night, Daddy called me and Park into the den. I figured he would lecture us on you. Lol. Nope, he surprised us. He's taking us on a surprise trip to the Caribbean. Can you believe that? Two weeks."

Holy shit! The phone slipped from my hand and bounced off the toe of my sneaker underneath the bed. "Dammit," I yelled to the empty room.

I had a hard time focusing my thoughts. Hetfield was getting them out of the country, and he had made the plans before Garrow and Jo Jo's meet. The son of a bitch.

I dropped to my hands and knees and reached through dust bunnies and wadded up tissue to fish my phone out from under the bed.

My thoughts turned to Amy Hetfield. How her innocence was being exploited. "When do you leave?"

"We are at the airport now."

The room spun around me. I looked up to the ceiling and

anchored my gaze on a coffee-colored water stain. I typed, "Don't go, Amy."

"Are you crazy?" She responded.

Probably. And I suspect at her age I would ask the same question.

Before I could respond she included, "Look, if you're still around when we get back, I'll still let you take me out."

"Don't go, Amy. You'll spend the rest of your life on the run."

"?"

"Have you heard what happened to Mr. Bigtree?"

Long pause. I have expected to get one of those text-not-delivered-messages.

I typed in, "What airport are you flying out of?"

Typing began from her side. Stopped.

I held my thumb over the send button, waiting to see what her message would be. When her typing did not continue, I hit send.

And then I got my response, "Leave us alone, Fuzz-ball."

Dammit, Hetfield. I threw my phone against the wall with such force it was a wonder it hadn't embedded in the plaster.

Damn, what would I do now?

I crawled across the bed and picked up my phone. Its screen had shattered, but the pieces remained in place.

I dialed Steve Whitaker. The plastic of my screen depressing with each punch of a number.

He picked up on one ring. "Dang, Koella. I speak to you more than I speak to my wife."

"Yeah, whatever. Look, I need you to help me get a flight delayed."

Silence from his side spread for a couple of seconds, then he cleared his throat. "Fuzzy, I'm trying to get you some time with the higher brass. That is an uphill battle. I'm only a correctional officer. Now, you want me to get a flight grounded? You are seriously overestimating my pull. We don't even have an airport in Franklin County."

"I'm guessing it's out of Massena."

He chuckled. "You don't even know?"

"Look, it's a long story," I said. "And the longer we sit here chatting about it, the greater chance a killer escapes."

"Fuzzy, I'm telling you. There is no way I will be able to ground a flight. Now do you want me to keep trying to get you an ear over at the Sheriff's office?"

I felt like I was running in waist high water. Trying my damnedest, kicking my feet, but getting nowhere. "Keep at it with the Sheriff," I said.

"Office, not--"

I cut him loose.

Headed for the door with my keys in hand. Just as I put my hand on the knob, there was a knock.

I opened the door to find Sonny LaPage standing in the doorway, wearing a plaid lumberjack's coat with a corduroy collar, and a green hunter's cap traced with white salt stains. He cradled a hunting rifle in the crook of his arm.

I'm pretty sure it was not the season. I stared at the gun, hoping it was an illusion.

Sonny LaPage didn't seem to register my concern. "Hey there, Fuzzy. My condolences on the loss of your friend, Jo Jo."

I opened my mouth to say something, but realized I had no words, and I couldn't stop looking at that damn rifle. This town was full of hunters. Good shots. One of those shots put one between Jo Jo Bigtree's eyes. It wasn't Sonny LaPage. I was sure of that, but the list was long of who that shot could have been. Didn't matter who pulled the trigger. Matteo Garrow set it up.

LaPage interrupted my thought process with something I hadn't expected, "I want to help."

I lifted my gaze from the gun. Sonny LaPage's eyes were slits, his mouth a slash, and the cartilage in his jaw bunched like cauliflower. He wasn't bullshitting. "Can you get me to Massena International in a hurry?"

"The airport? You aren't leaving, are you?"

I patted him on the shoulder. "Come on. We can talk about it on the way," I said. "And keep that thing pointing away from me."

SONNY LAPAGE MANAGED to keep us out of the ditch, as he fishtailed us onto the reservation. His rifle pointed barrel down at the floor boards rested uncomfortably against my thigh. I had him pull around the back of the Howlin' Wolf, but Tony American Horse's cruiser had disappeared. I should have taken his number when I had a chance. But there had been a lot of "should haves" on the case, and contemplating them got me nowhere. I pointed Sonny back onto Highway 37 in the direction of Massena.

He kept the needle on sixty through all the changing speed limit signs. None of which had read greater than fifty miles per hour. As we reached the other side of the reservation, the flashers of a Tribal Police cruiser shone in the rearview mirror.

"Goddamn Natives and their speed traps!"

"I don't think Native Americans have a monopoly on speed traps," I said.

Sonny looked at me with his slit eyes.

I smiled, and shrugged.

Tony American Horse's visage appeared in the driver's side window.

Sonny kept his eyes on me, and laughed. "All right, then.

Goddamn Natives and their fucking speed traps! Any better?"

I nodded. "There's one waiting at your window."

His eyes settled on me for a moment. Then he gave Tony his attention. The window slid town, and Tony's cop glare changed to good cheer when he noticed me in the passenger seat. "Where are you heading, gentlemen?"

I cut in before Sonny could answer. "Lead us to the airport, Horse. We have to get there before Hetfield's flight takes off."

He held his palms up. "Whoa, I can't lead a convoy into St. Lawrence County."

The police in upstate New York were the most concerned about jurisdiction I had ever encountered. "Okay, then let us go," I said. "A killer is going to get away."

"Killer?" Horse said. "Garrow killed Jo Jo."

Sonny LaPage's slit eyes opened and now were perfect marbles.

"And Hetfield killed Katie," I said.

Sonny LaPage's mouth opened in a toothless Oh.

"You don't know that--"

"And you can't prove Garrow killed Jo Jo," I said. "Now shit or get off the pot."

Tony frowned, and he held it there while he turned things over in his mind. He swatted the car door. "All right. Follow me."

Sonny LaPage watched me as Tony American Horse returned to his cruiser. "If you already know who all the killers are, why aren't we reporting it to the police?"

I pointed out the window to Tony's cruiser pulling past us, "We are," I said. "There's our police."

He shook his head and worked the wheel like a kid in a bumper car trying to get us back on the highway without sliding us into oncoming traffic. He lifted his chin, indicating Tony's car. "That isn't much better than school patrol, eh?"

"It's all we got, eh?"

He put the pedal down. Tony American Horse had his flashers on, and the needle settled on seventy. Tony had to have seen the rifle lying beside me, but he hadn't even acknowledged it.

I reached up and held on to the handle above my window. If I hadn't spent the last week hearing about Katie Couture's failings, I would have done the sign of the cross.

36

Horse pulled us right up to the front door. Left his flashers on and got out. Sonny thumbed his hazards on, and we crawled out of the pickup.

Nothing was said.

We hit the front door in a light jog.

The terminal was empty, except for the old gate agent and another woman young enough to be his granddaughter. Out on the tarmac, a sooty American Airlines prop-jet taxied out to the runway. Its wings bouncing with each expansion joint its tires hit, as if it were an elephantine egret flapping to take flight.

I continued my trot, as Tony American Horse and Sonny LaPage skidded to a halt just inside the doors. I stopped in front of Grandpa, and his prey.

She scanned me up and down. He dark brown, blood-shot eyes clashing with the blue eye shadow haloing her brows. At this distance, I could see the thick foundation pancaked on her face, and the missing teeth in her smile. She was closer to grandpa's age that I had originally guessed. She scoffed, "Another one who missed their flight, Teddy?"

I ignored her. "I need you to stop that flight, Teddy!"

Teddy leaned forward and held his hand behind his ear, palm out. "What's that?"

The charming old fart reminded me of Burt Lancaster as Moonlight Graham in *Field of Dreams*, but I didn't have time to wait on him to decide if he would step over the baseline. I grabbed a handful of his blue shirt, and felt a button pop loose. "I need you to call up to that plane, and ground it. There is a killer on that plane."

He looked over my shoulder. Tony American Horse came into view on my right. Teddy, whose name tag read Theodore Rattay, snickered. "I cannot do that, boys." Teddy jabbed a thumb over his shoulder, "Once we close the gate, we don't open it again. This flight isn't just closed, it's about to take off," he squawked.

I looked to Tony American Horse, but he just stood there with a politician's grin that would be the envy of Dave Hetfield. I gave Teddy another tug on his shirt, "You can pick up your radio, and tell the pilot to stop the take-off, and allow the police to enter the plane."

Teddy kept his focus on Horse.

I wanted to yank his fat ass over his stand.

His girlfriend whined, "I know you're just Tribal, but if you don't arrest this guy for assaulting Teddy, I'm gonna get the Sheriff's office down here."

Horse took my biceps in his hand, "Come on, Fuzzy. Take it easy. Mr. Rattay is right. There is nothing we can do."

I released my grip on Teddy's shirt, and pulled my arm loose of Horse's grasp. "Y'all are unbelievable. We are talking about a killer, here! Murder!"

Teddy's girl started punching numbers into her phone.

I stopped myself from swatting it free from her hand, because I figured we could use more cops.

A smile returned to Teddy's face, and he turned his attention to me. "It was only the Hetfield family on that flight. I'm sure you are mistaken."

I watched as the plane sped down the runway.

"I'm not mistaken," I said to Tony American Horse. "Find out where that flight was headed."

WE SPENT a half hour determining that the flight was heading to Pittsburgh by way of Ogdensburg and Watertown. I had ended up swatting the woman's phone out of her hand when she over exaggerated my manhandling of Teddy Rattay. Sonny LaPage and Mr. Rattay came to my defense and settled her down, when she attempted to claw my eyes out with her two-inch nails.

Eventually, I conceded.

There was no way that we were speeding over to any of these tiny airports before Hetfield and crew took off again. Tony American Horse had no pull with the Feds to get the flights grounded. And Steve Whitaker wasn't picking up the phone.

The three of us left Teddy Rattay and his friend there.

At the curb, beside our vehicles, Tony American Horse said, "We need to shift our attention to Garrow."

He was correct, but I couldn't let Hetfield go. "I want to take a look at Hetfield's place."

"Hetfield is gone, Fuzzy. Let's fight the battles worth winning," Horse said.

I knew better than to ask about a warrant. He couldn't provide one, and I couldn't give a shit. I gestured like I was checking my watch, and said, "Let's meet back at Jo Jo's office in two hours."

Horse shook his head, "Sometime today that place will be crawling with my kind," he grinned. "The Chief has been texting me through this whole ordeal. At some point, I will need to answer him."

"Okay, so what?"

"Keep the two hours, but let's make it your place at the Traveler's," he said.

I turned to Sonny LaPage, and said, "You still in?"

He squinted, and puckered his mouth. "You're damn right, I'm in."

"Let's go," I said.

37

Back home in South Carolina, the Hetfield residence with its faux-stone veneer and high-arched gallery would look like the home of a wealthy doctor or attorney. In the mobile home and tinned-roof cottage dotted landscape of Franklin county, it stood out like something erected by the Vanderbilt family. Sonny LaPage drove up a driveway lined with dead crab apple trees, and after a couple football fields stopped us in front of a three-car garage built to look like a carriage house connected to the main house by a narrow umbilical with floor to ceiling glass. The three garage doors each had a string of windows in the eye-height panels.

We hopped out of Sonny's cab. He carried his rifle over his shoulder.

"I don't think we'll need that," I said.

"If it's all the same to you. I'll let you debate whether we need it, and I'll keep it on the off chance we do."

I walked over to the garage doors with Sonny on my heels. We looked through the windows into the most organized garage I had ever seen. A spot for the Hetfields' SUV was empty, Amy's little green compact and Parker's canary yellow truck occupied the other two spaces. Parker's truck must have hunched over like an NBA player to make it through the doorway. Work benches lined each of the walls. Manual and automatic tools hung neatly on hooks from the walls above each surface. It would not surprise me to find out he had tagged all the equipment for proper maintenance tracking. The place was that tidy.

"He's probably never used a bit of it, eh?"

We continued over to the main house and climbed eight feet of steps up to a gallery with dead potted plants hung from the balustrade. The dead plants left over from summer stood in stark contrast to the tidiness I had witnessed at the garage.

"Mrs. Hetfield doesn't do much but look good on his arm." Sonny spat a thick glob of mucous onto the floorboards and reached for a brass knocker set in the center of the right leaf of the double-door entry. "Shall we?"

I produced a pocket knife and unfolded the blade. "I don't think knocking is necessary."

I slid the blade between the door leaves, until it stopped against the latch, pried with little care, and sprung the lock in a matter of seconds.

Inside the house, it was about as I expected. Two-story foyer with stairs leading to an H-plan second story. A lot of fake hardwood floors. Cracks at doorjambs, indicating foundation settling. Plastic laminate cabinetry made to look like wood. Dave Hetfield liked things "Huge", like our President. But he didn't bother himself with good.

We spent an hour digging through Hetfield's cabinets and drawers. Sonny wasn't sure what he was looking for, so he spent most of his time inspecting and admiring Hetfield's gun case.

Sonny determined with relative certainty that none of the weapons had been fired recently. "At least not since hunting season," he said. After seeing how Dave Hetfield cared for his tools, I wasn't sure how he could say with any certainty how long it had been since someone had used the weapons.

I spent my time digging through cabinets, drawers, and closets. I wasn't sure what I was hoping to find. But that was always the case in my work. I had learned that you keep pulling at every loose thread in the ball of yarn. Usually, it left me with a bird's nest, but sometimes in the center of the ball, you found the core that held it all together. I wasn't finding any core.

Tony American Horse was correct. Hetfield was a waste of time.

But I kept at it.

I found a Mohawk war club leaning against the back wall of Dave Hetfield's walk-in closet. It matched the one used to beat me and found at Katie Couture's crime scene. I ran my fingers across the polished wood of its shaft, up to the knobbed end which looked like the top of a newel post. I wielded the weapon like a hammer. Chopping it like an Atlanta Braves' fan. It had a nice heft to it, and the knobbed end felt powerful as it swung down. It was a dangerous, bludgeoning weapon. I still had no clue why it was in the basement with Katie Couture, as she showed no sign of blunt force trauma. I carried it with me as I rifled through the drawers of Hetfield's mahogany desk in the den.

I mostly found bills. A lot of them credit card bills. A lot near their limit. There were also coupon books for short-term, high interest loans he had taken out with some Tribal finance company. Hetfield was playing the shell game with his credit. Shuffling the shells around as fast as he could, so all the creditors had a difficult time catching the little red ball. Hetfield was in terrible straits financially.

Still not sure what any of that meant to me. To Gary Pressley. To Jo.

Tucked behind some hanging folder in the bottom drawer,

I found a metal box with a cheap clasp lock, and combination dial.

I used my knife to pry the clasp loose and opened it to find it packed with hundred-dollar bills. It wasn't a big box, but that number of bills had to put the total in the tens of thousands of dollars. Holding it there in my hands, I recalled that Jo Jo hadn't reimbursed me for my travel expenses, and I was probably not going to see any of my pay for this job. Anyone who tells you that money isn't everything, is skirting around a very real truth. Which is that money was something, and a pretty big something. I fought the temptation to balance my books and left the bills where I found them. But as I thumbed through them with a great longing, I caught the glint of something glossy beneath the wad of bills, and dug down beneath the money and slid free a photo I had seen before.

It was a duplicate of a picture Jo Jo had left for me in the evidence for the Katie Couture case. The one where Matteo Garrow carried a tote full of Native artifacts to a smiling Dave Hetfield standing beside the open hatch to his SUV.

Why did Hetfield have this picture? Was he there when Jo Jo met with Matteo Garrow?

Sonny and I made the trip from Hetfield's place to the Traveler's Rest in relative silence. The only words exchanged were when he asked why I had taken a photograph of Parker Hetfield's monster truck. I had shrugged and explained that you never know when something might become important. It wasn't the complete truth. I had taken the picture intending to show it to Gary Pressley to determine if it was the "high truck." I'm not sure why I didn't share that with LaPage, but I was happy when silence descended upon us again.

The picture I had found gnawed at my mind. It was

important, but I was unsure why. Obviously, it was proof that Hetfield and Garrow were cozier than they let on in public, but I had already known that. Even before Jo Jo had left the other copy for me. But Jo Jo left that copy for me for a reason, and now I had found another copy stowed away in Dave Hetfield's cash box. Coincidences like that typically add up to more than a coincidence.

Sonny climbed us up the incline to the Traveler's Rest, and in front of unit three, sat Stefanie Charles. Even in the relatively tame weather, it was well below freezing. So, she wore a heavy, quilted blue coat with a faux fur fringe, tight blue jeans, and knee-high, leather Han Solo boots. She sat on a metal folding chair, and a pile of cigarette butts at her feet counted out the time she had stacked at my front door waiting on me.

She squinted back the bright sunlight as she peered up into Sonny's windshield as the tires came to a crunching stop before her.

I hopped out of the cab before Sonny had killed the ignition.

"Stefanie, what the hell are you doing out here?" I strode to her. "You will freeze to death."

Standing before her, I noticed her colorless lips, and the way her hand shook as she put a cigarette between them. Something more than the cold had drained the life out of her eyes.

"What's wrong?" I said.

She took a deep drag on her cigarette and held it in her lungs for a good minute. Smoke slowly leaked from her nostrils. It gave her the visage of an angry bull. "You haven't checked your text messages?"

She was right; I hadn't. I dug in the front pocket of my jeans.

She wagged her cigarette at me as Sonny stopped beside me.

"What's up?" he said.

"You had Stevie Whitaker trying to get you an ear with the top brass?" She took a shorter pull on her stogie and blew the smoke out of the corner of her mouth.

"Sure," I said. "We aren't getting anywhere with Cliffie Hetfield. Especially, with his brother's fingerprints all over this."

"Yeah, when Stevie was asking around, he determined Cliffie hadn't made it in to work today. So, he sent a cruiser by Cliffie's place."

"He's out at his hunting camp."

Stefanie waved that off, too. Her lower lip trembled. "They found him," she sobbed. "He was in his trailer. He got himself shot." She looked to Sonny with watery eyes. "God, Mr. LaPage. What is happening to our little town?"

I caught her eyes shift before settling on Sonny. I said to him, "This isn't a random shooting. This is covering tracks. The work of a professional. How does someone in Ft. Covington, New York connect with a professional?"

"Ha," squawked Sonny Lapage. "You'd be surprised, Mr. Koella. We're a small town, but we're also a border town and with that comes crime."

I stepped past Stefanie Charles and opened the door to my unit. "Come on, let's get in out of the cold."

As I stood aside to let them enter, Sonny continued, "Why, even my next-door neighbor runs drugs and kids across the border. How else is he getting the money to build those race cars?"

I had no clue what race cars he was talking about. "Mr. LaPage, I'm talking about a professional, a button man."

He looked up at me as he passed. A quizzical look was on his face. "Buttons," he said. "What are you talking about?"

"A hit man," I explained. "The guy who presses your button."

He made his way to my bed and dropped there like he'd just pulled a double shift.

Stefanie Charles stood beside him, arms crossed and trying to rub warmth into her biceps. "We certainly don't have that type here in Fort Covington?" She looked down at Sonny propped on both elbows and leaning back on my bed. "Do we?"

He scratched the gray stubble on his chin. "I don't know," he said. "We definitely have an organized crime presence. Why, Chucky's auto repair shop has to be a front."

I didn't know who Chucky was, but Sonny LaPage was glorifying Ft. Covington. The only place he had ever lived. He lacked perspective, but that was okay. I needed to keep him focused on what he knew for sure. "I guess it doesn't matter. Professional or not. All signs point back to Matteo Garrow and Dave Hetfield."

They both looked at me with mouths open.

"What?"

"How can you be so sure?" Sonny said. "We want to be sure before those kinds of rumors get out."

I tossed my keys on the bed beside Sonny and unfolded the glossy photo I had brought from Dave Hetfield's place. I tossed it next to the keys and stepped over to the evidence box and removed the duplicate photo. I held it in front of me, "Jo Jo left this for me. Matteo Garrow unloading a tub of Mohawk war clubs on Dave Hetfield, his sworn enemy." I pointed at the other picture lying beside Sonny. "That one, I found at Hetfield's place beneath a stack of bills that would be envy of this crime syndicate Sonny says has set up shop here."

Sonny's brow furrowed, his eyes pinched, and mouth formed a tight frown.

A knock came at the door.

Stefanie Charles drew her arms tighter against herself, and wide-eyed, looked to me.

"Probably Tony American Horse," I said.

They both sighed.

I swung the door open.

And there he stood. "Sorry, I'm a little late," he said. "Matteo kept me over at Jo Jo's place longer than I figured."

I stepped aside. "Find anything?"

Tony removed his sand-colored cowboy hat and stepped into the room.

With the four of us in the room, the walls seemed to close in.

Horse stepped past me. "Not much to find." His eyes settled on the evidence box sitting on the bed. "But then you already knew that."

"Is Garrow still tied up over at Jo Jo's place?"

Horse nodded. "I'm sure he'll be there a while. He has to make an act of it or else it won't look real. Why?"

I ran my wounded tongue back and forth over my teeth. Each pass a little more painful, more toe-curling. I'm not sure what I hoped to find, but I shared what I was thinking. "I'd like to get a look at Garrow's place?"

Sonny LaPage sat up, shaking his head, "Now you want to toss a cop's place?"

Horse's eyes settled on mine. They were good cheered to match his smile. "Toss?" He asked. "What have you two been up to?"

How could this guy still be smiling with all this death? I changed the subject. "Forget that," I said. "Did you hear about Cliffie Hetfield?"

His head tilted to one side.

He hadn't.

I shared the little I knew, and he listened, rotating his hat in his hands. His thumb running lightly along the brim. When I finished, he gave himself time to process the fall of Cliff Hetfield, Dave's run out of town, and his boss's implication in all of it.

"If anyone has a connection to a button man, it would be Matteo." He said, "But I don't think he'd need one." He looked to Sonny LaPage. "There are plenty of good shots here in town. Do we know anything about the crime scene?"

I remembered that I hadn't checked my messages. I scrolled through the whole story again, as told by Steve Whitaker via text messages. Typos and all. "Nothing new here," I said. "But I don't need to know anything about all of that. I want to see Garrow's place."

"What do you hope to find?"

"Humor me," I said.

It was my way of saying, I had no clue.

WE DECIDED on Tony American Horse leaving his cruiser behind. He followed behind us in the passenger seat of Stefanie Charles's red compact. We made quite the motley crew, heading off to break into a police officer's place. Silence cloaked Sonny LaPage and I, again.

I gave Steve Whitaker a call.

He answered on the first ring. "Jesus, Koella, where have you been?"

"Busy," I said. "Look, Hetfield's on his way out of the country. Matteo Garrow is in on this, too. If you're interested in a collar, I can arrange it."

"A collar?" Silence from him now. Teeth clicking. "Fuzzy, how many times do I need to tell you? I am a corrections offi-cer. I don't make collars. I escort inmates to the showers. I make sure they aren't hiding shit up their rectums. I try my best to act like I'm not listening in on the conversations with their loved ones. It's not glamorous. It's what I do."

"You get any recognition for finding Cliff Hetfield?" I said.

"What?" He said. "I didn't find Cliff — "

"But you got some recognition, didn't you?"

"I don't give a shit about recognition!" He hung up on me.

Steve Whitaker was an honorable man. He didn't seek recognition, but he was lying if he said he didn't give a shit about it. I also didn't believe he was happy settling for escorting inmates to the showers.

As we passed the Casino on our right, Sonny jabbed a thumb at it. "You don't think that brings the grease-balls in?"

38

Matteo Garrow's place sat in an open field at the end of a winding dirt road lined with tar-papered shacks on one side and the Cedar View Golf Course on the other. The golf course was the flattest course I'd seen north of Florida. And the surrounding area provided little more topography. If anyone wanted to take out Matteo Garrow, they could do it from half a mile away. But I wasn't there to take out Garrow. The point being, however, anyone at Garrow's place or the vicinity knew our cavalry had arrived.

Sonny wheeled us up beside a tiny, single-car garage disconnected from the main house. Both buildings had gray, false-slate siding, which made the home fit in against the bright white of the snowy landscape.

Stefanie pulled up beside us. The inside of her car was all smoke, obscuring Tony American Horse's face. When he stepped out of the car, he coughed and cleared his throat.

Second hand smoke was a bitch.

The four of us huddled in front of Sonny LaPage's truck.

"Okay, now what do we do," Stefanie mumbled around a filtered cigarette which hung from her bottom lip.

"I see no cars, but since we're out here like sitting ducks, I'm gonna try knocking on the front door," I said.

"I'll come with you," Stefanie said.

As I stepped past the little garage shack, I noticed that the bottom edge of a wooden door on the side had rotted away, leaving what looked like thatching. Garrow had applied a padlock to the jamb which now hung loose and open.

I stepped to the door and gave it a light push.

Stefanie blew a plume of smoke along the side of my face as she looked over my shoulder.

"Do you mind?" I said.

She dropped the cigarette butt to the ground and put it out with the toe of her boot. "That some shop," she said.

Matteo Garrow's garage did not serve its intended purpose. He had fit it out to be a high-quality wood shop. Or at least it looked high quality to my novice eyes. I recognized some of the saws and sanding machines from my days in high school wood shop, but my expertise began and ended there. Much like Hetfield's garage, the place was immaculate. Benches lined the walls; table saws and planers took up the center of the floor. Not the slightest speck of saw dust marred the bright white epoxy painted floor.

I stepped into the room.

Stefanie stayed put and shrugged. "I have broken no laws yet," she said. "I'll stay on this side of the door."

I ran my fingers on the unfinished wood surface of one of Garrow's work benches. My fingertips came back free of any dust. "Where are the others?"

She looked over her shoulder. "Looks like they're knocking on the door."

I made a loop around the perimeter of the room. Testing each work surface for stray sawdust. I wasn't sure what I was hoping to accomplish by that, but I kept recalling how certain Sonny LaPage had been about Dave Hetfield's guns.

As I completed my trek around the room, I stepped to a sanding table at the center. Two manual sanders sat on the table, but again, my swipe of the table top was free of any dust. As I stepped to the table, my toe kicked something which shifted with the pressure of my boot.

I squatted down and saw a wooden crate. My breath left me, when I saw a replica of the cudgel that had been used to beat me. I took the club by its handle. It was knobby, unfinished. A wood splinter dug its way into the heel of my palm.

"What the fuck is that?" Stefanie called from the doorway.

I waved the club above my shoulder and smiled, "An ancient Indian artifact."

"The hell it is," she said. "That thing's been carved out of hardwood in the last week. If I'm lying, I'm dying."

Like I'd said all along, she was the smartest one of our bunch. I scanned the room for any other recent projects. There were some other crates with tops and padlocks securing the contents. I could have pried my way into any of them, but what was the point. I wasn't there to toss the place. I found the clue I needed. I carried it and myself back out of the garage.

As I did so, Tony American Horse and Sonny LaPage stepped off of the short front stoop. "Doesn't look like anyone's home," Sonny squawked.

I patted the business end of the club in my palm. It was lumpier than the handle. Still a work in progress.

Sonny's eyes settled on it. "What the hell is that?"

"It's what this whole charade is about."

"A war club?" Horse asked. "They only get brought out at the Pow-wow."

I held the club out to Horse, handle first.

He studied it and frowned, "This is not authentic."

As much as Horse wanted to leap frog Matteo Garrow in small-town politics, I could see the hurt in his eyes when he realized what he was looking at, and what it meant.

I shook my head. "Garrow and Hetfield were running a counterfeit artifact scheme. Selling these," I wagged the club. "As originals on online auction houses. Jo Jo left a picture for me. He must have stumbled onto their scheme. The same picture was at Hetfield's place behind lock and key."

Horse raised eyebrow. "So, you tossed his place?"

"Tossed is such a strong word."

"Yeah? So, you want to give Matteo's place a toss?" He clasped his hands together in front of his chest, almost in prayer.

My shoulders sagged. I don't work many cases where there's any true investigation. Taking pictures of some rich dude and his side piece of ass, or running stalkers off their all-time favorite stripper doesn't involve much investigation. So, when I work a case which involves more than a money shot with the camera or muscle, there is a rush of adrenaline when I put the pieces together. All I felt now was sadness.

IT WAS MID-AFTERNOON, and all of us had skipped lunch so we decided on some dive restaurant on the reservation called the Pot o'Gold. By the interior, the owners had yet to discover theirs. Fake wood paneling, worn indoor/outdoor carpet, and mismatched vinyl-covered tables and chairs gave the place a homey trailer park aesthetic. Back in Carolina, this place would serve the best barbeque in town. Here? I got a decent slab of some fish called haddock, lightly breaded. It had a flaky, white flesh, and if I wasn't cranking the gears in my mind on what to do about Matteo Garrow and Dave Hetfield and Gary Pressley, I probably would have enjoyed the fish. Instead, I pushed it around my plate, and tried to think.

We had the place to ourselves, but the chattering of voices still gave the impression of a school cafeteria. The conversation occurred around me, but I kept to my own thoughts. Stefanie tended towards, "What the fuck?" Horse preferred, "It isn't right." And Sonny LaPage's penguin voice rose above it all, "Why, it just isn't right."

Nothing had been right about all of this. Katie's affair with Parker Hetfield. Her murder. Gary Pressley's arrest. Jo Jo's murder. This shit with the war clubs.

Some pieces I couldn't get to fit together. I wasn't sure I ever would. Katie's murder and Jo Jo's murders seemed to be separate cases involving the same evil duo.

"So, what do we do now?" I said to myself as much as to the others.

The conversation halted.

"We need to confront Matteo with this," Horse said.

"With what?" Stefanie said. "Carved wooden sticks?"

I took a deep breath. "I think I confront Matteo Garrow," I said. "And I bring everything with me. His connection to Hetfield. The cover-up in Katie's murder. His meeting with Jo Jo on the night of his death. The fucking clubs. Everything."

"To what end?" Sonny LaPage said.

I shrugged, "Mine or his."

"Oh, hell no!" Stefanie said. "You will not bring this Dirty Harry shit up here." She crammed something that looked like chipped beef in her mouth. Swallowed it down, and smiled, "Not without me."

Oh, brother.

39

In the safety of Sonny LaPage's truck, I used a number provided by Tony American Horse to call Matteo Garrow.

He answered on one ring. "Garrow."

"Matteo, this is Fuzzy Koella. I think we need to talk."

"Is that so?" He said. "How did you get this number?"

I lied, "Jo Jo gave it to me last night right before he met you. He told me to use it if something went wrong."

His breath came heavy over the phone. I could almost feel it crawl down my neck.

"I can't imagine anything more wrong than my friend's death, so I'm doing what he asked, and using the number."

"So, you have used the number. Now what?"

"I think we need to meet, Garrow," I said.

"What for, Koella?" He only gave me a second before continuing. "As you know, I kind of have my hands full with your buddy's death."

I could feel Sonny LaPage's eyes jabbing the side of my face. I pointed out the windshield to remind him to keep his eyes on the road.

"That's what I think we need to meet about, Matteo. I stopped by your place. You have a nice wood shop there."

There was a pause. The click of his tongue against his teeth. "There's a tree stand that the Cookes hunt at during the season."

"What the fuck are you talking about, Garrow? You don't really expect me to stroll out to some deer stand in the middle of nowhere like a sitting duck while you peer down your scope?"

I looked to Sonny LaPage.

And he stared me down with bulging eyes as he slid us off the road. Snow crunched beneath the tires as we came to an abrupt stop.

I had forgotten to fasten my seat belt, and the side of my head smacked the windshield and my bruised ribs crashed into the dashboard.

"What's this about a deer stand?" Sonny said.

Almost as if he overheard Sonny, Matteo Garrow answered, "If you want to meet, that is where it has to be, Koella. And do not bring the old man."

"How the hell am I supposed to find some random deer stand?" I said. "And who the hell are the Cookes?"

"You are a resourceful guy, Koella. You will find it."

And the line went silent.

I felt a warm, wet, sticky liquid trail from my temple down the side of my face. Just what I needed, another trip to the ER in my future.

"What this about the Cooke's tree stand? Why, that's the best hunting spot in the county."

"He wants me to meet him there. Tonight. Alone."

"Well, you ain't doing it," he said. "You'll meet him, but it won't be alone."

STEFANIE HAD PULLED off the road onto the shoulder two hundred feet in front of us, and a white and navy cruiser, like I saw on my trips to the Malone correctional facility, approached at great speed. As it pulled even with Stefanie's car it squealed as its tires searched for a dry patch of pavement to grip onto. The car spun one hundred eighty degrees across the road into our lane and pulled slowly to the side of the road. It was the niftiest car maneuver I'd seen this side of a Rockford Files episode.

A blood droplet formed and hung from my brow. I squinted my eyes closed and wiped my forearm across my forehead keeping my eyes free of my blood. When I opened my eyes, I saw the stern face of Steve Whitaker in the police cruiser's cab.

I had collected quite a motley crew of north countrymen.

"Who the hell is this?" LaPage screeched.

"Steve Whitaker, at Malone corrections."

LaPage's lips jutted out like a duck's bill. He bobbed his head rapidly. "Good guy," he said.

I agreed, but what was he doing here?

Whitaker watched over his shoulder as a snow and salt covered pickup drove by, and then when the highway was clear of traffic he crawled out of the driver's side of his car, and walked around the front of his car in a stride straight out of Fort Jackson. His holster was empty.

I'm not sure why I noticed that, but it didn't make me feel good.

Sonny lowered the driver's side window. "Why, Stevie, you gave us quite a scare with that car stunt you just pulled."

Whitaker had his biceps tucked tight to his side. He only wore his long-sleeved uniform. His teeth chattered when he looked past Sonny LaPage and said, "I'm in."

I looked to Sonny and saw nothing but confusion. "In?"

"That's right. I heard they found messages on Cliff

Hetfield's phone. From Dave Hetfield and Matteo Garrow. They've been pulling strings on this all along."

"So, Pressley is home free?" I said.

Sonny LaPage's toothless smile wiped the feel of sticky blood from my face and halted the pain at my side.

"I understand they're working the paperwork for his release right now," Whitaker said.

There was no smile on his face.

"I want Hetfield," he said. "And I want Garrow."

Tony American Horse unfolded himself out of Stefanie Charles's tiny car. He shrugged into a dark, brown leather jacket and donned his beige cowboy hat. The son of a bitch was smiling again. He said something I couldn't comprehend, and Whitaker turned to look at him.

Whitaker looked at me sideways as he nodded to Horse. There was an uncertainty there that I had never seen before in Whitaker.

"What are you doing here, Tony?"

Horse stepped toward us and into earshot, "Funny, I was going to ask you the same thing," he said.

Whitaker rocked back on his heels and hooked both thumbs into his belt loops like an extra in a John Wayne film. "Your boss has been up to no good, Horse. He's going down this time."

Horse's smile remained. "Don't I know it, Stevie."

Whitaker's jawline pulsed with energy, but he remained silent.

"And I'll be right there in line," Tony said.

Whitaker laughed. Shook his head.

"You should have been Native, Stevie. Maybe you wouldn't be stuck cleaning out the bedpans."

I didn't have the patience to watch them play out old rivalries. "You say you're in, Whitaker?"

He nodded. His eyes never left Tony American Horse. "What about you, Horse? Are you in?"

Horse chuckled and broke Steve Whitaker's stare. Shook his head, at some inside joke. When he lifted it again, he said, "I'm in."

"What's this about 'in'?" Her voice called. Stefanie Charles bundled up in her heavy coat and sucking on a fresh cigarette had made it half the distance to us from her car.

We all looked at her. Humor in our eyes.

"What?" she said.

It was the last bit of humor any of us would find in some time.

———

STEFANIE CHARLES HAD FINALLY GOTTEN me back to her place, a single-wide trailer in a place called the Lazy Brook RV park. The place was old, its siding in need of pressure washing. Its roof sagged beneath the weight of the snow, but even in the blankets of snow I could tell Stefanie kept a tidy yard. The inside was tiny and tidy.

She watched as we poured into what served as a living room off the front door. She dropped her cigarette down to the porch's floor and put it out with the toe of her boot. Then, bent over and picked it up.

The floor sagged beneath my steps, but as far as mobile homes went Stefanie Charles's place was an ace.

Much like the outside, she kept the inside in order. Bookshelves lined the walls, stuffed with "Cat who solved" mystery books. Not even the faintest scent of tobacco smoke lingered in the air. In fact, not a lone dust mote drifted in the air.

"Nice place, Stefanie."

She cocked an eyebrow, "I knew I'd get you back here before you headed back south. But I didn't think it would be for this Rambo stuff."

Our rag-tag group made its way into her dining room. Sonny, Horse, and Whitaker took a seat around the pressed wood table.

I remained standing as Stefanie ducked into the refrigerator. She dug various beer brand bottles out and placed them on the Formica countertop. When she emerged, she said. "Okay, if any of you pretty boys want a glass for your beer, tough shit."

A knock at the door erased the smile from her face. She mouthed, "Who could that be?"

I shrugged and went to answer the door.

With my back to them, I heard Sonny sharing Garrow's plan to meet me in the deer hunting fields.

I opened the door and gazed into the bushy face of Billy Howe.

His mustache crawled up his cheeks. Crumbs from his last meal hung to the ends. Flushed pink flesh peered out from the facial hair, put there either by the cold or time spent on a barstool at the Legion. When he spoke, the smell of his breath confirmed it was the latter. "How you like me now?"

I laid a hand on his beef shoulder. "Billy, that depends what you are here for."

Through the tangled mess of his beard and mustache his lips pursed to a button, and his brow dropped his eyes to his feet.

I patted his shoulder. "Come in," I said. "We can use you regardless of why you're here."

That lightened his mood, and he stepped into the living room.

"Why, Billy Howe, what are you doing here?"

He shrugged his massive shoulders and sheepishly hung

his head. "I saw you all pull up. I heard about Jo Jo and figured I want in on this."

I looked at the knuckles of his right hand and saw the fresh scabs he had earned on the night of my beating. They still bothered me, but if he'd had anything to do with my beating why would he be here?

Stefanie took a seat at the table, and Billy and I stood beside the friends at the table. Sonny and Steve continued developing a plan. Tony American Horse sat arms crossed across his chest and nodded approval. His politician's smile stuck like glue on his face.

Billy Howe leaned over and whispered "Yeah, I want in on this."

I draped my arm over his shoulder and said, "Billy Howe, I like you quite a bit, right about now."

40

My appeals to leave Stefanie Charles behind fell on deaf ears. I had no desire to add another woman's death to the tally on this case.

But she insisted, "Fuzzy, honey, I've been hunting these fields all my life. First with my daddy, God rest his soul, and then with every man I've dated in my adult life. I was a better shot than most of them, and I don't doubt I'm a better shot than you."

With that she had marched into the trailer's lone bedroom and returned with a thirty-aught-six deer rifle with polished stock every bit as nice as the weapon Sonny LaPage cradled in his arms, now.

We had all crawled into Sonny LaPage's truck. Stefanie squeezed in the cab between Sonny and Horse. The rest of us kneeled in the bed.

As my damp knees went numb, Sonny pulled us off a dirt road brushing his tires against the frozen dead stalks of a cornfield.

The driver's side door creaked open, and Sonny hopped

down, and stepped around to the rear, and lowered the tailgate.

"All right, Fuzzy, it's like we agreed. Haul your ass up into the cab and enjoy the heat. Give us until eight-forty-five to get into our perimeter, before you head to the tree stand."

"And what direction would that be?"

Sonny pulled some goggles up on the crown of a camouflage ball cap he was wearing. "See how the truck is pointed? Just walk a straight line in that direction. But keep your wits about you, I wouldn't put it past that son of a bitch Garrow to ambush you on the way there or shoot you like a deer from the stand."

"What's with the goggles?" I said.

"Son, did you listen at all to the plans? These are night vision glasses. They'll come in handy if we have to shoot."

It was only then I noticed that Steve Whitaker and Billy Howe had similar glasses propped on the bills of the black caps they wore. I winked at Sonny, "Let's not shoot unless it's necessary."

"Fuzzy, don't fool yourself into thinking Matteo Garrow plans anything less of you than he wanted of Jo. If you can keep that at the front of your mind, and just leave the shooting to us. We might make it out of here tonight."

Nothing like a little reassurance.

Whitaker and Billy crawled out of the bed. Both looked at me and nodded.

It reminded me of the treatment I got out of my CAU teammates when I carried a no-hitter into the ninth inning of a game my sophomore year.

I left them and hurried up to cab to catch Stefanie Charles before she exited.

Horse climbed down from the cab.

I opened the driver's door on Stefanie.

She dug into a purse a few inches larger than the pack of smokes she sought.

When I hopped into the seat beside her, she jolted upright, and turned to face me.

"Fuzzy, don't do that to a girl? I'm a nervous wreck."

"Stay here with me in the cab, and when I head off on my death trek, just stay here."

She screwed a cigarette between her sticky pink lips, and mumbled around it, "That ain't how it works, Fuzzy. The plan has us marching in from all corners of the perimeter. If I don't take my position, you may just be making that death walk."

She was right. She'd been the smartest of us most of this case. Tonight was no different. Still, I couldn't have her out there putting her life on the line trying to save mine.

She cut me off before I could appeal and snatched the cigarette from her mouth and planted her pasty lips to mine. She tasted of boiled cabbage and menthol. When she peeled her lips from mine, and leaned back, her simian smile wide on her face and pink lipstick stains smeared across her two front teeth, she winked at me and said, "You might not want to tell your Veronica about that."

Nor did I not want to tell Veronica about it, I hoped Billy Howe or the others hadn't seen it. I wiped the sticky paste from my lips, and scraped my tongue against the wounded roof of my mouth, trying to erase the taste of her last meal.

She leaned into the passenger door and swung it open. As she stood on the running boards, one hand on the top of the door, she slid her rifle from the rack with her other. "Don't do anything stupid, Fuzzy."

It sounded just like something my friend Jimmy Alou would say, or my Uncle Rod, or my mother.

I waved her off, "Go if you're going to, it's getting cold in here."

She shook her head, "You Southern boys are wimps."

And with that, she slammed the door, and joined the huddle near the tailgate where Sonny LaPage quarterbacked them through the next play.

I wondered if it made sense sitting there in plain sight in the dead fields, pouring exhaust into the night sky. But I didn't consider it long, there was no way I'd sit there for the better part of an hour with no heat.

In the rear, I saw Sonny LaPage clap his hands, and they broke the huddle, and strode in a loose line down the dirt road like an offense approaching the line of scrimmage with the game in hand and time expiring. As they reached the extent of the headlights, their silhouettes broke in different directions. I watched Stefanie's fragile black shape march with confidence into the cornfields to the right.

Night vision glasses? What the hell were these dudes doing with night vision glasses? I didn't want to know, but I'm glad they had them.

I wondered why I didn't?

WHEN THE TIME CAME, I cut the engine and pulled my light coat tight across me. I turned the headlights off and sat there in the darkness allowing my eyes to adjust to the darkness. When the pitch black faded to dark gray, and I could discern the dark shapes of the dead corn forming short cliffs on either side of the road, I hopped down from the truck. I patted my lower back and felt the hard steel of the revolver Sonny LaPage had lent me.

And then I sloshed through the melting snow puddling on the surface of the dirt road.

I twisted my right ankle twice, and my legs were numb to the knees with the splashing water by the time the parked cruiser came into focus at the edge of tree line. I stopped and listened to a silence like death.

Somewhere out there was my motley crew. And I'm sure a few of Garrow's guys.

I squinted my eyes and searched the trees and settled on a rectangular shape perched there in the dead trees. If it had been summer, I would never have seen it. Even in daylight. But it was there, alien among the black, spindly branches.

Empty.

The entire walk I had feared that Garrow would be sitting up there sighting me in his rifle, and just pick me off like a buck. Somehow the sight of the empty tree stand ran cold shivers up my spine.

I patted my lower back again.

And the cruiser's searchlight flashed on, blinding me.

I kept my hand at my back and worked my fingers around the grip. The world was still black, and I tried to blink my eyes back to life.

"Do not be a dumb ass, Koella," the monotonal voice of Matteo Garrow filled the field. "Both hands out where I can see them. And empty."

My bladder seemed to fill with each word from him. Great, Fuzzy, piss your pants and then get shot. Somehow, I didn't think Garrow's shot would find the right shoulder that always seemed to attract bullets. I released my hold on the pistol, and lifted both hands shoulder height, palms facing out.

My blinking eyes had brought nothing but piercing light, and greenish ghost images. "How about going easy on that light, Garrow?"

"Step forward, Koella," he said. "Keep the hands up where I can see them."

I did what he said and walked in the light's direction as

slowly as possible. Unsure of where my crew was, I wanted to give them all the time they needed.

As I got within fifty yards of the light, I tested holding my hand out before my eyes to shield against the blinding light.

"Keep coming, Koella. Jesus, you're like an old lady."

"You come out here and try walking blindly in this shit," I said. As I got closer, I could feel warmth coming from the light.

He said, "Okay, Stop."

He angled the search light away from my face just enough so I could make out his diminutive frame. It gave me the slightest hope he would not shoot me right there.

"I'm wondering, Koella. If you are any smarter than your friend."

"I'm wondering how much of a pussy you must be to lead a man out into the cornfields, and shoot him like a coward, when you find out he's got you by the balls."

"It appears you are no smarter," he said.

Silence descended upon us. My arms ached from holding them out shoulder height for so long. I tried easing them down.

The sound of the hammer cocking pierced the silence.

"Back up with them, Koella." The crunch of a footstep on the frozen snow came from his direction.

I held my hands up again, "Make this quick, Garrow, or come and get my gun. My arms are sore."

"You said you had pictures," he said. "Is it the same shit Jo Jo tried to peddle?"

"Jo Jo was trying to come clean," I said. "It took courage for him to come to you, and I know he came to you with more than pictures."

"Is that so?" More crunching footsteps. "And if it took courage for Jo Jo to come to me. What about you?" He said, "What did it take for you to come here tonight?"

"Anger."

The crunching steps stopped, and he stood before me silhouetted against the bright light. Even in the glare, his smile was brilliant like black light. "Did you bring the pictures with you?"

"You think I'm an idiot?"

He shook his head, "The two of you are something else. You know that? All of this hero shit over a dumb homeless kid, and a diseased whore of a nun."

My fists clenched of their own will.

He raised an automatic pistol with a barrel the length of a baby's arm and centered it on my chest.

It was the kind of thing that left a hole there was no recovering from. My throat clenched to swallow saliva that was not there. "Easy with that thing, Garrow. I don't think you want another murder rap to beat."

His eyes bothered me. I wasn't sure if it was my vision still adjusting to the spotlight, but they were like onyx marbles jammed into his sockets. The only white I could see was in the glistening reflection of the light against the polished black.

"You should not have broken into my shop, Koella," his smile glowed purplish-white. "Not even Bigtree pulled such a stupid stunt."

"He would have gotten around to it. He was a bright guy."

"Don't go making him a martyr." He jabbed the gun at me.

I closed my eyes and waited on the blast announcing my death. When it didn't come, I snuck a peek at him.

The black marbles stared back at me. The stoic face returned. The one he and Jo Jo favored. "He wanted to fucking blackmail me. Can you believe that?" His mouth pinched and nostrils flared like a feral rodent. "All those years, I kept his secret. And he thought he would turn me over for fifty-K over some stupid picture."

"You're full of shit, Garrow. Jo Jo only wanted absolution. Maybe that's blackmail. Maybe it's not. But don't stand there waving a gun at me trying to sell me on some bullshit."

"Koella, you may be a good investigator. You're charming, and can get people to open up to you. But you are a piss poor judge of character." The smirk crawled back onto his face.

I wanted to swat it clear from his face, but I had to remind myself of the widow-maker he held in his fist. "Hardly so, Garrow. You aren't half the man Jo Jo was."

"Why?" he said. "Because I tried to make money for my tribe? Have you looked around Hogansburg? Really looked? Have you seen the blight? The depression?" He dropped his head. So, I could not see his eyes. The gun remained locked in on my heart. "This nation in all its prosperity has turned its back on us. We're left with a casino, our sole source of employment. And another half built one. Abandoned because the funds ran out. So, yeah, I jumped in bed with Hetfield. What of it?"

"Katie Couture is dead. A kid is stacking yours and Hetfield's time. Don't try sounding honorable when you're out here waving a gun and Hetfield is sipping some fruity drink in the Caribbean."

He raised his head at that.

He didn't know? "Who's the bad judge of character now?" I asked.

He still trained the barrel of his pistol on me, but now it trembled.

"You know what I haven't figured out, Garrow?" I paused, but when he didn't answer, I continued. "What the hell was one of your counterfeit war clubs doing down in that basement with Katie Couture?"

His head hung and shook back and forth. "Typical white man stupidity. Hetfield liked to scare Sister with that thing. When he remembered he had left it there, it was too late.

Katie was weak, and she died. The kid had found her. Hetfield, like a dumb ass drove back to retrieve the club in the most recognizable vehicle in town."

"Again, I ask you. Who's the bad judge of character now?"

"You tell me," and shouted, "Horse, come on out now."

There was a metallic ping like a stone hitting the cruiser's fender followed by the clap of a rifle firing. Matteo Garrow's eyes dilated enough that the marbles were ringed in white.

I dropped to the ground and log-rolled through the icy snow in the cruiser's direction. My legs slammed into Garrow.

He landed in the snow beside me and splashed the white powder all over me.

My eyes stung with the icy crystals, but all I could think of was Matteo Garrow waving that oversized rod at me. I continued to roll. Closing my eyes against the wet splashes of snow and the images of Garrow and his weapon. When my head banged against the underside of the car's door, I flattened myself as much as possible and squeezed underneath the chassis.

Only then did I chance a peek. Matteo Garrow crawled to his feet like a drunken, geriatric bear. His hands were empty.

I released breath I hadn't realized I was holding. A puff of steam lingered in front of my face.

Garrow patted the ground at his feet. But that wasn't the sight that caught my attention. Out beyond him, some fifty yards, two dark shapes wrestled. The shape of a hunter's rifle held in each of their outstretched arms above their heads.

I pulled my knees up to my chest and rotated on my hip so I found myself in a taut fetal ball crammed between the two front tires of the cruiser.

There was another clap of gunfire from the direction of the wrestling shadows.

I closed my eyes and took three deep breaths before looking out from the tire.

Garrow approached slowly, one hand held out before his eyes to guard against the glare of the light. The gun hung like a tire iron from his other. He scanned the length of the cruiser. "Where did you go, you bastard?"

Glass popped and shattered. Then the clap of the rifle. The world went empty.

I heard Garrow drop to his knees and crawl in my direction.

I unfolded myself and slid out feet first from the other side of the car.

I heard the shooter slide the bolt back on his rifle. Then another clang as a bullet slammed into the body of the car.

Was it Horse? The son of a bitch sold me out, and now he was trying to fill me full of lead. I had no time to ponder it as Garrow's feet and knees sloshed through the puddles at the front of the car.

I squatted in a catcher's crouch, beneath the car's window. All of my weight was on the balls of my feet, and I was no catcher. I wouldn't be able to maintain the position for a long time, but kneeling wouldn't help what I planned to do.

I pictured Matteo Garrow crawling around the front hood of the car. He'd probably lead with the gun hand.

And he did.

But I waited, resisting the urge to chop the gun from his hand.

As he emerged from around the front fender, the world seemed to slow to half-speed. I launched from my crouched position driving all of my power through the balls of my feet. Somehow, they held true on the slushy turf. I hit Garrow on the point of the chin with my dropped shoulder. There was the sickening crunch of a broken jaw, and I followed through trying to take his head off at the shoulders.

I landed on the same shoulder three yards beyond Garrow and rolled back up into my catcher's crouch.

Matteo Garrow lay there unconscious, his chest rising and dropping rapidly.

I crawled to him cautiously.

Footsteps crunched through the crusty snow in all directions. The shooter's steps were coming at a slow trot.

When I got to Garrow, I unwrapped his grip from the pistol, and searched his belt for his handcuffs.

The shooter's footsteps stopped at the hood of the car, just over my shoulder. "Geez, Fuzzy. Did you kill him?"

I looked up into the smiling face of Tony American Horse. Even in the adrenaline and violence of the moment, he looked like a Native American used car salesman.

TWO DAYS later I was on a five-stop flight home. Tony American Horse had spotted Matteo Garrow's favorite deputy Hack Brouchard moments before Garrow had called Horse's name. Horse insisted that it was in his plan all along to lead Garrow into believing that he was entrapping me, when in fact he was betraying his boss. I couldn't tell if he told the truth or not with that stupid look on his face, but I gave him the benefit of the doubt based on his disarming of Hack Brouchard before he could set his sights on me. That turn of events I could not discount. Brouchard was the sharp-shooter that had taken down both Jo Jo and Cliff Hetfield on Matteo Garrow's orders.

The others rounded up two other deputies Garrow had set up as snipers while Tony and I cuffed the slumbering Garrow.

I remembered little else of the ensuing days outside of the blond paneling at the Legion.

Before I left, I stopped in to see Stefanie Charles and tried to pay up for an additional week to give Gary Pressley a place to stay. Stefanie waved off the suggestion and lied and said Jo Jo had paid in advance till the end of January. It meant Gary had a relatively warm place to stay for several weeks. So, I let the lie stand.

The last leg of my flight was in a DC-9 jet out of Washington-Dulles. I had the bulkhead seat on the single seat side of the plane, and I spent the trip in that peculiar haze of half-sleep consciousness I only seemed to manage in planes and hospitals.

My tongue still had the queasy texture of raw hamburger meat.

In what seemed like five minutes after take-off our pilot set us down so gently that he only loosened the filling in one molar. I squeezed out of the fuselage, and into the umbilical which attached us to the terminal. The air seemed warm, almost muggy, after all the time spent in the apocalyptic winter landscape of Fort Covington. The airport seemed larger than it had when I left it to fly up north. Kids no taller than my waist ran weaving in and out of the traffic of jet-lagged passengers. The wheel on my roller board jammed, and I almost did a full out Pete Rose slide across the frayed carpet tiles. The culprit was one of those metallic souvenir pins that had stuck between the wheel and its well on the suitcase. It was blue and gold and inscribed American Legion Post 1418.

I don't know how it got there, but it brought a smile to my face.

But that smile did not quite match the one I'm sure appeared as I took the escalator down to the baggage claim, and saw Veronica standing there, heels tight together like someone from the Royal family, wearing a yellow dress that came to her knees, and the big floppy white hat I had bought her on our trip to Florida. Even at the distance, her ice crystal blue eyes sucked all the breath from my chest.

Beside her Mr. Singh stood, smiling like a kid that had just convinced his parents to allow him another piece of dessert.

As I stepped off the escalator, he jabbed a thumb at Veronica, winked, nodded his head, and turned up the smile a few watts.

I hadn't taken him to be a dirty old man until then. Then I remembered how I hadn't taken a breath since I had seen her. And I completely understood.

"Hey, you," she said.

I stopped a few feet short of her, and we smiled at each other.

When we had worn that out, she frowned and put her fingertips to her lips, "What happened to your face this time?"

I forced myself to peel my eyes off her, and turned to Hab Singh, "Hi Mr. Singh. To what do I owe this pleasure?"

He looked at Veronica, and she nodded. "Oh yes, well forgive this intrusion, Mr. Fuzzy. It's just I came by your place there at the marina to drop off this."

He waived a white envelope, meant for letters. The kind you never see anymore.

"You see?" he said. "Miss Veronica was there, and when I told her why I had come to visit, she insisted that I join her in picking you up."

In my peripheral vision, I saw Veronica's crooked grin.

I turned to her, "Okay, well what is it?"

One of her eyebrows rose.

Mr. Singh slid the envelope into my hand. "You look, Mr. Fuzzy. I told you there would be a bonus."

I opened it while I watched Veronica. She wasn't showing her hand.

I removed the loose piece of paper inside. A check. Made to me for five thousand dollars.

I thought about the costs of my trip north, which would never be reimbursed because my client had been killed. I thought of the otherwise slow off-season it had been for me. And I thought about the little black drops of oil I had been seeing on the pavement where I parked my truck.

I looked at the check again and turned and wrapped my arms around Mr. Singh in a big bear hug.

"Oh dear, there is no need. There is no need," he protested.

EPILOGUE

Two months later, I still hadn't lived down hugging a little, old Indian man before hugging my girlfriend, but an incredible thing happened. I discovered I missed my newfound Northern friends. So, I called Sonny LaPage.

His squawking voice was a comforting reminder of the people from the north country. He explained how Matteo Garrow and his three deputies were all awaiting trial. He didn't know the charges, but he assured me they were going away for a long time. The deputies were turning on Garrow, and Sonny suspected Garrow would get life in prison.

Derry Trong had set up "one of those online fundraising things like eBay", and the community raised enough money to put Gary Pressley up at Unit 3 at the Traveler's Rest for the rest of the year. LeRoux's Filling Station had hired Gary to stock shelves on a part-time basis. He still didn't speak much, but he wasn't on the streets and he had a warm bed to sleep in every night. The *Ti bon ange* would be okay.

Stefanie Charles must like Billy Howe now because they were a number. Audrey LaPage piped in from the background to inform me Stefanie could do so much better. I wasn't so sure. Billy seemed like a stand-up guy, even if I never figured out how he got those scabs on his knuckles.

Tony American Horse had taken over as interim-Sheriff for the Akwesasne Tribe. They would have an election for Matteo Garrow's permanent replacement "after the snow melted." To no one's surprise, Horse had already started his campaign.

Katie Couture's two surviving daughters remained in West Virginia with an Aunt for whom nobody in the Fort had anything good to say.

When the discussion turned to Dave Hetfield, there was silence on the line. "Mr. LaPage?"

"I'm here. You know I think no one has heard from him."

They had already forgotten him.

Sonny LaPage signed me off saying, "You need to come up for a visit when the snow melts in May, Fuzzy. You won't believe the difference."

May? These people were insane for living up there.

That night I dreamt of Katie Couture. Her pale and frail features in stark contrast with the bold red doors of St. Mary's of the Fort Church as she swept the front stoop. Then she stopped, as if she felt my presence, and turned and smiled at me. She looked like a young Grace Kelly, back when she was making all of those Hitchcock films, before she became Princess Grace. Her face was free from the guilt of the sins of her past. It lacked the grief of losing a son far too young. The return of the *Ti Bon Ange* had not haunted it. Hers was a simple, innocent beauty. That of a north country girl.

ABOUT THE AUTHOR

Anthony DeCastro is a life-long fan of detective fiction. He is thrilled that he now gets to share his own stories with the world. *North Country Girl* is his second novel.

Anthony loves hearing from his readers. Please visit him on the web at:

www.tonydwritespulp.com
www.facebook.com/tonydwritespulp/

9 781733 653305